"Let's get out of here, Jes," Korda said, heading back into the main building from the observation platform. "I've changed my mind about scouting further. We'll get back to the Fort, find the world key, and finish the job we came for."

"And what job might that be?" said a hissing voice.

"Jes, this is no time for games," Korda said, spinning in the direction of the voice.

"Boss, I didn't say anything." The PDA bobbed forward a few inches. "*It* did!"

Korda blinked in astonishment, his hand dropping to his blaster. A hulking bipedal reptile stood at the end of the corridor, effectively blocking his exit. It wore a metallic tunic emblazoned with the emblem of Urbs and carried a large laser cannon—the type that usually took a human both arms and a tripod to manipulate—tucked lightly under one arm.

Roger Zelazny and Jane Lindskold's
Chronomaster™
A Novel

Jane Lindskold

Prima Publishing

ISBN: 0-7615-0422-2
Library of Congress Catalog Card Number: 95-72002
Printed in the United States of America
96 97 98 99 EE 10 9 8 7 6 5 4 3 2 1

*This one is for the good folks
at Intracorp and DreamForge,
too numerous to name, who made it possible.*

Foreword

Time has passed so quickly since the time Intracorp approached DreamForge Intertainment to work with two of the finest science fiction writers of our day, Roger Zelazny and Jane Lindskold, on the design and development of *Chronomaster,* a groundbreaking graphic adventure.

As fate would have it, *Chronomaster* was one of Roger's final projects, and thus, holds special meaning with all members of both companies who worked to develop this adventure. Whether you have been a fan of Roger Zelazny's writings over the years or are just now discovering them the excitement and fantasy he has brought to science fiction will never be duplicated.

Now, thanks to Jane Lindskold, their story and vision is continued through the creation of the *Chronomaster* novel. Her story will take you through pocket universes and worlds filled with magic puzzles and plots as Korda embarks on his quest to return justice to the stars. We thank Jane for her undying devotion to Roger and his dream.

We hope you enjoy the journey!

—Intracorp Entertainment, Inc.
DreamForge Intertainment, Inc.

I

A rain of liquid silver, the meteor shower streaked around the sleek elegance of the starship. On the bridge, Rene Korda, the ship's captain, owner— and, indeed, sole living occupant—watched the storm of stone and metal, imagining that it tinkled against the hull much as rainwater had rung against the tin roof of the house in Tennessee where he had been born.

He was drowsing when a perky female voice broke his concentration.

"Hey, Boss! We've got an incoming call from some-one who identifies herself as the Regional Representative for Old Terra!"

"I'm busy. Tell her to go away."

"Boss! The call is coded 'Urgent.' Don't you think you should at least talk with her?"

"I'm listening to the rain—"

"Sugar Pop! It *is* coded 'Urgent.'"

"Very well, Jester. Give me a minute's delay and then put the Rep through." The captain swiveled his seat so that he would be sitting upright when the call was connected.

From the armrest he deployed a mirror and checked his appearance. Average height, gray-blue eyes, blond hair cut short. He did not show his age, the three long centuries linking him to the boy from Tennessee. Of course, he'd paid enough for the drugs that gave him those years and made sure he would not show them.

"Call coming through, Boss," Jester's voice said. "You might want to put the mirror away."

Rene Korda did so, almost regretting—and not for the first time—giving his ship's computer permission to sass him. He had nearly rewritten the personality program a dozen dozen times, but had always halted. What other friend remained to him?

The woman whose image appeared on the viewscreen was attractive if one liked the flamboyant cosmetics now fashionable on Old Terra—which Korda didn't. Her hair was confined in a tight headdress and her figure concealed by the loose robes of a high-ranking government official.

"Do I have the honor to speak with Rene Korda, captain-owner of the *Jester*, Universe Maker of the First Rank?"

"That's me."

Korda did not volunteer to help the conversation along. The Terran Regional Representative had interrupted his reverie. Let her do the work. It had been a long time since he needed to cater to the whims of government officials.

The Terran Regional Representative did not seem annoyed by Korda's abruptness. Silently, he awarded her two points for poise. She knew enough to put her personal reactions aside in order to do her job.

"Mr. Korda, my name is Conchita Devenu. I am the Regional Representative for the government of Old Terra and associated planets."

"Delighted," Korda said, although his tone said he was anything but.

Conchita Devenu continued. "Recently, a very sensitive matter has come to the attention of this office. Our research shows that you are the best person to deal with this difficulty."

Korda leaned slightly forward in his chair. "I am retired, Representative Devenu. That means that I do not deal with 'difficulties.'"

Conchita Devenu's face showed emotion for the first time, but the annoyance that flickered across her painted features did not touch her voice.

"We are aware that you have retired, Mr. Korda. However, when we fed data about this problem into our computers and requested recommendations on who would be best able to solve the problem, your name headed the list by a fair margin."

"I am flattered," Korda said, "but I am not taking any work."

Representative Devenu nodded curtly. "Very well. I have a proposal for you. Since you have been kind enough to take my call, I request that you humor me long enough to permit me to outline this problem. If you are interested, you can take the job. If you are not interested, perhaps you can recommend someone who could. This would at least help us to narrow down the computer's other choices."

"So there are other choices," Korda said.

"Yes," Devenu replied, "but their percentage chance of success was by no means as high as the one given for you."

"I see." Korda considered. His mood of quiet meditation was broken and, if he was honest with himself, he had to admit he was interested in what problem would be urgent enough that the Representative would attempt to call him out of retirement. "Very well, I will do you a favor and listen."

Representative Devenu smiled a tight-lipped, professional smile that looked as if it concealed an urge to tell Korda where he could take his favor. Her words remained calm and polite.

"Thank you, Mr. Korda. I will flash your vessel a standard confidentiality contract. When you have read and accepted it, we will talk further."

The screen went black.

"Boy-o-boy, Sugar Pop!" the voice of the *Jester's* computer said. "I think you really ticked her off!"

"Quite possibly," Korda replied. "Has the contract come through?"

"It's here and I've scanned it," Jester said. "It looks good, Sugar Pop."

"Give it my seal and return it," Korda said, "and, Jes?"

"Yes, Boss?"

"Don't call me 'Sugar Pop.'"

"Right, Rene." There was a slight pause, then, "The confidentiality contract is off to Representative Devenu."

"Put her through when she signals."

"Gotcha, Sug . . . Boss."

Conchita Devenu's expression, when she reappeared on the screen, had lost any trace of annoyance. She curled her lips in a polite smile.

"Thank you for your prompt response, Mr. Korda. Shall we proceed with the briefing?"

"Go ahead," Korda said. "I will listen carefully."

Devenu gave another polite smile, then, with a glance at a notescreen, began to speak. "Within the last half standard year, two pocket universes belonging to private owners have been put into unauthorized stasis. We were notified by merchants who could not enter each universe on prearranged trade missions."

"Of course they couldn't," Korda said. "If a universe has been put into stasis, time within has ceased to function there. No one without a specially prepared ship could get in."

"Precisely," Representative Devenu said. "I have been authorized to hire an expert to enter those universes, find how to reactivate them, and, if possible, hunt down and capture the saboteur responsible."

"Wait a minute," Korda said. "Why is the government of Old Terra involving itself with pocket universes? As far as the physics go, those universes are wholly independent entities. Don't they have independent jurisdiction?"

"An intelligent question, Mr. Korda," Representative Devenu replied. "Under the provisions of the Treaty of Mars, pocket universes are independent entities within their borders. However, to facilitate cooperation between the areas outside pocket universes and the pocket universes themselves, extra jurisdiction is given to the governmental systems that hold the rights to the void space in that region wherein the universe's entry point is located."

"And these two universes," Korda said slowly, "presumably have their entry points in Terran space."

"That is correct," Representative Devenu said. "Since the merchants who could not enter the universes are protected under the trade provisions of the Treaty of Mars, we are authorized to investigate. Preliminary investigations showed that stasis was in effect. That having been established, we sought an expert and so contacted you."

"I understand," Korda said, rubbing his jawbone. "Pray, continue."

"The legal situation does have its awkward aspects," Devenu said. "The Treaty of Mars grants jurisdiction over the space outside the pocket universes and imposes Terran law on interactions between the universes and any entity outside their borders. However, some could argue that actual entry into the universe is a violation of the rights granted by the Treaty."

"I see," Korda said. "Interesting."

"Our legal experts," Devenu continued, "have interpreted the law as protecting those who would do legitimate business with the pocket universes."

"Those merchants again," Korda said.

"Correct," Devenu nodded. "Since their business was prearranged and they stand to lose with the universes in unplanned-for stasis, the legal department has argued that our government is authorized to make an in-depth investigation. However . . ."

"You would prefer that, if I take this job, I do not overemphasize my connection to the government of Old Terra," Korda finished for her.

"Precisely."

"An interesting restriction," Korda said, "but reasonable. Is there anything else I should know?"

"Not much more," Representative Devenu said. "Our computers have indicated that you are the ranking specialist on both terraforming and the creation of pocket universes who also holds Terran citizenship. You are the best person, professionally and legally, to solve a problem that may—without exaggeration—threaten the continued existence of hundreds of thousands of sentient beings."

Korda considered. It would be false modesty on his part to deny his abilities in his chosen fields. He had begun as a terraformer—an artist in the sculpting of planets not merely to make them habitable, but to fulfill the whims and wishes of his clients. From that it had been a logical development to learn how to create pocket universes.

The training had taken half a century, but he had considered the decades well spent. Afterward, he had created a handful of pocket universes, crafting every detail, from the essential laws of physics to the fauna and flora on each planet. A pocket universe was a microscopic thing on the scale of the real universe—not much larger than a solar system, but for a human the sensation of creating one was godlike.

With more wealth than any one man could spend and virtually immortal due to the access his wealth gave him to advanced medicine, Korda had retired to design a universe of his own. However, for nearly a decade he had been drifting from place to place around Universe Prime, Jester his only friend, forever searching for a hint of what he wanted in a universe of his own.

Suddenly, the attraction of listening to imaginary rain against the ship's hull diminished. Korda wondered what had become of the man who had dreamed first of sculpting worlds, then universes. Surely, there had to be something of that self remaining in his weary soul.

"Mr. Korda?" the anxious note in Representative Devenu's voice made Korda realize that he had fallen silent for a good while.

"Sorry, Representative," Korda said. "Woolgathering. The province of the long-lived, I fear. If I choose to take on this investigation, what is the government offering me?"

Conchita Devenu's expression brightened. For the first time, Korda realized that the official was genuinely worried about the fate of the yet-unidentified pocket universes. Feeling as if ice was melting around his own soul,

Korda listened.

"You can pretty much name your fee," Devenu said. "Additionally, we can offer you some start-up support in the shape of equipment and access to databases for research."

"Let's see," Korda said. "I don't really need money and I have a fine ship . . ."

"Don't you know it, Boss!" Jester interrupted.

" . . . But I wouldn't mind making my life easier around tax time. Would the TRG's generosity extend to a remission of my taxes for the next century?"

Conchita Devenu nodded, a smile touching her lips as she realized that Korda's fee would not touch her departmental budget. "I can approve that without going to the committee. Is there anything else?"

Korda nodded. "I would like an official writ saying that anything I do in this job which could be construed as illegal will be reviewed in light of the urgency of the situation. Perhaps I could temporarily be given a law enforcement officer's badge."

"I can do that," Devenu said, "as long as you don't think that this writ is giving you carte blanche to commit murder or other crimes. And I must remind you of the need for confidentiality in this situation."

"Consider me reminded," Korda assured her. "I simply want to be able to call on you if I find myself unexpectedly running afoul of the local law. Now, back to business. I notice that you haven't told me anything about the universes in question."

"That information is classified for anyone except the one who takes on the job and a limited number of my staff members here," Devenu said, her tone guarded.

Korda discovered he still knew how to put on a reassuring manner. "Consider me on the job, Representative."

"You'll take the job!" The Representative forgot her dignity long enough to bounce in her seat, then regained her composure. "Thank you, Mr. Korda. Thank you!"

"You've piqued my interest," Korda said. "Now, flash me a contract so we can get to particulars."

"A contract will take a few hours to draw up," Devenu said. "Flash me a letter of agreement and we will work out the details later."

"It's on the way," Korda said. "Jester?"

"I'm on it, Boss."

Devenu looked agreeably surprised at the turn of events. She tapped a few icons on a screen off to one side and then turned to face Korda.

"The two universes in question are called Urbs and Aurans." She paused expectantly.

"I can't say that I've ever heard of them," Korda said, "and that in itself is a bit odd. I'm retired, but I've been keeping up with the trade journals."

"Interesting indeed." The Representative paused to make a note, then continued. "The entry point to Urbs is closer to your current position. Aurans is somewhat further."

"Do you have any indication who was the designer

for either one?" Korda asked.

"I fear not," Devenu said. "This information was not required for our registration files. Let me give you what I do have."

"May I record?"

"Please do," Devenu answered, then started in surprise.

When the Representative had given her agreement to have the conversation recorded, the *Jester* had manifested her persona icon on one of the holopads on the bridge.

In a fit of whimsy, Korda had designed the persona icon to complement the name of his ship. A petite figure no more than a foot tall, Jester was cute, but too mischievous to be conventionally beautiful. She was brightly clad in close-fitting yellow and purple checked leggings and a tight hot-pink leotard. The sleeve details of the leotard picked up on her yellow and purple leggings. Her wild blond hair evoked a jester's cap. The only things missing were the bells.

She sat cross-legged on her holopad, an old-fashioned stenographer's notebook on her knee.

"I'm ready when you are, Sug . . . Boss," she said, giving Devenu a perky smile.

Devenu recovered her poise with remarkable grace. "I see that you and your vessel have all sorts of hidden qualities."

Korda sighed, "In *Jester's* case, that at least is true. To business?"

"Indeed," Devenu glanced at her notescreen. "The

access point for Urbs, as I mentioned, is the closer of the two. As the name hints, the universe is fully urbanized. It has a single Earth-normal sun, several planets, and an asteroid belt. A cross-check of our immigration records shows that a comparatively small number of humans have requested visas."

"However, this does not rule out nonhuman inhabitants or inhabitants from outside Terran space," Korda said, thoughtfully.

"True," Representative Devenu agreed. "The largest portion of imports into Urbs consists of raw metal ore, premade electronics, and the like. The largest portion of their exports is completed, customized mechanical devices."

"Fascinating," Korda said. "Do you have an owner's name?"

"It is registered to a consortium called God's Pockets," Devenu said. "I checked out God's Pockets and learned that none of the board members is listed by name."

"That is evocative," Korda said. "Is Aurans possibly also owned by God's Pockets?"

Devenu nodded. "It is indeed. I've about exhausted my information on Urbs. Would you like me to go on to Aurans?"

"Please do," Korda said. On her holopad, Jester made a show of flipping to a clean page in her stenobook.

"Aurans is listed as being designed around a binary star system," Devenu began. "There are three major bodies: a gas giant, a large semidesert world, and a smaller earthlike body. Immigration from Old Terran space is minimal. Imports include cryofrozen embryos of exotic animals, artwork, and a large number of historical relics and reproductions. There is a sidenote that physical laws are not Universe Prime standard."

"Do your records say what they are?" Korda asked eagerly.

"I fear not," Representative Devenu said. "We could not require that detail be listed. All we have is a notation ordering incoming ships to signal a satellite for a briefing."

Korda rubbed his hands together briskly, realizing that he felt more alive than he had for a long, long time. This could actually be fun.

"If that is all the information you have on tap now," Korda said, "I will let you go so I can begin my own research. You can draw up our business contract."

Devenu bowed politely toward the viewscreen. "Is there anything else I can do?"

"Yes. See if you can find anything more about God's Pockets. Did they have any other universes made? How did they pay for them? Anything we can learn may help me with Urbs and Aurans. I may be able to contact their Board and get formal permission to enter."

Representative Devenu frowned. "And if the Board refuses you permission?"

"Then we give them twenty-four hours to reactivate those universes. If they don't, I still go in under the provisions of the Treaty of Mars." Korda grinned at her. "Don't worry, Representative. I'm not trying to back out of the job."

Devenu smiled in return. "I never believed that you were. Good luck with your research and I shall be in touch."

"Thanks," he replied. "Korda out."

Jester set down her notebook, which conveniently vanished. Rising to her feet, she stretched, wriggling in a distracting fashion.

"What next, Sugar Pop?" she asked.

"Just what I told Representative Devenu," he said. "Research. I may be able to figure out who the designers were just from what I know about styles in pocket universes. I even have some guesses already."

"Who?" Jester said, hopping from pink-booted foot to pink-booted foot. "Tell me, Sugar Pop!"

"Not until I've done some more research," he said. "I don't want to look the fool. Oh, and, by the way . . ."

"I know," Jester sighed. "Don't call you 'Sugar Pop.'"

Korda winked at her. "Right. Now, let me get to work."

As he sat down in front of the library console, Korda realized he was humming softly to himself. Apparently, he no longer needed meteors to make music. He was finding it within himself.

II

Some hours after his discussion with Conchita
Devenu, Rene Korda turned away from his library
console.

"Jester, I need you to place a call for me."

Promptly, Jester appeared on her holopad. There was
a switchboard in front of her and she wore a headset that
somehow managed not to flatten her hair.

"Number, please," she said nasally.

"Charlie Bell," he answered. "You should find him in
the Universe Designers directory. He was one of my
instructors at the Academy and we worked on a few projects. He's retired now, but last I heard he was living on
Venus."

Jester wrinkled her nose. "Venus is awfully hot."

"Ah, but Charlie's a terraformer, just like me. I don't
doubt he's made himself comfortable."

Jester's hands moved as if she was plugging in phone
connections. Intellectually, Korda knew that the starship's
communications system had already begun signaling
Venus. The ship's call would be relayed from satellite to

satellite first in-system, then orbiting the planet, before it reached Charlie Bell.

Had they been outside the Terran solar system, the call would have been difficult to make. Had Bell dwelt within a pocket universe, especially one with nonstandard physics, such a simple call would have been impossible.

"I have Charlie Bell on the line," Jester said, still affecting the nasal whine.

"Put him through," Korda said, suppressing a sigh. Jester would play. She wouldn't be Jester if she didn't.

"Rene!" Charlie Bell seemed genuinely pleased.

He hadn't changed much since Korda's days at the Academy. His white mustache still flopped walrus-like, its profusion seeming a deliberate defiance of his bald head. Like Korda, Charlie Bell was wealthy enough to afford antiaging drugs, but he had begun the course later and he was about a hundred and fifty years Korda's senior—the centuries did catch up with one after a while.

"Rene!" Charlie continued, "I could hardly believe it was really you when the call came through. How have you been? I heard you retired."

"That's right, Charlie," Korda said. "Your example was too good not to follow. Besides, I was getting fed up with some of the unimaginative design specifications. If people wanted to live on Old Terra, why didn't they just stay there?"

"Perhaps they wanted room to grow, political and social freedom; there are lots of reasons," Bell said. "Not everyone wants to live in a work of art. You know that as well as I do. Have you designed your private universe yet?"

Korda shifted uncomfortably in his chair. "No, not yet. I can't seem to work out just what I want."

"I know the feeling," Bell said. "When I was working just for myself, suddenly there were too many options. Fortunately, my wife wanted to be near our eldest daughter and Fria has settled on Venus to do thermascapes. It took the decision neatly out of my hands, and I can't say I'm sorry."

"Yeah, well . . ."

Korda didn't know quite how to answer. He had never found a woman to settle down with and raise a family. His only marriage had ended in divorce. Idly, he found himself wondering if, just as with a pocket universe of his own, he found it easier to dream than to make a commitment.

Bell seemed to sense Korda's discomfort, for he changed the subject. "I can't believe you called me after all this time just to chat. What's going on?"

Relieved, Korda turned to business. "I called to ask if you know anything about a pocket universe called Urbs. Its access point is in Terran regional space."

At the word Urbs, Bell's relaxed, welcoming manner vanished. Suddenly formal, he turned an unfriendly gaze on Korda.

"Urbs? I may have heard of it. Why do you ask?"

"I heard about it from some people," Korda said, concealing his surprise at the change in Charlie's mood. "I thought I recognized your design work and decided to look into it."

"I see." Charlie fell quiet for a long moment. "Yes, I did design Urbs, but I can't say anything about it. I signed a confidentiality contract even more restrictive than the usual. I probably shouldn't even admit to designing the place."

Korda studied his old friend. "God's Pockets drew up this contract?"

Bell arched a wispy white eyebrow. "That's right. They paid well, too, in case that's your next question. They were even able to get Nizzim Rochtar to do some work for them and you know how expensive alien designers can be. Now, Rene, I won't say anything further about the job. Nada. Nicht. Zero. Zilch."

"I understand," Korda said, frowning slightly.

Charlie had grown a bit pale. Was that fear in his eyes? What could the people at God's Pockets have said to him that could make him so edgy?

Politely, Korda turned the conversation to more neutral subjects: mutual friends, Charlie's swamp orchids, Korda's travels. When they ended the call with various promises to stay in touch, Korda was more puzzled than ever. He knew little more about Urbs, but he was beginning to suspect that God's Pockets was at least as interesting as what had happened to two of their universes. He wondered if Representative Devenu would turn up anything further about them.

"Jes, I'm going to take a break for a sandwich and a cup of coffee. While I'm at it, look up the number of a universe designer named Nizzim Rochtar. She's an alien and may not reside in Terran regional space."

Jester twirled happily on her holopad. "When I locate where to call her, should I go ahead and get it started? It may take a while to make out-system connections."

"Do it, Jes, and bill Representative Devenu for the connection charges. In fact, you might want to see if we can link the call through the government channels. They could be more efficient."

"I'm on it, Sugar Pop!"

Korda sighed. Easing himself out of his chair, he headed off to the galley.

He was halfway through his second salmon and Swiss with German mustard on rye when Jester popped into existence across the table from him. She was wearing her phone operator's headset again.

"I've finished the link up, Boss," she said. "Nizzim Rochtar should be available to talk with you inside of five minutes."

Korda washed down the last of his sandwich with a mouthful of dark beer. "Wonderful! I'll take the call on the bridge."

"Hey, Great and Powerful Maker of Universes," Jester called after him. "Wipe the mustard off of your nose!"

Korda did so. Staring at the yellow smear on the back of his hand, he decided that moments like this, when Jester's initiative saved him from making a fool of himself, were worth a fair amount of teasing.

The call from Nizzim Rochtar came through just as he was easing himself into his chair. Due to the distance involved, there was a slight lag between the reception of the image and response. Korda used it to study the alien.

She was quite small and resembled nothing so much as a kangaroo rat. Perched rakishly between her ears was a flowered straw hat. A cigar hung from the corner of her mouth.

"Greetings, highly ranked, most important designer of universes," Nizzim Rochtar said. Her voice was high and somewhat squeaky, just as Korda had expected. "What may this lesser-ranked one do for you?"

Korda placed a hand over his heart and bowed. "This one has contacted the wise Rochtar to request information on a segment of the art in which Nizzim Rochtar is known to have no peer. I speak, of course, of the designing of desert worlds."

Nizzim Rochtar took her cigar from her mouth. Setting it in an ashtray shaped like a small volcano, she also bowed with a hand over her heart. Beside her, the cigar smoke drifted up the cone of the volcano, so that it appeared about to erupt.

"This one is pleased to hear the great Korda so name her an expert. I would be happy to assist him in whatever small way I can."

Korda had used the delay to frame his response. "I heard of a universe called Aurans. From the description, I believed it to be the artwork of Nizzim Rochtar. I placed a bet on this and now I humbly await your confirmation."

Nizzim Rochtar twirled her whiskers around one paw. "Yes, this one did design the universe called Aurans. Of course, professional confidentiality prevents me from discussing the details of my design, even with one so august as you. I would need a signed waiver from the universe's owners."

"That would be an organization called God's Pockets," Korda said. "Would you have an address where they can be contacted?"

Lifting the cigar from the shadow of the volcano, Nizzim Rochtar puffed on it to get it burning again while she considered his request.

"I fear I do not have a contact address for my former employers," she squeaked at last. "However, perhaps Clia T'rifit does. I understand that she undertook to design several universes for God's Pockets."

Korda made a note of the name. "Thank you. I shall owe you a meal next time you visit my region."

Nizzim Rochtar blew a smoke ring. "Perhaps the great Korda would permit me to use his praise of my desert worlds in my dossier. That would please me greatly."

"I would be honored," Korda said. "I spoke only the truth."

After a few more exchanges of compliments and flattery, the call was terminated.

"Wow! That call is going to run up the national debt," Jester commented. "Do you want me to locate this Clia T'rifit, Boss?"

"Would you, please?" Korda said. "I've heard of her work, but she burst on the scene about the time I was getting ready to retire so we never had any personal contact. Still, she seems to be our last lead unless Representative Devenu discovers something else."

Leaning back in his chair, Korda studied the ceiling. He was impatient to be moving, to start the hands-on portion of his job. However, he knew that research now could save him considerable trouble later.

He was almost as fascinated by his impatience as he was by the problem that Representative Devenu had set before him. How had he been willing to confine himself to the narrow boundaries of his starship for so long when there was an entire universe—hell, a series of universes—out there for him to enjoy?

"Boss, I have a contact number for Clia T'rifit. It's an Earth number and on the night side of the planet, but the listing does say to call any time."

"Place the call," Korda said. "We may just get an assistant at this hour, but maybe not."

"I'm on it," Jester said. "The call is through."

Korda straightened his chair, returning his gaze to the viewscreen. The face staring out at him was nearly expressionless, dark, and somewhat foreboding.

"May I speak with Clia T'rifit?" Korda said. He was certain that Nizzim Rochtar had used the female pronoun.

"Clia T'rifit has died," the man said, his stone-faced expression not altering a whit. "I am in service to the attorneys for her estate."

Something clicked into place in Korda's brain. He wasn't addressing a human here, but an android. No wonder calls to Clia T'rifit could go through day or night. Korda permitted himself to look shocked.

"Dead? How did she die?"

The android tilted his head stiffly; quite likely he was running the question through his programming before answering. Single-task androids were rarely as clever as multi-task creations like the *Jester's* computer program.

"Clia T'rifit died when a fire broke out in the building where she had offices."

Korda frowned. "Was it accident or arson?"

The android tilted his head again. "The official ruling was that the fire was accidental. The building was quite old and the insulation was not up to code. There was some question, however, as the fire seemed to begin simultaneously on the floors above and below, as well as on those with the T'rifit offices."

"So all her records burned, too," Korda said thoughtfully.

"That is correct. All that was not stored in vaults was destroyed," the android replied. "Were you a client of the T'rifit firm?"

"I was planning on becoming one," Korda evaded. "I had heard about her work from organization called God's Pockets. They sent me to her saying that I could check her work using them as a reference."

The android's pause was longer this time. "I regret to say that client confidentiality forbids us to discuss

Clia T'rifit's work. If you return with written or videoed confirmation from God's Pockets, we can discuss this issue further. Good evening."

Korda blinked in surprise as the call was terminated without further formalities.

"Jes?" he said. "Do you get the impression that everyone we've spoken with is scared stiff of God's Pockets?"

Jester appeared on her holopad, sitting cross-legged, her chin resting in her hand. "Yeah, Boss, I do. I'm just a computer, but there is definitely a pattern developing."

"It's strange," Korda said. "Universes created for God's Pockets are the victims of our saboteur. The company must have lots of money or they couldn't have contracted for several private universes, but no one we've spoken with knows anything about them. Strange."

"That's saying it, Sugar Pop," Jester said. "Why don't you catch some shut-eye? I'll wait for Representative Devenu's call."

Korda rose and stretched. "Sounds like a good idea. Give me some warning before you put her through. Got it?"

Jester grinned wickedly. "You mean you don't want her to see that you sleep in the buff?"

Korda did not deign to reply, making his retreat with what dignity remained to him. He had gotten a solid eight hours sleep and was in the galley sipping strong Irish breakfast tea when the call came from Representative Devenu. Deciding that he was too comfortable to move, he had Jester route the call to the galley.

"Good morning," Conchita Devenu greeted him. She was definitely more friendly than she had been the day before. "I have some of the information that you requested."

There was a faint "ping" in the background of the galley and Jester, a chef's hat perched jauntily atop her hair, appeared on the nearest holopad.

"Your scones are ready, Sug—" She stopped speaking, acting as if she was aware of Representative Devenu for the first time. "Well, hello! You don't mind if he finishes breakfast do you? He's just a mess if he doesn't eat right."

Representative Devenu's eyes widened, but she managed a dignified nod. "Of course, I don't mind. Can I brief Mr. Korda while he eats?"

Jester grinned and tossed off her hat. It vanished as it hit the holopad and her notebook appeared in her hand.

"Brief away," she said. "I take all the notes anyhow. He lives the life of the wealthy—"

"Jester," Korda said sternly—or at least as sternly as one could with a plate of clotted cream, strawberry jam, and scones occupying both hands. "Shall we stop teasing the good Representative and get to work?"

"Sure, Boss." Jester sat cross-legged on her holopad.

Representative Devenu shook her head in amazement, but forbore from commenting further. Angling her viewscreen so that she could consult it more easily, she took a deep breath.

"Mr. Korda, God's Pockets is proving to be quite a mystery. I had several members of my staff researching the company from the time we terminated our call yesterday. Despite the full resources of the Terran Regional Government, they were unable to discover who precisely is behind the Board of Directors."

"Pray, continue," Korda said.

Conchita Devenu flipped her palms apart in a gesture of helplessness. "God's Pockets lists a variety of companies and persons—both human and alien—as members of the Board of Directors. However, our research shows that every entity listed is a front for someone or something else. We checked these as well and the web simply became so complex that we were forced to give up the cause as hopeless."

"Wise," Korda said. "If they were that careful, we could end up triggering some warning system."

Representative Devenu looked relieved. "I am pleased that you see things that way. I was concerned that my staff and I would seem less devoted to the truth than we should be."

"Not at all," Korda said. "I did some investigating of my own, and I'm certain that God's Pockets has some interesting secrets."

"You must tell me the results of your research," Devenu said. "Let me finish first. I really don't have that much left to tell."

Jester perked up. "I'm still copying, Representative."

"Uh, thank you, Jester." Devenu shook her head, then consulted her notes. "Our one success was that we learned that God's Pockets has registered not two, but seven pocket universes. Why don't I just give the basics now and I can beam your computer . . . I mean I can send Miss Jester the details later."

Korda nodded agreement. Jester wiggled happily on her holopad.

"That would be great, Representative," she said. "After all, we may not need them. Why waste your time?"

"True," Devenu said. "The universes contracted for by God's Pockets are as follows: Urbs, Aurans, Fortuna, Verdry, Cabal, Jungen, and Dyce."

Korda scratched the back of his head thoughtfully. "I believe I've heard of Fortuna. It's something of a Mecca for hard-core gamblers. I've never heard of any of the rest."

"Well, you're ahead of me," Devenu said. "I'd never heard of any of them and they're within my jurisdiction. They don't seem to have much contact with Universe Prime. Now, can you tell me what you learned?"

"Certainly," Korda said. "As with you, it wasn't much, but what I did learn ties in nicely with your work. Urbs was designed by a fellow named Charlie Bell. We've been friendly acquaintances for centuries, but when I brought up the subject of God's Pockets, he clammed up. My guess is that he was scared."

Representative Devenu frowned. "Fascinating. Would you say that Mr. Bell was a person to scare easily?"

Korda shook his head. "No, not at all. He's a fine designer. You can't scare easily and work in this field. My next call was to an alien named Nizzim Rochtar."

"He charged the call to your office," Jester cut in.

"That's fine," Representative Devenu said.

"Nizzim Rochtar," Korda continued, "is known for her work with deserts. Charlie Bell hinted that she had done work for God's Pockets, so I asked her about Aurans. She mentioned having designed it, but just like Charlie Bell, she adamantly refused to discuss it."

"I suppose that is her obligation under the client confidentiality provisions," Devenu said.

"True," Korda replied, "but—between you and me—"

"And me!" Jester piped in.

"And you," Korda agreed patiently. "Universe designers are artists, in a way, but our art is a specialized one. We don't often get a chance to discuss the details with people who would understand them. Usually, when two designers meet, there is at least some discussion of projects. Aurans, for example, had a binary star system, two habitable worlds, *and* alternate physics. Nizzim Rochtar should have been itching to do a bit of bragging."

"But she didn't," Representative Devenu said, "and neither did Charlie Bell about Urbs. I see your point. Is there anything else?"

"There is," Korda said, "and it may be the most disturbing element of all. Nizzim Rochtar did give me the name of another designer who'd worked for God's Pockets—a Clia T'rifit. When I tried to call her, I got an android instead. She's dead—recently, the victim of a suspicious fire that not only killed her, but also destroyed most of her records."

Representative Devenu frowned. "You suspect that she was murdered?"

"It does seem possible," Korda said. "Especially now that you have discovered that God's Pockets had other universes made. Quite possibly, Clia T'rifit designed one or more of them. From what I recall, she was quite a hotshot."

"God's Pockets does seem to merit further investigation," Devenu said.

"Can I ask you not to start that investigation for a while?" Korda said. "At least until I check out Urbs and Aurans?"

"Are you afraid that they will come after you?"

"Perhaps," Korda said. "I've been alive for a long time. I know that people who take care to hide something also tend to protect their secrets. Let's not give them any warning."

Devenu nodded. "I agree. First and foremost, this unauthorized stasis needs to be looked into. God's Pockets can wait until later. I will let you work unhindered."

"Uh, Representative?" Jester said, unnaturally diffident. "Before the Boss signs off, could you send me his contract? I want to make certain it's in order before he goes blasting off into danger."

"But of course," Representative Devenu said. "And if you ever get tired of working for Mr. Korda, I hope you will consider working for me. You seem quite a bit more advanced than the average computer."

Jester beamed at the praise. "Thank you very much,

Representative, but I could never leave Rene. He'd be lost without me."

Korda sighed and buried his face in his hands. "Given your praise, there will be no living with her, Representative. Not that there was much leeway before. I'll report as soon as I know something."

"Thank you," Representative Devenu said. "I'll send that contract along. Good luck to you both."

"Thanks," Korda said. When the screen went black, he turned and shook his finger at Jester. "Jes, you are impossible!"

"But I'm great, too, aren't I?" She twirled on one toe. "You couldn't do without me, could you, Sugar Pop?"

Korda tossed a scone at her. It sailed through the holographic image and broke against the wall.

"Don't call me that!"

III

S omething like twenty hours later, Korda set course
for the access point into Urbs. Its proximity made
it the logical first choice, but Korda would have chosen it anyhow. There had been nothing in Representative Devenu's notes to indicate that he could expect
abnormal physics. To start, he preferred as few surprises
as possible.

Much of the last day had been spent outfitting the
Jester for this venture. In addition to the usual supplies
of food, clothing, weapons, and ammunition, he had
stocked his equipment pack with some tools that would
have puzzled anyone but another person skilled in universe design.

First, and perhaps most immediately important, came
his supply of bottled time. This was a device that gen-
erated a personal temporal field. With it the user negat-
ed the stasis effect for the wearer and whatever else was
in immediate proximity. Bottled time had its drawbacks.
For one, it was a power hog, so effectively that Korda
could only carry a limited supply. If he was not very care-

ful, he could find himself running out of time and joining Urbs in its unwelcome stasis.

His second piece of gear, the resonance tracer, was only useful to a trained universe designer. The resonance tracer, when placed on magnetic north on a planet, supplied a reading of the planet's entire magnetic field. For most people, the resulting readout would be a useless blur of lines and numbers. However, a trained universe designer could interpret those lines and numbers and use them to find the location of the world key. "Universe key" would have been a better name for it, but "world key" was a holdover from terraforming. From within the world key a universe designer could alter the basics of the universe. Most tellingly, only from within the world key could a universe be put into stasis.

Korda's last piece of specialized gear, the universal tool, was theoretically available on the open market. However, UTs were so expensive that they were custom-made. A universal tool had the capacity to key directly into the physical laws of a universe and then function according to those laws.

This ability was of inestimable value. With a good UT, travelers never need worry about being helpless within an environment. Rather like a Swiss army knife, the universal tool contained a hammer, a screwdriver, and sundry other items—all guaranteed to work no matter what was the physical makeup of the universe. However, the last function of a UT was what ran up its price.

A genius named Abbot Epi had come up with a way

to permit the universal tool to "read" a pocket universe's physical design and then come up with the optimal tool for that environment. In the greater canvas of Universe Prime, this function of the UT was inert, but in the comparatively smaller area of a pocket universe it functioned beautifully. Often, the function that the UT chose for itself was a clue to the physics of a given universe.

"We're approaching the entry point for the universe of Urbs, Boss," Jester said, her tone a bit more formal than usual. "Are you ready?"

Korda set aside his tools and strapped himself in the command chair on the bridge. "I'm ready, Jes. Let's start by scanning the vicinity. Then we'll move in."

"Gotcha," she said. There was a moment of silence, then, "Boss, I've located a beacon of some sort right by the entry point. It doesn't seem to have a weapons mount."

"Good job, Jester," Korda said. "Signal it and let's see if the beacon has anything to tell us. It could be the equivalent of a welcome mat."

"Or a warning," Jester said. "I'm signaling."

The beacon's reply came almost instantly. "Entry to the Universe of Urbs is restricted to those with prearranged business. If you are interested in doing business with this universe, please contact the offices of God's Pockets on Old Terra. Thank you."

Korda nodded. "Good. Now, Jes, put up our shields and take us in closer. Let's see if the beacon changes its tune."

"Shields up, Oh Great and Powerful Maker of Universes," Jester said. "We are approaching the beacon. I've left the comm link open."

"Warning!" the beacon said. "You are entering the private space of the Universe of Urbs. Transmit your official visa at this point. If you do not have an official visa, you may apply for one at the offices of God's Pockets on Old Terra. Please consider this your final warning. If you cross the entry point, you will be fired upon."

Korda frowned. "We're going to risk it, Jester. If the merchant report was correct, Urbs is in stasis, so we shouldn't have anything to fear from their weapons."

"How did the merchants know that the universe was in stasis, anyhow?" Jester asked.

"My guess is that they tried to pass the entry point and found they couldn't get in. Long-range scanners would have shown that the planets were not revolving or moving in their orbits. A solar system is much like a clock if you know how to read it."

"That's cool!" Jester said. "How are we going to get in?"

Korda smiled. "Remember this morning when you were complaining that my alterations to your structure were tickling you?"

"Yeah?"

"Well, I've fitted the ship with its own bottled time unit. Essentially, you can run it off your drives. As long as we make certain you don't run out of fuel, you're going to be better off than I am—you'll have a virtually limitless supply of bottled time."

Jester's hologram appeared, an uncharacteristic expression of concern on her pixy features. "But what about you, Rene? What if you run out?"

"I'll just need to be careful not to run out," Korda said. "You can help me by tracking my use of bottled time and informing me through the PDA when it gets low."

The hologram grinned happily. "You mean I get to use my Personal Digital Assistant link and come with you?"

Korda resisted the impulse to pat the hologram. "That's right, Jes. I'm going to need your help, especially your link to the ship's main computers."

"Boy-o-boy!" Jester said. "Well, Boss, shall we cross the entry point?"

"Shields up?"

"Yep!"

"Bottled time activated?"

There was a slight pause while Jester located her new ability. "Got it, Boss!"

"Then let's go. Keep it slow and steady and run the cameras. We need to take a good look at what this universe has to offer."

As the *Jester* glided past the still protesting beacon, her shields momentarily flared lime green. The control panel registered a faint sense of resistance, then they were through.

Displayed before them as they traveled inward was a solar system consisting of four planets and an asteroid belt orbiting an Earth-normal yellow sun. Although even the naked eye should have been able to see movement within the asteroid belt, everything was as still as a photograph.

Korda glanced at the readout screen, speaking aloud more from habit than from a need to inform Jester of what her own instruments were telling him.

"Let's see," he said. "The two outer planets are gas giants. The next planet is in an Earth-equivalent orbit and appears to have a breathable atmosphere. The innermost planet has a thin atmosphere and a high metal content. The asteroid belt also shows a high proportion of metal ores."

"Where do you want to start, Boss?" Jester asked.

"In order to find the world key," Korda said, "I need to set the resonance tracer on magnetic north of the most likely world. From here that looks like the one with the breathable atmosphere."

"Can we call that one Urbs, just to make things simple?" Jester asked.

"Technically," Korda said, "it is Urbs Two, but I'm willing to concede the point for simplicity's sake. Let's do a quick fly-by of the inner world and then head into Urbs. Stay clear of the asteroid belt whenever possible. Our bottled time is going to reactivate those babies and we don't know their velocities."

"I hear and obey, Great Master," Jester said. "I'm taking us in."

The fly-by showed them that Urbs One was a barren planet devoid of any habitation. The planet's surface was scored with strip mines. Processing factories turned raw ore into bars of gleaming metal. Other factories were apparently devoted to turning the raw metal into machinery.

"It looks like the place is fully automated," Jester said, her tone touched with awe. "That's an amazing feat."

"I'm almost as amazed that with an entire planet to mine," Korda said, "this universe still imports metals. The demand must be enormous. They probably mine the gas giants for materials as well as fuel."

"Fuel!" Jester said. "That's a good thing to remember. We should tank up before we leave. Maintaining the bottled time has put me at about half-efficiency."

"That bad," Korda said with a frown. "I thought I did a better job with the installation. I'll tinker with the link-up later. Meanwhile, I don't think we have much to worry about. Once we put down on Urbs, you can put the star drives on standby."

"Good planning," Jester said. "Traveling on in-system drives, we're going to take about a half hour to get to Urbs. If you want, you have time to grab something to eat."

"I hear and obey," Korda said with a chuckle. "I've a taste for fettuccine Alfredo and a green salad."

Appearing on the holopad in the galley, Jester shook her head in dismay. Once again she had donned her chef's cap. She waggled a diminutive wooden spoon at him.

"You really should watch your cholesterol, Rene!"

Korda went to program the food processor and discovered that Jester had already done so, in the process adding a slice of chocolate-raspberry torte to the menu.

"You should talk, Jes," he said, amused as always.

She winked at him and twinkled out. Korda was just finishing the torte (with a glass of milk), when she reappeared on the holopad.

"We're approaching the planet of Urbs, Boss. I've been scanning as we closed and you've got to see this place. I don't think there is a square mile that has been left in anything like a natural state!"

Korda hastened to the bridge and played back the scanner recordings. What Jester had said was true. Urbs was completely urbanized. The only green spots were obviously parks or planned farm areas. Even the shorelines of the oceans looked as if they had been stamped out with harbors neatly placed at convenient distances from each other.

"No wonder Charlie Bell didn't want to brag about this one," Korda muttered. "It's creepy!"

Shaking himself, he tapped into the navigational computer.

"Jester, set us down near magnetic north. There appears to be a garden of some sort in that vicinity, so you should be able to avoid damaging anything."

"Aye-aye, Captain!" she said.

Then the hum of the engines changed and the *Jester* began her descent through the atmosphere onto the sleeping planet of Urbs.

IV

W e're down, stabilized, locked, and the ship's personal defense program is loaded," Jester announced. "Ready to hop, Sugar Pop?"

Korda sighed, but he was too excited about being planetside to bother reprimanding the computer. While he was giving his gear a final check, a little globe, not much more than six inches in circumference, sped up and hovered about the level of his shoulder.

In keeping with the general theme he had created for the *Jester*, Korda had designed the computer's Personal Digital Assistant to resemble a smiley face—a purple and turquoise smiley face.

The PDA's broad grin nearly bisected the sphere and served as a limited clamp so that the PDA could pick up and carry a variety of small items. Right now, a pair of what appeared to be sunglasses dangled from the grinning mouth.

"Brought you your shades, Sugar Pop," Jester said, her voice emanating from the PDA. "Don't want you to get wrinkles around your eyes."

Korda accepted the "shades." Although superficially

they did resemble a pair of mirrored sunglasses, the device did a great deal more, for the glasses provided his link to the *Jester*. They served as a screen on which he could view, on command, information downloaded from the ship's computer or from the PDA itself. That they also looked pretty cool didn't hurt at all.

He slid them into place, marveling, as always, that they did not distort his vision. The PDA buzzed around him, chortling happily.

"I've packed the resonance tracer with your things," she said. "And I made you a couple of sandwiches for lunch. Are you ready to go?"

Korda shouldered his equipment pack. Actually, even with the help of the PDA, Jester could not have packed anything for him. Sometimes he suspected that she would enjoy having a set of hands of her own, perhaps a full android body.

He had considered the possibility, but had always drawn back in trepidation. Jester got into enough mischief without hands and feet. What might she do if she had a complete body? His life—no matter what universe he settled in—would never be the same.

Keeping his thoughts to himself, he swatted at the grinning PDA. She dodged easily.

"Come along, Jes," he said. "I want to get a look at this garden while we have plenty of daylight left."

"I'm right with you, Boss," she said. "Do you want me to swoop ahead and take a look at the garden?"

Korda shook his head. "No, I don't want to use the

extra bottled time to keep you active on your own unless we have to. Remember, this entire universe is in stasis. Nothing should be able to sneak up on us—the only things that can move will be those inside our bottled time sphere."

"So we just go strolling in the garden," Jester said, her tone slightly doubtful. Korda had programmed her to be concerned for his safety. "If you say so, Rene."

The garden was quite large, neatly bordered by a wrought iron fence sectioned by rough-hewn stone pillars. Two impressive pillars flanked the gate, supporting a stone arch. Set into the arch's apex, a brass plaque read: "The Garden of Honor."

Within the garden, Korda could see flower beds, ornamental ponds, and various statues. Most of the statues had a rather martial flavor. There were warriors in armor, in star-trooper reflec, in military uniforms taken from numerous human cultures. Korda glanced at the compass reading on the inside of his glasses.

"Wouldn't you know it," he said. "The largest statue in the place is right on magnetic north. I should've known Charlie Bell wouldn't design the place for easy access."

As Korda strode through the gate, the PDA bobbing at his shoulder, an enormous raven that had been perched on one of the pillars cawed and sprung into the air. The leap of its flight took it outside the confines of Korda's bottled time and it froze in place, still on the wing. Until time was restored, it would continue to defy both logic and gravity.

"Wow!" Jester said, bringing her PDA to huddle by Korda's ear. "That was really weird."

Korda nodded, but his attention was on the statue that blocked magnetic north. Clad in silver armor that looked vaguely medieval, it towered at least thirty feet tall and was proportionately massive. It bore a sword in one hand, a blaster in the other. Although its features were concealed by an oddly shaped helm, it evoked a feeling of undefinable sadness, as if it mourned all those who had fallen in battle without the least regretting the necessity for war.

"I'd hate to blow it up," Korda mused. "Charlie must have worked in a way to move it. Perhaps there's a grav platform built into the base."

He was climbing onto the statue's pedestal when, with a slight creaking sound, the statue came to life.

"It's not a statue at all!" Jester said. "It's an enormous robot!"

"When my bottled time came close enough, the robot activated," Korda agreed. "It's a risk, but I'll stay within range. I may be able to convince it to move off of the pedestal."

The gigantic robot had now located them. Tilting its helmeted head slightly, it directed the attention of its dark eye-slits toward them.

"Welcome to the Garden of Honor," it boomed.

"Uh, thanks," Korda said.

"In ancient days, the heroes of the Fort held fast," the statue continued, its tones making Korda's ears ring.

"Before the press of the enemy, they never retreated. Here, Deter commemorates their sacrifice."

"Deter?" Korda said, resisting the impulse to rub his ears. "Is that the name of this planet?"

"Deter is the ruler of this universe!" the robot boomed indignantly. "He is the great commander who guards and guides us all through danger and strife! What kind of infidel are you?"

Seeing the enormous metal boot stirring as if the armored robot would grind him underfoot, Korda hastened to find an appropriate reply.

"I'm not from this universe," he said lamely. "Deter hired me to do some repair work for him. Unfortunately, you're standing right on the place I need to set up my equipment. Could you move to one side?"

"Ever did the heroes of the Fort hold fast," the robot said. "I shall not stir for a mere civilian!"

"But I'm here at Deter's request!" Korda protested. "You would not be retreating, just stepping to one side."

"I shall not stir for a civilian," the robot repeated stubbornly. "You shall not fool me."

Korda stepped away so that the robot would fall back into stasis. Rubbing his tortured ears, he sat on one of the benches. The PDA buzzed up and rested lightly on his shoulder.

"Blowing the damn thing up seems like a waste of good artwork and robotics," Korda said, "but I can't let it stand there and keep me from accessing magnetic north."

"I don't suppose that you could set the resonance tracer on its head?" Jester suggested.

"No good," Korda said. "The resonance tracer would need bottled time to function and the bottled time would activate the robot. I'm willing to bet anything that the robot's blaster works perfectly."

"Yeah," Jester sighed. "How about the UT? Will any of its settings help?"

Korda took out the device. "I can't see that the hammer or screwdriver will be of any help, but let's check the variable setting."

He touched a button and a faintly humming rod of blue light about as long as a knife blade sprang forth.

"A Force Rod," he said, "useful for all sorts of minor welding and repair jobs, but I'm afraid it doesn't have the punch we'd need to deal with this robot. In any case, even if it did have the power, I can't imagine the robot sitting by while we cut away at its base."

"Well, it was worth checking," Jester said.

"I wonder," Korda said, after a thoughtful pause, "if we could find this Fort the robot mentioned. Maybe I could get one of the 'heroes' there to come and talk with the robot."

"Gee, Boss, I don't know," Jester said. "There seems to be a whole lot of cities on this planet. I don't know how we could find one fort out of all of these buildings."

Korda rose to his feet. "There may be a depiction of the one we need here in this Garden of Honor. It would fit with the general mood. Will you stroll in the garden with me, lady?"

Jester giggled. "But of course, noble sir."

As they walked through the garden, they brought a whisper of time with them. Fish leapt from the ornamental ponds, flowers swayed in breezes that vanished seconds later, fragments of bird-song reached their ears.

None of the other statues proved to be robots, although Korda tested his bottled time on each as they walked by.

"That's further proof that we're meant to be able to move that big guy," Korda said. "If this garden was intended as a robotic tour of Urbs' martial history, then others would have their spiels as well."

"It's weird," Jester said. "This is a pretty new universe, right? How can it have a history of battles?"

"Good question," Korda said, "but actually, it's pretty simple. We just got what the robot was programmed to believe. If its programmer gave it a history of centuries of battles, then, as far as it is concerned, there've been centuries of battles."

"Right!" Jester said. "That was dumb of me."

"Not really," Korda said. "There are other possibilities as well. Time in this universe could run faster than that in Universe Prime. Charlie might have finished his work, say, fifty years ago, but if the time was set at four times normal, then two hundred years would have gone by."

"Wow!" Jester said. "Do you think that's the answer?"

"Honestly," Korda said, "no, I don't. Human life is

short enough, even with life-prolonging drugs. I can't believe anybody would voluntarily choose to burn their life up more quickly. I think an artificial history makes more sense. Speaking of which . . ."

The PDA bounced in the air. "I see it, Boss! There's a diorama over there!"

The diorama was something rather like a relief map built into beautifully sculpted terrain. It depicted a battle in progress.

Isolated from its surroundings by a ravine, a dark, blocky fortress stood besieged—almost certainly, the Fort. The enemy had gathered its forces on a rocky, barren plain on the far side of the ravine. Missile launchers were trained on the Fort. Soldiers with rifles and rocket launchers crouched in hastily dug trenches—presumably ready to shoot any who emerged from the Fort's protecting walls.

"Jester, I want you to scan the survey we took of the planet and see if you can locate the original of that Fort."

"I've already located it," the PDA reported smugly. "I'm projecting you a picture now. There's something you should see."

The image that appeared on the interior of Korda's glasses was virtually identical to the diorama, with one telling exception. Bodies lay sprawled on the rocky plain, a missile fired toward the Fort had been halted in mid-arc. The Fort itself had laser cannons deployed, defending a small cadre who had established a beachhead on the plain.

"That's very strange," Korda said. "The evidence would

seem to show that the battle is still in process!"

"Yeah," Jester answered. "Are you still certain you want to go there?"

"No," Korda replied, "but the alternative is admitting that Charlie Bell could design a blockade that I can solve only by resorting to brute force. My vanity, if nothing else, is on the line. Besides, how dangerous can a battlefield in stasis be?"

"The Fort is on the other side of the planet," Jester said. "We can get there most quickly by taking the ship."

Korda nodded. "Then that's what we'll do. Let's make certain that our flight plan and landing path won't activate any live ordinance. I'm beginning to suspect that on Urbs there may always be a battle raging."

This time, Korda did not let the *Jester's* computer fly the ship unassisted. Figuring that two alert minds were better than one, he strapped himself into the pilot's console. Realistically, he was actually taking the co-pilot's console, since the *Jester's* computer had reflexes far faster than those of any human.

Watching through the scanner link, Korda studied the cities spread out below. Most showed some sign of battle damage: bomb craters, the burned-out shells of buildings, permanent armament placements. In some, the sudden cessation of time had halted active battles.

Oddly, the uniforms worn by the soldiers were rarely repeated from region to region. Technology levels shifted as well. In some places the equipment was ultra-modern, in others, the warriors fought with sword and shield.

"Jes," Korda said thoughtfully, "I have an odd thought about this planet. It's almost too weird, though."

"Try me," Jester said. "I'm good at weird—I like you, don't I?"

Korda decided to ignore the comment. "At first I thought that we had stumbled on a world at war, but the mixture of technologies and uniforms suggests a nastier possibility."

"Yes?"

"What if this world is one vast war game?" Korda asked.

"Your thesis fits the available data," Jester said hesitantly, "but why would any sane person do that?"

"Who is saying that the person who ordered Urbs designed is sane?" Korda countered. "Wealth is a requirement. Sanity is not. That would certainly explain why Charlie Bell was so nervous when asked about his employer."

Uncharacteristically, Jester did not have a quick, sassy answer for him. Korda was trying to decide whether this made him more or less apprehensive when he felt the engines shift to signal an impending landing.

"I'm going to bring us in on the same side of the ravine as the Fort," Jester said. "I can't see any advantage to landing in the territory held by the Fort's enemies."

Korda nodded agreement, his own attention reserved for the ground-level scanners. The flat open plain surrounding the Fort looked so very tempting. What had kept the enemies from bombarding the Fort at closer range?

The near-omnipresent stasis made scanning difficult—the absence of time also meant the absence of heat, of sound, of the myriad little indications that he would usually use to detect danger points. As the situation stood, if he was not careful, he would not know there was danger until his own ship's bottled time activated it.

"Coming in," Jester announced. "Sixty seconds to ground contact. Bottled-time contact in forty-five seconds."

On the peripheral borders of his shades, Korda was aware of time ticking down. The flatness of the plain, its deceptive openness, still troubled him. The countdown was at twenty-two seconds when he suddenly yelled.

"Jes! Pull us up now! That's a minefield!"

The engines roared protest as the *Jester* pushed skyward. Korda felt his neck snap back at the sudden g-force. Only his padded headrest saved him from whiplash.

Below, the flat plain waited, deceptively innocent and calm, but Korda knew that had he waited only a few seconds more, even launching into the heavens might not have saved them. Once the bottled time activated the buried explosives, the backwash from the engines alone would have been enough to set them off.

Rubbing his hand along the back of his neck, he smiled. "Good job, Jester. You have better reflexes than I do."

"Thanks, Boss." The hologram appeared, smiling shyly,

her arms behind her back. She pulled out a bouquet of flowers and made as if to hand them to him. "And thanks for saving me. Those mines really would have smashed up my underside."

Korda touched the holographic bouquet. Of course, nothing was there, but the hologram seemed pleased that he had accepted her "gift."

"Is there any other good place for us to land?" he asked.

"I'm scanning," she said. "There's a field out beyond the copse of trees that borders the battlefield. I see a few deer on it—in stasis—so I'd guess that it isn't mined."

"Probably it's beyond the parameters of this particular war game," Korda guessed. "Let's try setting down there. I don't mind walking the mile or so back to the Fort. If I'm careful, I won't activate any of the enemies with my bottled time and I can talk with the defenders."

This time the *Jester* set down without incident. With the PDA bobbing at his shoulder, Korda trudged across the field toward the forest. Here he could see touches that definitely showed Charlie Bell's style. A waterfall cascaded over some rocks in a brook, falling from pool to pool with artifice too perfect to be entirely natural. Iridescent blue butterflies sipped nectar from ice-white flowers.

Charlie made pretty worlds. It must have really burned him to see this one turned into a war zone. Korda wondered how his old friend could have taken the contract. Perhaps he hadn't known what was planned until it was too late—or too dangerous—to back out.

Heading back to the Fort, Korda tromped through the wooded copse far less quietly than he would have liked—comforted by the fact that no one outside his time bubble could hear the noise. Once he reached the battlefield, he skirted the stasis-bound soldiers.

"When I reactivate time here," he muttered to himself, "the killing will continue. Does that make me a murderer?"

From the vicinity of his shoulder, he heard Jester snort disapprovingly. "I don't see how you could think that, Sugar Pop. Whoever started this war should worry about the morality of it, not you."

"I know," Korda said. "That is the rational answer, but look at that young man." He gestured to where a soldier lay on his side, one leg twisted at a right angle to his torso, blood frozen in mid-gush from a wound in his side. "When time resumes its flow, he will bleed to death in a few moments. Do I have the right to do that to him?"

"Do you have the right to leave the rest of this planet in stasis?" Jester countered. "Do you have the right to leave everyone here vulnerable to whoever triggered the stasis in the first place? Let me remind you, Great and Powerful One, whoever turned this place off didn't do it for the good of the universe of Urbs."

"Jester, we have no idea why Urbs has been put into stasis. I firmly expected to see evidence of grand scale theft, but all I see is a universe apparently devoted to war games—and that the games have stopped for now."

"Maybe the saboteurs are playing their own war

game," Jester suggested. "If so, they've won this move."

"That doesn't explain why similar action has been taken against Aurans," Korda said, shaking his head. "No, whatever the saboteurs' motives are, they are larger than the games that Urbs plays. What has me puzzled is that the saboteurs have at least one trained universe designer on their team. They must be paying very well to get his or her services, yet I do not see how they are making a profit. Of course, we have barely sampled the universe . . . . I babble. I simply don't have enough information to make a reasonable guess."

Korda walked a few paces before continuing. "I don't like having to act without knowing more of the situation. And I dislike knowing that when I carry out the job Conchita Devenu hired me to do, that young man and others like him will die."

The PDA buzzed in front of him, so that its smiling face was staring directly into his eyes.

"Tell me, Rene, how did you ever become a universe maker if you have such incredible scruples?"

He batted at the PDA. "Youthful arrogance, I suppose. Perhaps the scruples weren't there all along. Perhaps they developed with age. For all my supple skin and youthful appearance, I am centuries old, Jester. I hope I have learned something in all those years."

The metal sphere bobbed to the edge of the time field. "I just hope you haven't started thinking so much that you'll get yourself killed while you're puzzling out the ethics of a situation."

Korda smiled sadly and gestured at the torn bodies on the battlefield. "There are far worse ways to die, Jester. I can promise you that."

They finished crossing the battlefield in silence. At the edge of the ravine a solid metal pillar-shaped scanner held a solitary vigil. When they were close enough that the bottled time activated it, it flashed a terse readout.

"Bridge access restricted to loyal soldiers of the Fort. Stand and be recognized."

Korda frowned. "I guess they won't want visitors. How am I going to convince that stupid robot to move?"

"There's a rocket launcher on the battlefield," Jester said. "That would probably do the trick."

"No," Korda said decisively. "I was just talking about my discomfort with using battle as a solution for all problems. I'd feel like a real hypocrite if I did that."

"Then what are you going to do, Boss?" the voice from the PDA sounded plaintive. "We're going to run out of bottled time if you keep wandering around out here."

Korda checked the time-supply readout on the inside of his mirrored glasses. The amount available had dropped, but there was plenty left.

"I have an idea," he said. "Just watch."

Slowly, trying his best to ignore the carnage around him. Korda returned to the battlefield. He found a dead soldier who had fallen with the banner of Urbs still clutched in one hand. The standard bearer had been killed by a shot that left his black plasteel uniform fairly undamaged. Korda carefully removed the soldier's full-face helmet and looked into his dead eyes.

"I need to take your uniform, Lieutenant," he said, "for the good of Urbs."

The soldier stared blankly, but Korda felt a bit better about his looting as he stripped the young man's uniform from him. On impulse, he pulled the battle standard from under its fallen bearer as well. Then, gently, he closed the soldier's eyes.

"How do you know if you have the right stuff, Boss?" Jester asked.

"The device," he indicated the design, an irregular crescent set with two small circles silk-screened on the standard, "matches the device on the scanner and on the Fort."

"I get it," she said. "Good thinking! Now, can we go back to the ship?"

"I think so," he said. "I don't see any need to get into the Fort now. With these I should be able to fool the robot into believing I'm a soldier from the Fort."

The *Jester* made the trip back to the Garden of Honor swiftly. Korda barely had time to change into the soldier's uniform and brush the worst of the dirt off the standard.

"How do I look, Jester?" he said, checking his reflection in a mirror.

"Really dangerous," she said. "What is it about a man in uniform? Gets a girl every time."

Korda refrained from commenting that a ship's computer could hardly be qualified as a girl. Jester would not appreciate the reminder. She might even get sulky.

Why had he set himself up for problems like this?

The raven cawed and took a few more flaps in its interrupted flight as Korda passed beneath it. After the near silence of his passage, the sudden hoarse sound made Korda jump.

"Good thing that's all it did, huh, Boss?" Jester commented slyly through her PDA.

Korda groaned but otherwise decided that dignity forbade an answer. Approaching the robot, he struck what he hoped was a military pose.

"Welcome to the Garden of Honor," the robot boomed. "Heroes of the Fort are ever welcome in this place."

Good, he had fooled it. Now for the tricky part.

"Comrade in arms," he said. "I bring you new orders from Lord Deter. You are needed on the battlefield. I am to take your post here."

There was a grinding of metal against metal as the robot turned its helmeted head to study him.

"That is highly irregular," it said.

Inspired, Korda held out the standard from the Fort. Despite his best efforts to clean it, it was still rather bedraggled.

"The battle rages fiercely," he declaimed, thinking that he sounded rather like an old war movie. "The men at the Fort need this to inspire them to carry on. I cannot travel the distance quickly enough, but with your great size . . ."

"Say no more, brother-in-arms," the robot boomed.

"I will carry the banner to the Fort. Guard my post well!"

"I will!" Korda said. Joy that he had been able to do this without damaging the steadfast metal soldier gave his voice true intensity. "I promise!"

The robot stepped from the pedestal. Wanting it fully clear, Korda moved so that his bottled time would keep it active for a few more steps. What should have happened was that, when the time field was withdrawn, the robot would lumber to a halt. What actually happened was far more frightening.

A beam of yellow-white light flashed out, striking the robot in the center of its glistening chest armor. For a moment, the metal warrior simply froze in place, then it was limed in a yellow-white field. There was a flash that burnt itself into Korda's retina even as his shades adjusted to compensate. When he blinked the spots from his eyes, the robot had vanished.

"Something blew it away!" Jester said, her voice trembling. "One shot and it was gone! Rene, it could have hit you!"

"I know," Korda said. "Either the height of the robot threw the aim off or whoever it was meant to take out the robot all along."

The PDA bobbed to face him. "You know what this means, Boss, don't you?"

Korda nodded. "It means that there is someone else active in a universe that is supposed to be completely frozen in time."

"And whoever it is has some pretty big guns," Jester

added. "Let's get that resonance tracer set up. The sooner I have you safe inside the ship's armor the better I'll feel."

Swinging his pack from his shoulders, Korda hauled out the resonance tracer. "Jester, for once, I couldn't agree with you more."

V

Back aboard the *Jester*, Korda recharged his harness of bottled time and then concealed it as best as he could under the trooper uniform. It made the lines a bit bulky, but he thought it would pass. The resonance tracer's reading, perhaps predictably, led Korda back to the Fort. To his supreme satisfaction, the Fort's scanner activated the mechanical bridge without hesitation.

"Come on, Jester," he said, as the metal platform started to extend. "We have places to go."

"And people to see," she said. "This is getting easier. Perhaps the shot that blasted the robot was a fluke. I was really worried while you were out there in the open, but nothing happened."

Korda decided not to tell her that the robot's unseen assailant might have chosen not to fire because a shot at Korda on the battlefield could have ruined the scanner or some other part of the elaborate diorama. Jester was very good at logical deduction, but she didn't have a human's capacity for morbid imaginings.

His shoulders were tense as he walked out over the bridge half-expecting to feel the impact of a bullet or laser, but he passed unmolested. The scanner at the Fort's massive blast doors recognized his uniform, opening the portal just enough to let him enter.

Once he was inside and the doors safely closed behind him, Korda pulled out the resonance tracer's direction finder. The resonance tracer itself, when activated, was too bulky to carry around, but the direction finder fit easily in one hand. A simple readout indicated the location of magnetic north.

"That corridor and possibly down," Korda said, already walking that way. He glanced over his shoulder. The quiet of the stasis-held building was eerie. He was also too aware that an enemy using bottled time could quite easily sneak up on him. There would be no sound to give away the other's position until they were close enough for their time spheres to overlap. The knowledge did not add to his confidence.

He strode down the silent corridors, trying hard not to keep looking over his shoulder. Each time he passed a door, he checked the direction finder. Time after time, the flashing arrow led him deeper and deeper into the heart of the Fort.

"Does this place give you the willies, Boss?" Jester asked.

"Yes, it does," he said honestly.

"Me, too," she said.

"How can a computer get the willies?" he asked, somewhat exasperated.

"Probabilities indicate that this building conceals

dangers to your health and well-being," she said promptly. "And that gives me the willies."

"Great," he said. "Just let me know if you spot any of these probabilities becoming realities . . . ."

His voice trailed off. While they talked, he had continued walking toward the heart of the Fort. Now, in a room to his left, he saw a strange and macabre sight.

A dark-haired, olive-skinned man clad in flowing desert robes was standing with his back to an armored section of wall, his hands bound behind him. Another man, this one in the uniform of Urbs, stood in front of him, apparently frozen in the act of tying a blindfold around the first man's eyes. Four soldiers with rifles held at ease waited across the room. A fifth rifle leaned against the wall.

"That's a firing squad!" Korda said.

"Looks like it," Jester agreed.

Korda walked a few steps into the room, carefully keeping his bottled time from activating any of the people within.

"Boss? What are you doing? The world key isn't that way!"

Korda continued into the room. "I can't leave a man to be shot!"

"Why not?" the Jester said. "He might deserve it."

"Jester . . ." Korda growled.

"Sorry, Boss." The voice from the PDA actually sounded contrite.

Korda examined the tableau before him. The prisoner

stood close enough to the man with the blindfold that
Korda could not activate one without activating the other.
Fortunately, the firing squad was positioned far enough
across the room that they could remain inactivated if he
was careful.

However, these were not figures of plastic or clay. They
were living, breathing people and if he made the wrong
choice one or more might die.

Decision made, Korda advanced on the prisoner. The
instant his bottled time touched the pair, the man with
the blindfold raised his arms to complete the interrupted motion.

"Hold it right there," Korda bluffed, his voice steady.
"I have a blaster aimed at your heart."

The Urbs soldier stiffened, then turned his head
slowly. "How did you get in here? Guards!"

The prisoner looked no less surprised. Korda imagined how *he* would feel if one moment he was preparing to be executed and the next he found a stranger
coming to the rescue.

"Your guards cannot come to you," Korda said to the
soldier. Without taking his eyes from the astonished soldier, Korda spoke to the prisoner. "Come over here beside
me."

With understandable alacrity, the prisoner moved to
obey. Seeing Korda was unarmed, the guard dove to where
his rifle leaned against the wall. As soon as his leap carried him outside the radius of Korda's bottled time, he
was frozen in midair.

"By Allah!" the prisoner swore. "That is astonishing. What manner of sorcerer are you? Did Sheikh Dwistor send you to save me?"

Korda grinned and shook his head.

"I am no sorcerer. I simply took advantage of the guard's ignorance. Had he not tried to attack me, the result would have been much the same. I would have stepped out of his range and the stasis would have claimed him again—although in a less spectacular fashion."

"Stasis? Again?" The prisoner was clearly confused. "I do not think that you are Dwistor's man. Who are you?"

"My name is Rene Korda and this," he answered, gesturing at the PDA hovering over his shoulder, "is Jester. Who are you?"

"I am Tico Higgins of Aurans," the man said, with a curious glance at the PDA.

"Glad to meet you, Mr. Higgins."

Korda offered his hand. Hesitating for only a moment, Higgins gave him a firm handclasp, then he bowed deeply from the waist.

"I am also pleased to meet you, Mr. Korda." He smiled, formality vanishing, his teeth twinkling white within his dark beard. "Actually I am more than 'pleased'—I am delighted! Had you not come when you did, I would most certainly be dead."

"Perhaps not as soon as you might think," Korda said, leading the way out of the room. "I wonder what the firing squad will think when they find you vanished?"

"Possibly they will think I am a sorcerer and conjured

myself away," Higgins said. "The people of Urbs have always been wary of the sorcery of Aurans. We can't seem to get through to them that the power does not work outside the specialized physics of our universe."

"So the physics of Aurans permits magic," Korda said. Already his impulsive rescue attempt was reaping rewards.

"That's right," Higgins said. "It's not the flamboyant, flashy magic of Cabal. It manifests more in creatures and physical anomalies. Still, we have our share of sorcerers. I never bothered to disabuse the Urbanites of their belief that I was one."

Korda found a comfortable bench and offered Tico Higgins water and rations from his pack. Higgins accepted both. The PDA rose to the highest limits of the time bubble, spinning slightly as she kept watch.

"They kept me without food and water in the holding cells," Higgins said around a mouthful of vita-bread. "I suppose they thought they could weaken my will and make me confess. They forget that a desert dweller is accustomed to doing without food and water. Still, we take it when it's offered and there is no pleasure in doing without."

"Why were they holding you prisoner, Higgins?" Korda asked. "From what you said before, I had the impression that you had visited Urbs frequently."

Higgins spread his hands and shrugged in puzzlement. "I have no idea, Mr. Korda. Sheikh Dwistor has frequently sent me here on diplomatic missions. We trade with Urbs in raw metals and silicon chips in return for machinery. I was negotiating with the Minister of Trade when some guards marched me off to a jet flyer and took me to the Fort."

"Did they say what crime you were accused of, Mr. Higgins?" Korda asked.

"Espionage!" Tico Higgins flung up his hands. "Me! I have been a trusted emissary from Aurans for years."

"Still, they must have had a reason for believing . . . ." Korda rubbed his chin. "Tell me, what were the questions they asked you?"

Higgins frowned. "They wanted to know about my 'other ship.' I have no ship but the one that bore me here from Aurans and that one remained in the hangar in Ground Zero."

"Ground Zero?" Korda asked.

"The capital city of Urbs," Higgins explained. "An expression of Deter's peculiar sense of humor. I asked the Minister of Trade about it once and he said that in a nuclear war the capital city is always at ground zero. Deter, apparently, had no desire to hide from that knowledge."

"Deter . . ." Korda mused. "Have you ever met him?"

"Sands! Yes, I have." Higgins shuddered as if the memory was not a pleasant one. "He's nothing but a brain— a brain in an antigravity case. All of his communication is done through mechanical devices."

"A brain in a box, ruler of an entire universe." Korda shook his head in puzzlement. "Somehow I expected something else—a tank, a war robot, a missile. Given the Urbanite obsession with war, why would Deter settle for something so mundane?"

Higgins shrugged. "Asking questions like that is not part of my job. My job is to arrange trade negotiations for Dwistor. Certainly the situation on Urbs isn't going to make *that* any easier."

Korda rose from the bench and packed away the remains of his supplies. "Do you want to help me reactivate this universe?"

Higgins looked him squarely in the eye. "Let me put it to you another way. I have a duty to Aurans. If I stay here and help you, I may learn things that Urbs would rather not have a stranger know. Therefore, I endanger not only my usefulness to my ruler, but my own life. I am engaged to marry a lovely young woman who will mourn if I fail to return. Do you think I should remain?"

"No one needs to know you helped me," Korda countered.

"We cannot be certain of that," Higgins said. "No, I cannot help you. If you insist, you may as well march me back in front of the firing squad."

Korda shook his head. "I could not do that. I could simply walk away from you here. You would return to stasis. Then, as soon as I succeeded in my mission and time returned you could make your escape."

Higgins studied him. "That's a long shot for a man with no vessel and no weapons."

"True," Korda said, "but still better odds than a firing

squad."

"I accept that." Higgins leaned back against the wall. "Very well. Walk away. I will even wish you luck—and mean it."

Korda studied him, remembering the missile blast that had come from nowhere to destroy the robot in the Garden of Honor. If he left Tico Higgins here he would be putting the man at risk—a stupid thing to do after saving his life.

Rene Korda sighed. "I think the wisest thing for me to do would be to escort you to your ship at Ground Zero. I can supply you with enough bottled time for you to clear the universe. After that, you're on your own."

Higgins beamed as he leapt to his feet. "Allah is wise and merciful! He sends his servant a protector in the darkness of Urbs. Korda is the servant of the great God!"

Even Jester, who had been unwontedly silent, had no clever response for this outrageous claim.

The *Jester* carried them unmolested to the city of Ground Zero. The city was a lovely, futuristic place, but like so much of what Korda had seen on Urbs, it was structured for war, not for peace.

Tidy signs indicated the location of bomb shelters. Soldiers wearing the Urban emblem stood at intersections, deadly blaster rifles slung from shoulder harnesses. The vehicles that hovered frozen over the streets were armed and armored, as if in preparation for a riot or an invasion.

Even the monorail that twirled and twined about the city's glass and steel towers, like a string of pearls in a debutante's hair, bore concealed laser canons.

"Ground Zero," Jester announced over the ship's intercom, "though it looks more like a death zone to me. I'm bringing us in on a landing pad on the building Tico indicated was the capital center—and don't worry. This time I scanned for mines."

Korda patted the arm of his chair. "Very good, Jes. I'll take Tico to his ship, collect whatever information may be useful, and then we'll head back to the Fort and finish our job."

"Right!" The PDA bobbed out of its holding rack. "And I'll be ready to keep you out of trouble all the way."

Tico Higgins led the way across the rooftop landing field to a lift-shaft. Over one shoulder he had slung a pack with a supply of bottled time for his own ship.

"This lift has self-contained power," he said. "One of Deter's men was bragging about it one day. A hit on the central power unit would only slow functions down, not stop them."

"For us," Korda said, moving up to the control panel and punching a button, "it means that our bottled time will still make machinery operate. Good."

The lift carried them almost soundlessly several levels down, across, and then down again. Tico Higgins kept a wary eye on the readouts, as if fearing that if he looked away the elevator might carry him somewhere else entirely.

"You seem edgy," Korda observed.

"Dread," Tico Higgins replied succinctly. "I fear that I will never leave this place alive. There may be no magic in Urbs, but still I feel as if my doom is near."

The PDA brought its smiling face close to Higgins'. "Don't worry, Tico. You'll be home to the deserts and your sweetie soon enough."

"I hope so." Higgins paused. "My report will not please Dwistor. He is a fair man, in his way, but very touchy about what he perceives as slights to his honor. If he decides that my arrest was such a slight, he could enter into war with Urbs and I fear we would lose such a war. We play at battle with swords and archery. Urbs knows nothing but war in many forms."

The lift stopped with a faint thump. Higgins hurried forth almost before the doors had opened. Korda followed with equal haste lest the anxious man find himself inadvertently exceeding the limits of the bottled time.

"We'll help you mount the bottled time on your ship," Korda said. "Then you must be on your way as quickly as possible. You only have a limited amount of time."

"How odd it is when metaphor becomes literal truth," Tico Higgins commented. "There is my ship—the little khaki vee-wing. I call her the *Whirlwind*."

"Pretty name for a pretty ship," Korda said.

"And a reminder of my home," Higgins said. "Whirlwinds are sometimes useful for transportation—a thing you might remember if you come there."

Korda wrinkled his brow in puzzlement, but Higgins did not give him time to ask questions. Already he was opening up the ship's engine panels. With Jester supplying instructions relayed from the *Jester's* library, the two men made short work of mounting the bottled time in place.

"Good luck," Korda said as Higgins climbed into the cockpit.

Higgins, safe now within his own bottled time, waved cheerfully. "I will trust in Allah. Luck is a capricious deity. Thank you for the service you have done me. Perhaps we will meet again!"

Korda stepped clear of the ship, still waving. It would not do for him to be too close when Tico Higgins fired up the *Whirlwind*.

"Boss?" Jester asked as they rode the lift to an observation platform from which they could see Higgins safely away. "Can I ask you a question?"

"You already have," he said, then relented. "Yes, what do you want to know?"

"Why didn't you ever tell Tico Higgins that Aurans was in stasis? If the Terran Regional Representative's report was true, he's going to get home and end up frozen."

"True," Korda said, "but if I told him while he was here, he might have decided that Urbs was in some way guilty and gone on a vendetta. He seemed a pleasant enough person, but people react oddly when they believe their home is in danger."

"Oh," Jester said, the PDA holding still in the air as if the computer was deep in thought. "That was a good idea."

"Thank you, Jes," Korda said. Then he raised a hand and pointed. "There goes Tico, safely away despite all his feelings of dread . . . ."

His words trailed off. Even as he spoke, red beams of light shot from the clouds. Tico Higgins turned the *Whirlwind* on her side in time to miss all but a grazing shot. Trailing a faint plume of smoke, the spaceship gained altitude and speed.

Other bolts of laser light shot forth, but none appeared to touch the ship. Within seconds, the *Whirlwind* was lost to sight.

"Maybe I shouldn't be so quick to mock his intuitions," Korda said slowly.

"Boss, who shot at him?" Jester's tone was worried.

"Perhaps the bottled time we mounted on the *Whirlwind* was enough to activate an automatic weapons platform," Korda said. "These Urbanites must have all sorts of autodefenses. Right?"

"Right," Jester said, but her tone said she was not convinced.

Considering the course of recent events, Korda was not certain that he was, either. He glanced toward the sky. Under stasis, it was still. Clouds hung like fluffy bits of cotton glued onto blue construction paper by a kindergartner. Yet behind that calm vista lurked weapons capable of blowing a starship from the skies.

"Let's get out of here, Jes," Korda said, heading back into the main building from the observation platform. "I've changed my mind about scouting further. We'll get back to the Fort, find the world key, and finish the job we came for."

"And what job might that be?" said a hissing voice.

"Jes, this is no time for games," Korda said, spinning in the direction of the voice.

"Boss, I didn't say anything." The PDA bobbed forward a few inches. "*It* did!"

Korda blinked in astonishment, his hand dropping to his blaster. A hulking bipedal reptile stood at the end of the corridor, effectively blocking his exit. It wore a metallic tunic emblazoned with the emblem of Urbs and carried a large laser cannon—the type that usually took a human both arms and a tripod to manipulate—tucked lightly under one arm.

The two human guards flanking it looked so small and ineffective that Korda had to forcibly remind himself how dangerous the blasters they held leveled at him were.

All three of them stood within faintly glowing halos of bottled time. Apparently, as Tico Higgins had indicated, the Urbs military really did prepare for all eventualities.

"Do not move or we will vaporize you," the reptile said, "and dig what information we need from the computer in your ship."

"You just try," the PDA muttered furiously. "I'll show you what for!"

"Hush, Jester," Korda said. "Let me handle this."

He lifted his hands, turning the palms outward so that the reptile and its human goons could easily see that they were empty.

"You have the advantage of me," Korda said smoothly. "I fear that I do not know who you are or what I have done to merit your attention."

The reptile bared needle-sharp teeth at him. "I am Grrn'scal of the Council of the Wise. You are a spy and an invader."

Korda shook his head. "I am not a spy."

"Do you deny that you assisted the spy from Aurans to escape?" Grrn'scal's voice rasped unpleasantly.

"Tico Higgins was a trade negotiator," Korda said. "I merely helped to prevent the irremediable wrong that would have occurred if your firing squad had executed him."

"So you admit to assisting him!" Grrn'scal's tone was smugly satisfied. "Very good. Your trial shall not unduly waste the time of the Council of the Wise."

"Trial?" Korda said. "For what?"

"For spying," Grrn'scal said. "I thought you understood that, foolish human."

"But I just told you I have done nothing wrong!" Korda protested.

Grrn'scal only chuckled, an unpleasant sound that would not have been recognizable as humor if his guards had not smiled.

"Put your hands on the top of your head and march!" Grrn'scal ordered, waving the nose of his laser cannon as if the weapon weighed nothing at all. "We cannot keep the council waiting."

Looking down the barrels of three weapons, any one

of which could quite easily end his tenure in this universe—
or any other—Rene Korda folded his hands on top of his
head and marched.

"Lead on, gentlemen," he said. "I look forward to
meeting the Council of the Wise."

"Liar!" the PDA whispered in his ear like the voice
of his conscience.

"You're right," Korda whispered back. "But what else
could I say?"

VI

Grrn'scal took him off to a holding cell where he kept Korda waiting for several hours—long enough that he began to worry that his bottled time would run out before he could get back to *Jester* and recharge his supply. When his guards refused to give him either water or food, Korda knew that the wait was meant to break his nerve. In response, he leaned his head against the wall and pretended to doze.

At last they opened the cell and marched him to the Council Chamber. The Council of the Wise met in an oval room. A variety of efficient but somehow beautiful control panels embellished the walls. An oval table of polished silvery metal dominated the center of the room. Around this table were seated what had to be the councilors.

Korda noted with some relief that the room had its own supply of bottled time and knew that his personal unit had switched to "stand-by" as soon as he crossed the threshold.

Grrn'scal's human lackeys positioned Korda on a raised platform at the foot of the table. Then they snapped a pair of electronic cuffs on him and fastened his wrists to a railing at the front of the platform. Given the number of weapons pointed at him, Korda did not think it wise to argue. Instead, the PDA nestled almost out of sight near the back of his neck, Korda turned his attention to studying the assembled councilors.

They were an eclectic lot. On the right side of the table sat an elegant brass-toned humanoid robot, a human wearing the hooded cassock of the Sages' Guild (from which a length of white beard emerged), and an alien with three eyes.

On the left side of the table sat another cassocked figure, but something about the odd lumps and bulges within the official cassock made Korda suspect that whoever—or whatever—wore the garment was other than human. To the right of the alien Sage was a large chair, specially reinforced. Korda was only slightly surprised to see Grrn'scal snap off his bottled time and take this seat. The reptile set his laser cannon on the table, angling its barrel directly at where Korda stood.

However, Korda only gave peripheral attention to the five councilors, for at the head of the table hovered a box holding a creature who could be no other than Deter. The grav case was an opaque mottled green that gave only slight hints of the brain within. Various waldos extruded from the case. Right now, one was occupied with a recording device; another held a flat information disk.

Motioning for his two guards to take posts outside the council room door, Grrn'scal slid a second information

"Some of the merchant companies in Terran regional space that regularly do business with Urbs became concerned when they could not make contact with your universe," he said. "They investigated far enough to see that the universe was in stasis. Since they had not been informed that there would be an interruption in the normal shipping schedule, they assumed that there was trouble."

With a slight bow to Deter, the bronze-finished robot rose. Now that it was standing, Korda could see that it had a vaguely female shape. Its voice when it addressed Korda was light and melodious.

"Korda, why were you contacted rather than another universe creator?"

"As your own records note," Korda replied, "I am one of the best in my field. As you may know, reactivating your universe would take someone with specialized knowledge and skills."

"So would turning a universe off," Deter said, after the robot had resumed its seat. "How do we know that you are not merely hiding the fact that you are the one who deactivated the universe?"

Korda frowned. "Surely you can check my story. Your own recording devices on the borders between your universe and Universe Prime would confirm when I entered this universe."

"Cameras can be gimmicked to give a false report," Deter said. "Do any of the councilors have any other questions before we move into the charges against the prisoner?"

The human Sage bowed to Deter and then rose. The

hood of his cassock fell back, revealing a white-bearded face almost too perfectly noble and wise. Wings of white hair fell to his shoulders. His blue eyes were clear and lightly framed with lines.

"I do, my lord," he said. "Korda, you have been retired for the last decade. What about this job—assuming for a moment that we accept your explanation that you were indeed hired to investigate the stasis in Urbs—could draw you from retirement?"

Again Korda opted for a half-truth, although he suspected that his answer would completely alienate Sage Qyil. It could not be helped. These people were sensitive about their universal security. Knowing that Korda had taken the job in part for the challenge of deciphering their safeguards and proving himself at least as talented as the mysterious saboteur would not make them feel at all comfortable.

"They offered me a great deal of money," he said. "Although I am wealthy, my dream is to someday craft a universe of my own. I am beginning to see that I have expensive tastes."

Sage Qyil shook its head—or were those heads under the cassock? The human Sage, however, nodded as if satisfied. He bowed again to Deter.

"No further questions, my lord."

"Thank you, Marcus." Deter said. "We will now proceed to the reading of the charges against the prisoner. Councilors, refer to your readers for full text of the laws and punishments regarding these crimes."

Using the distraction while the councilors turned on their readers and called up the appropriate files as cover, Korda subvocalized a comment to Jester through the microphone in the fabric of his collar.

"*This entire room is under bottled time,*" he said. "*Can you locate the activation unit? If we can turn it off, then we may have a chance to escape.*"

"RIGHT," Jester said, her words printed on the readline in his shades. "BOSS, REMEMBER THAT YOUR BOTTLED TIME WAS DEPLETED IN THE HOLDING CELL. YOU'LL HAVE LESS THAN AN HOUR TO GET BACK TO THE *JESTER* BEFORE IT RUNS OUT."

"*I remember,*" Korda assured her. "*Check your memory against the route we took to get here. You can guide me out by the fastest path.*"

"GOTCHA," she promised. "BOSS, THERE'S SOMETHING ODD ABOUT THIS COUNCIL. LOOK AT DETER'S GRAV BOX WHEN ONE OF THE COUNCILORS SPEAKS. SOMETHING CHANGES . . . ."

Anything else she would have said was cut off when Deter rapped the gavel that he held in one of his waldos against the table.

"Rene Korda, the charges against you include trespassing within a private universe, espionage, sabotage, and interfering with officers of the law in the course of their authorized duties. How do you plead?"

As much as he wanted to imitate an actor in a video drama and send a ringing "Not Guilty" into the council chamber, Korda knew he could not. Technically, he was guilty of at least two of the charges presented and had already as much as confessed to them.

He took a deep breath. "Lord Deter, I plead guilty to two of the charges: trespassing and interfering with officers of the law. Of the more serious charges of espionage and sabotage, I plead not guilty."

There was a stir among the various councilors. Clearly, they had expected him either to surrender or to bluster.

Deter spoke. "According to the laws of Urbs, the prisoner is entitled to a representative from among our numbers. Marcus, since you are human, I appoint you to represent the prisoner."

Korda relaxed marginally. He had expected Deter to name someone else—perhaps Grrn'scal, who had yet to stop glowering at him, or the three-eyed alien who had been sitting as passively as a wax dummy. Sages were known throughout inhabited space for their wisdom and training in a wide variety of subjects.

His momentary relief faded as quickly as it had arisen. Sage Marcus was a member of Deter's Council of the Wise. Certainly, Korda could expect little more than well-governed neutrality from him.

Sage Marcus rose and bowed to Deter. "My lord Deter, I thank you for giving me this responsible position. I will do my best to respect your laws while defending my client."

Deter rapped the table with his gavel. "We may as well settle first the charges to which the prisoner has pleaded guilty. R-2F, please present the case for trespass against the prisoner."

The bronze-finished robot rose, bowed to Deter, and began. "The prisoner, one Rene Korda of Earth, pleads guilty to the charge that on or before the present date, he did enter the universe of Urbs without authorized permission of Lord Deter . . . ."

As her pleasant, melodious voice continued outlining the charge in exasperating detail, Korda allowed his gaze to drift away from her to Deter's gravity box. What had Jester meant when she said there was something odd about it? It looked just as it always had—opaque plastic with shadows within, waldos holding a variety of objects . . . .

R-2F finished speaking, bowed to Deter, and reseated herself. Korda barely noticed, his attention completely given to studying Deter.

Deter spoke next. "Sage Marcus, would you present any defense of your client. Please remember that if his trespassing can be justified within the laws of Urbs, then his sentence will be less severe."

"Thank you, my lord," Sage Marcus said, prefacing his remarks with the customary bow. "My client claims that . . . ."

Marcus droned on, repeating Korda's tale of being hired to investigate Urbs for some merchants. Hardly hearing the flow of the words, Korda stared at Deter, willing Marcus to finish speaking so that he could confirm the suspicion that was growing in him.

When Marcus finished, the Sage bowed and resumed

his seat. Korda watched carefully.

Yes! He had it!

He watched as Deter directed Grrn'scal to present the case against Korda for interfering with officers of the law. Now that he knew what to look for, the change within Deter's grav box was obvious. Each time Deter indicated a new speaker, the shadow within the grav box lightened, as if the brain within was suddenly no longer there!

Impatience grew as he listened to the farce of the trial unfolding. One by one, the charges against him were examined, Sage Marcus presented counterarguments, the prosecuting councilor cross-examined, and then Deter moved the court onto the next charge. It was brilliantly done and had Korda not seen through the deceit involved, he would have been terrified, for it was quite evident that he was going to be found guilty on all four charges.

Anger replaced terror, however—anger and a certain peculiar gratitude that Deter wanted to present this sham trial. At least the trial was giving the PDA time to make her stealthy examination of the council chamber.

Sage Marcus was presenting his argument against the charges of sabotage when the PDA bobbed up behind Korda's ear.

"BOSS," she printed on his readline, "I'VE LOCATED THE BOTTLED TIME FOR THIS ROOM. IT'S ALMOST DIRECTLY BEHIND YOU. IF I HAD TURNED RIGHT INSTEAD OF LEFT I WOULD HAVE FOUND IT ALMOST RIGHT AWAY."

She seemed so forlorn that Korda wanted to smile at

her in reassurance. Right now, he couldn't afford to give the show away.

"*Good work*," he subvocalized. "*Drop down out of sight below the level of the table and see if you can figure out how to undo these cuffs. Whatever you do, stay out of sight.*"

"GOTCHA, SUGAR POP," she answered, covering her descent behind the bulk of his torso.

Korda spoke aloud, completely ignoring the flow of Sage Marcus's words. "Hey, Grrn'scal, I think Marcus is going to have trouble with everyone's charges but yours. You're about as lousy a speaker as I've ever heard."

His eyes slightly narrowed, Korda watched Deter's grav box. Yes, there it was. Darkening as the brain returned to home base for a moment, then lightening as Deter teleported to Grrn'scal.

Jester had put him onto it—Korda owed it to her. Without the computer's suspicions, he would never have caught on that there was no "Council of the Wise"—there was only Deter manipulating a variety of mechanical bodies. The ritualized bow was to permit Deter time to teleport between bodies. Probably each mechanical body had its own series of automatic motions so that no one would notice when they were empty. Any silence would be taken as respect both for Lord Deter and for the serious nature of the business at hand.

"Korda!" Grrn'scal roared, his fangs flashing as he scooped up his laser cannon. "I could blow you away as a fit reward for your impudence."

"Why don't you?" Korda taunted. "Your boss is going

to have me shot anyhow. Why don't we get it over with so you can get on with whatever other important business you people have—like trying to decide who can suck up to Deter best!"

Grrn'scal roared with inarticulate anger. The cannon leveled its aim.

Feeling slightly foolish, Korda started hopping up and down in the prisoner's box, jumping as high as his cuffs would permit.

"Boing! Boing!" he laughed. "It's a kangaroo court and you all are a bunch of dumb bouncing bunnies! Some rulers for a world of warriors!"

As he had hoped, this last was too much for Grrn'scal —or rather, for Deter. Korda saw the reptile's massive finger tighten on the trigger, saw the tip of the laser glow. Then he dropped, falling to the floor in midbounce.

The laser beam shot over his head, coming so close that he felt his hair crackle. His bouncing, however, had shown him the precise limits of motion that his cuffs permitted and he escaped injury.

From the sudden lack of sound and the change in the quality of the echoes, Korda knew that he had succeeded in making "Grrn'scal" blow out the room's bottled time. Now all that remained was escaping.

Jester's PDA floated alongside the cuffs and played a quick electronic waltz.

"They're off, Boss," she said. "Let's blow this popshop!"

He rose and, with effort, scooped up the laser cannon

in both arms.

"We're going to need to deal with the guards outside this room," he said. "You open the door for me."

"Right!"

It is amazing how much a laser cannon big enough to hole an armored tank does to convince people to be reasonable. At Korda's polite request, the two guards threw away first their weapons, then their bottled time—effectively putting themselves into stasis.

Korda retrieved the latter and took one of the hand-held blasters the guards had discarded. The laser cannon was too heavy to be truly useful, so Korda left it on the floor—first fusing the triggering mechanism with the Force Rod setting on his UT.

As an afterthought, he took the medals and officer's insignia from one of the guards' tunics. If Urbs was as bound by military hierarchy as he was coming to believe, they could come in handy.

"Now what?" the PDA asked.

"We do the job we were hired for and reactivate this universe," Korda said.

"You mean you're not going back in there and shooting Deter?" Jester asked, her voice plaintive.

"No," Korda said, starting off down the hallway. "We weren't hired to do that. By his lights, Deter may have even been in the right."

"But he was going to have you killed!" Jester said.

"True," Korda agreed, "but by luring him into Grrn'scal's body I was able to deactivate his ability to move through stasis. Remember? Grrn'scal turned off his bottled time when we came into the council chamber. I'd guessed that Deter would have some on standby in his own grav box, but I gambled that he wouldn't have outfitted each of his 'bodies' that way."

"Quite a gamble, Sugar Pop," Jester said admiringly.

"Not really," Korda said. "If he had been equipped with bottled time I still should have had the jump on him and could have taken his laser cannon then."

"And if you couldn't have gotten to it in time?" Jester asked.

Korda chuckled. "I would have dived under the table and hoped that Deter didn't want to shoot his own council chamber up any more than he already had."

They regained the *Jester* without further difficulty. After launching them back into the stratosphere, Jester appeared on her holopad. The expression on her pixie features was pensive.

"Boss, do you really want me to set course for the Fort?"

Korda nodded. "That's where the resonance tracer told us the world key is located. Don't forget. I have a job to do."

"But Urbs is . . . ," Jester gestured widely, waving her hands. "Urbs is such an awful place. Shouldn't we just leave it shut down?"

Korda leaned back in the bridge command chair, trying to seem relaxed, although Jester's question had hit on some of his own discomfort. His interview with the

Council of the Wise had only added to his feeling that the motives of the saboteurs must be more complicated than he had first supposed. Still, even though his profession was highly specialized, he couldn't begin to guess who might be the universe designer involved. As his research had shown, even the best of his colleagues could be hired simply for a large fee.

"I know that Urbs doesn't seem like a great way to use a universe, but the laws do allow for freedom of choice. If I don't do my job, I'm condemning an entire civilization to indefinite imprisonment."

"But—"

"No buts, Jester," Korda said firmly. "Whoever deactivated Urbs has access to bottled time. At the very least, by reactivating the universe, I'm going to make indiscriminate looting a lot harder."

"But, Deter has bottled time," Jester said. "Couldn't he reactivate the world key?"

"Possibly," Korda said, "but it's a specialized job. Not everyone who knows how to fly a starship knows how to fix the engines."

"You do!" Jester said, flirtatiously. "And it tickles when you recalibrate my settings!"

"Jester," Korda said, refusing to be distracted, "my point is that Deter may not know how to reactivate his universe. I do. Get it?"

"Yes, Oh Great and Powerful Master of Time and Space," Jester sighed. "My readouts tell me that we're coming in on the Fort. Do you want me to set us down outside the woods?"

"That seems wisest." Korda rose from the command chair. "I'll go get my gear and put my Urbs uniform back on."

"Aren't you going to stop for lunch?" Jester asked.

"Not now," Korda said. "This job should go smoothly enough now. I'll eat once we're en route to Aurans."

Although Korda kept alert for possible assassins or soldiers, they regained the Fort without difficulty. Once inside the black metal walls, he pulled out the direction finder and flipped it on. The little arrows blinked obediently.

"Jester," he said, "this time we'll use the extra bottled time so you can scout ahead. Make certain that you stay clear of any people or electronics."

"Right," she said. "I wouldn't want my bottled time to make them active."

"I'll be following, so don't get too far ahead," Korda cautioned.

"Right!" she repeated. Then the grinning sphere buzzed off down the corridor.

With suspiciously little trouble, they made their way to a lift-shaft whose doors opened obediently when Korda paused in front of them.

"Which way, Boss?"

"Down," Korda said. "All the way down, I'd guess."

At each level they paused, but the direction finder's arrow pointed steadily into the bowels of the Fort. When they reached the lowest level and the door slid open,

Korda stepped out into the corridor and then paused.

"Do you hear that, Jes?" he whispered.

"Voices!" she said, somehow managing to make her mechanical eyes seem wider. "Someone here has bottled time."

"Probably one of Deter's emergency measures," Korda said. He motioned the PDA ahead. "You scout, but be sure to stay out of sight. Deter's soldiers may shoot first—especially if they've been notified of our escape."

The PDA flitted down the corridor. He followed more slowly. A few moments later a message line marched across the bottom of his shades.

"BOSS, I WANT TO BEAM YOU AN IMAGE. THIS IS TOO WEIRD FOR WORDS."

Immediately following the message, an image took form in the shades' interior. Although it was superficially quite solid and complete, if Korda tried he could see through the image. A single command would banish it completely.

He saw a round room nearly overwhelmed by a shielded reactor and flanked by two balconies. On each of the balconies stood a man in the uniform of Urbs, a complex control panel in front of him. Far from being the impassive drones Korda had grown accustomed to finding on Urbs, the two soldiers were shouting angrily at each other.

"Keep away from that button. If you press it, you'll shut down the reactor and I'll have to start it up again before I can follow my orders!" the one on the right was shouting.

"Follow your orders!" the one on the left rejoined. "Joe! Have you thought about your orders? If you follow them, the reactor will blow and destroy everyone in this region—maybe everyone on this planet!"

"I know my duty, Frank," Joe responded. "Our planet has been invaded. We must destroy it rather than give it over to invaders."

Korda began advancing down the corridor as the men continued to argue. Soon he could hear their words with his ears as well as through the audio projectors in the earpieces of his glasses.

"Let our armies defeat the invaders," Frank pleaded. "What else are they meant for? What else have they trained for? Surely Lord Deter will give conventional military tactics a chance before stooping to mass destruction."

"My orders come from Lord Deter himself," Joe said, "as you know very well. Civilization can be rebuilt from the ashes of our great sacrifice."

Frank looked as if he might launch himself at Joe. Korda decided he'd better intervene quickly, before Joe had a chance to push the button.

He strode into the room, making certain that his uniform tunic was straight and that his newly obtained officer's badge and metals were clearly visible.

"Sir!" Frank was clearly relieved when Korda appeared. "Have you come to rescind the order?"

"Order?" Korda snapped, in what he hoped was a

superior officer tone of voice.

"The order to detonate the reactor, sir," Frank said. "It came through about fifteen minutes ago. I've been trying to convince Joe that we should wait until we have confirmation, but he insists that an order is an order."

"And what is your excuse for asking questions?" Joe said snidely. Clearly his self-assurance was bolstered by the presence of an officer.

"The message could have been a false one," Frank said. "We haven't been able to raise headquarters in Ground Zero since it came through. There's interference of some type."

Korda reflected silently that the absence of time would prove to be an ideal jamming field, if a bit hard to effect in most instances. While the two soldiers had presented their cases, he had scanned the room. The direction finder gave no further indication of where he should go, so the world key must be here.

"BOSS! YOU'VE GOT TO DO SOMETHING!" Jester printed on his readline.

Korda nodded. "*I know.*"

He studied the soldiers, thought about what he had learned about Deter, about the civilization on Urbs. His hand steady, he raised the handheld blaster he had taken from one of Grrn'scal's men.

"Frank, step back from that console or I'll shoot. You should know better than to question the orders of Lord Deter."

"But—"

"Step back," Korda motioned with the barrel of his weapon. "Just as the heroes of the Fort stood fast in ancient days, so must we now."

Frank's eyes widened in terror, his mouth shaping a perfect "O" as he realized that Korda intended to support Joe. Beneath Korda's ear, the PDA was bobbing frantically.

"Boss! You've gone crazy!" Jester wailed.

For his part, Frank dove toward the button on his console that would deactivate the reactor.

"If I'm going to die," he shrieked, "I may as well die for something I believe in! Maybe I can delay this insanity!"

Reluctantly, for he admired the man's devotion to ethics, Korda pulled the trigger. A bolt of blue light caught Frank in the center of the chest. Like a puppet whose strings have been suddenly cut, the solider slid to the floor.

Korda leveled his weapon at Joe. "Press the button, Joe."

The PDA was orbiting Korda now, a small, fast moon around a vast primary.

"Boss—Boss—Boss—Boss—Boss!" The plea came out in a stream so fast it sounded like one word.

Joe nodded to Korda and saluted. Then he pressed the button.

The circular chamber flashed retina-searing white and then dull, bloody red. Beneath Korda's boots, the floor shuddered. A wind, hot and stale, blew from all directions. When it ceased, the room was transformed.

It was still circular, but the balconies were gone. So was the reactor. In its place stood a familiar control panel—the world key. Hovering in the air above them all was Joe, but he no longer seemed human.

He spun face down, viewing them from a face in which only the eyes lived. Limbs dangled loosely, making him seem grossly distorted, as if he had become a four-footed creature. Korda raised his blaster and took aim.

"Deter."

"That is correct, Rene Korda." The voice held the same unpleasant twanging as it had in the council chamber. "I tried to frighten you away by shooting the robot in the Garden of Honor but you remained unafraid. You freed the Auransan spy and yet stood before my judgment as if you were an innocent, daring claim that you acted for my own good. Even after you escape my guards, you persist in invading to my universe's most sacred core. Why?"

"I told you," Korda said. "I was hired to start time running again and—if possible—to find the person or persons who did this to you."

Deter's chuckle sounded like two discordant chords being played on an out-of-tune banjo.

"Still you say that. Very well. Start time again in my universe."

"And what will you do to me when I'm done?" Korda asked. "Why should I do you a service if I am going to be executed afterward?"

"Good point, Korda," Deter chuckled again. "Very

well. I hereby dismiss any and all charges against you on the condition that you reactivate my universe and leave with the minimal amount of further interaction with my people or property."

"That minimal interaction includes returning to my ship and flying away from Urbs?" Korda asked.

Deter bobbed in the air, Joe's limbs flopping grotesquely as he did so. "It shall be so defined. Get to work. I weary of dwelling in this simulacrum. I would have access to the others without the need to resort to the clumsiness of bottled time."

"How did you get out of Grrn'scal's 'body'?" Korda asked, moving to the world key controls.

"I had carried with me a small vial of bottled time," Deter answered. "It was not sufficient for me to pursue you, but it was sufficient to enable me to teleport back to my gravity box."

Korda started tapping buttons and setting patterns on the world key. "I guessed it had to be something like that."

Unwilling to talk further with the strange ruler of Urbs, Korda turned his full attention to informing the world key that time could be reactivated. As he reprogrammed the device, he found himself admiring the training of whoever had done the deactivation sequence. It was skillfully done, with minimal wasted code. Whoever his opponents were, they were certainly formidable.

When time ripped back into the surrounding space, Korda rose and gave Deter a brief, ironic bow.

"My job is done. I beg your lordship for permission

to depart."

"Go," the disembodied brain said, "and never return."

"Gladly," Korda said. "C'mon, Jes."

"Right with you, Boss."

As they left the subterranean chamber, they heard a faint thump as Deter abandoned Joe's body for some more suitable vessel. Glancing behind him, Korda could not restrain a shiver of almost atavistic fear as he saw the crumpled form twisted on the floor.

They reached the *Jester* without incident. Soldiers, both within the Fort and on the battlefield, eyed them curiously, but, perhaps because of Korda's uniform, no one interfered.

"I'm getting us off of here *pronto*," Jester announced as soon as Korda and the PDA had come aboard. "I don't know how long Deter's grace period will last."

"Do it!" Korda said, dropping into the bridge command chair. "I'll change out of this uniform as soon as we're out of Urbs."

He felt the rumble as the *Jester's* thrusters shoved them away from the ground and into the clean heavens above.

"Where do I set course for next, Boss?" Jester asked.

"We'll refuel, then set course for Aurans," Korda said. "Let's hope that the universe that gave us Tico Higgins is a bit more pleasant than Urbs."

Jester appeared on her holopad. From one of her memory banks, she had created a harem costume for herself. The diaphanous pink trousers ballooned out from the ankle and nipped again at the waist. Her vest was in the same yellow and purple check as her usual jester's costume. Bells jingled from wrist and ankle bracelets.

"Next stop Aurans!" she said, winking at him. "Land of sand, magic, and other wonders. Right, Sugar Pop?"

Pressing his face into his hands to control his laughter, Korda lacked the breath to reprimand her.

Interlude

Deter's private spaceship, the *Endgame*, was large and bristling with weapons. That there were more weapons than even a trained observer might realize was Deter's secret pride.

As a disembodied brain, he did not need more than a small life-support capsule to be comfortable. The ship had been built without cabins, without a galley or exercise station. All the space that would normally be given over to those necessities of organic comfort had been filled with powerplants and missile racks. In unbiased tests, expert analysts had usually misestimated the firepower of the *Endgame* as less than half of what it actually was.

But as he programmed the launch and departure sequence for his ship's computer, Deter did not feel the joyful savagery that being in his ship usually gave him. First the stasis, now this Rene Korda. He felt certain that Korda had been lying, that some of the colorful events in Deter's past were catching up with him at last.

Once he was out of the universe of Urbs, Deter prepared a message missile. He doubted he could beat Korda to Aurans if, as he suspected, that was Korda's destination, but a message missile set to burn itself out in a one-way journey could travel faster than any manned ship—or even a brained one like the *Endgame*.

Deter cast his message in cool, formal language. It would not do for Dwistor to believe that he was nervous. This was simply information sent as a courtesy from one ally to another. Yes.

> To: Sheikh Dwistor of Aurans
> From: Deter of Urbs
> Greetings. The universe of Urbs was put into stasis by person or persons unknown. Reasons for this undoubtedly hostile action unknown. Time restored to Urbs by one Rene Korda of Terra. Motives unknown but suspect. In interest of our common past, I send you warning. Warning is also being forwarded to Alachra in Fortuna. I am progressing in *Endgame* to Aurans for private conference on whether our cell needs to pass warning elsewhere.

Had Deter possessed a head, he would have nodded sharply with satisfaction as he reread his message. There, enough to warn Dwistor, enough so that skinny, costumed, pretend warrior could not say that Deter had failed in his duty to their alliance.

He checked his course plot, reduced his speed slightly. There was no need for him to hurry overmuch. Let Dwistor deal with events as Deter had, it would make him less volatile, more receptive to counsel.

Deter signaled his computer to download some information stored in files so secret that, even at the speed of thought, Deter spent five minutes removing the security safeguards. Then he began to review a history of the Pasqua wipeout, a military atrocity still shrouded in mystery—largely because, as far as he knew, everyone who had witnessed it was now dead or a mindwiped slave.

Everyone, that is, except for Deter of Urbs and six others.

VII

Korda was rested and alert when Jester announced their arrival at the entry point for the universe of Aurans. He put aside the biography he had been reading.

"Hey, Jes, I bet you haven't figured out where the name 'Aurans' comes from," he said.

Obligingly, Jester manifested on the bridge holopad. She still wore her harem costume with such obvious pride that Korda hadn't had the heart to tell her to revert to normal programming.

Besides, she looked cute.

"No, I hadn't bothered to work it out, Sugar Pop," she said. "Where did the name come from?"

Korda tapped the biography. "Back in the mid-twentieth century, Earth had the second of what it called 'World Wars.' One of the most interesting figures to come out of that war as a man called T.E. Lawrence—better known as Lawrence of Arabia. Most of his work during the war was with the Arab peoples. They had some difficulty pronouncing his name, so they called him 'Aurans'—their pronunciation of 'Lawrence.'"

"That's kind of cool," Jester said. "But what good is knowing something like that?"

"Sometimes quite a bit," Korda said. "The owner of this universe may have chosen the name by accident, but I don't think so. His interest in T.E. Lawrence may give us some insight into his thought patterns."

The hologram nodded, but Jester's attention was on bringing the ship to the entry point.

"There's sort of a 'Keep Out' sign at the entry," she announced, "but my scanners don't show any active weapons."

"Very well," Korda said, "bring us in. Put an image of the universe on the bridge screen as soon as there's anything to see."

"Aye-aye, Captain!"

Although Korda tensed his hands over the auxiliary piloting controls, the *Jester* entered the universe of Aurans without difficulty. In front of him, the bridge screen displayed their destination.

Dominating the whole was a binary star. The burning globes danced around each other bound by the pull of their mutual gravity. Examining them, Korda knew that if one speeded up time so that their motion could be observed faster than real-time, their interdependent orbits would resemble an infinity symbol etched in fire on the black heavens.

Now, due to the work of the unknown saboteur, they were frozen in stasis, their dance no longer warming the universe.

Three planets orbited the binary star, their orbits beginning far enough out that the heat from the double suns would not burn them dry.

The first was larger than Earth, golden brown with desert sands. Saturn-like rings of broken rock girdled it. The second was blue and green, like Earth. Although it lacked the first planet's spectacular rings, wispy bits of cloud white drew the eye, making it seem cool and inviting. The third planet was a gas giant striped in yellow, red, and orange.

"Scanning shows that both the first and second planets have evidence of habitation," Jester announced. "The first planet is only sparsely populated; the second shows several major cities."

"Set course for the first planet," Korda said. "My bet is that's where they hid the world key."

The hologram spun to look at him, harem bells jingling as she turned.

"Why, Boss? The other planet is so much more earth-like and pleasant. Even with its orbit, the first planet is going to be quite hot. I wouldn't want to spend time there."

"Ah," Korda said, "but the owner of *this* universe would. Remember, it's named for Lawrence of Arabia—who spent the best part of his life with desert peoples. Besides, Nizzim Rochtar—a famous desert designer—built this place. And Tico Higgins was dressed for the desert."

Jester rested her chin on the tip of one finger, then

nodded. "Yes, I think you have something, Sugar Pop. Shall I bring us down on magnetic north?"

"Somewhere close," Korda said. "I expect that magnetic north itself might be booby-trapped in some way."

Jester chuckled. "And whatever else you are, you're not a booby. Right, Sugar Pop?"

Korda mimed tossing something at her and the hologram blinked out.

Sand. Sand. Sand in his boots. Sand forcing its way past his glasses to get into his eyes. Grit working its way into the very pores of his skin.

The sandstorm had blown up the moment he stepped out of easy reach of the *Jester*. Korda spat dryly. There was sand in his mouth, too.

The howl of the desert wind would have made conversation with the *Jester* impossible except for his throat mike and the shades-link. Now, despite the aching dryness in his mouth, he tried to shape a question for Jester.

"*Jes, can you guide me back to the ship?*"

"NO GO, SUGAR POP."

In spite of the lightness of the response, Korda could tell that the computer was worried.

"*Why not? Give me a pattern of audio tones to follow. Make them louder as I get closer.*"

"I THOUGHT OF THAT!" The computer seemed offended. "PROBLEM IS, THE SAND HERE IS SEEDED

WITH SOME PARTICLE THAT'S INTERFERING WITH MY COMMO SYSTEM. AS IS, I'M ONLY REACHING YOU THROUGH A WIDE-BEAM TRANSMISSION. FIGURED THAT WITH THE STASIS, NO ONE WOULD BE LIKELY TO EAVESDROP."

Korda frowned. He forced himself a few more steps in what he hoped was the right direction before answering.

"*So I'm lost*," he said.

"THAT'S ABOUT IT, BOSS," Jester agreed via the readline. "I MEAN, I KNOW ROUGHLY WHERE YOU ARE—SOMEWHERE IN THAT SWIRLING CLOUD OF SAND—BUT I CAN'T REACH YOU AND YOU CAN'T SEE TO FIND ME."

"*Great.*"

Korda considered his alternatives. He could disconnect his bottled time. When it went off, the sandstorm should die down, too. Then Jester could figure out a way to retrieve him. The problem was that whatever the ship did would involve reactivating the sandstorm.

His other alternative was obvious. He'd just have to put one foot in front of the other and hope that he walked out of the sandstorm—or that the winds died down—before his supply of bottled time ran out. If that happened, Jester would end up rescuing him anyhow.

Some vague feeling that he should at least go out fighting kept him struggling against the sand and wind. His shades protected his eyes from the worst damage, but his exposed skin was scoured raw by the swirling particles.

His ears ached from the shrill wails of the wind.

Half delirious, Korda was trying to convince himself that the wind wasn't really laughing at him when the toe of his boot struck something solid. It was too small to be the side of the ship, but when he bent to touch it he found not a rock or a bit of wood, but something smooth and gracefully curved.

Kneeling beside it, Korda pulled his find from the sand. The wind's howls rose in intensity, blowing him a few steps, but he kept his grasp on the . . . his hands traced the curves . . . it was a bottle with a long neck, rather like a wine bottle.

The urge for a cool drink overwhelmed any caution that remained to him. Korda held the bottle near his mouth and pulled the stopper. As he tilted the neck of the bottle to drink, he became aware of a feeling of disorientation. His knees weakened and he tumbled to the sand unconscious.

When Korda awoke, his first thought was that he had suddenly been struck deaf. Then he realized that what he was hearing was silence. The wind was no longer howling. He was no longer being bombarded with sand. The storm was over.

Or was it?

Korda rolled onto his stomach and pulled himself to his feet. He was in a pleasant garden. A deep pool of cool water invited him to drink. Palm trees bore sweet, fat dates in their feathery fronds. When he walked toward the pond, birds sang arias as they fluttered beneath the golden sky.

Golden?

Korda craned his neck and looked as far up as he could. What he saw confirmed his first impression. He had not escaped the sandstorm. Somehow he had penetrated into its heart. On all sides were swirling walls of golden sand that peaked in a cone far overhead.

With a chill, he realized that the storm would not have died down. If he had not been lucky enough to stumble into its heart, he would have wandered in it until his bottled time ran out or he was worn into nothing.

But had it been merely luck that brought him here?

Korda went to retrieve the bottle he had stumbled on in the midst of the storm. It was nowhere to be found. The only evidence that it had ever existed was the imprint of the top where he had held it firmly grasped in his right hand.

"Jester?" he called experimentally.

There was no answer. The PDA still bobbed near his shoulder, but it did not respond. Apparently, the force of the storm was completely cutting off communication between him and his ship.

No more brilliant thought occurring to him, Korda decided to walk to the pool. Perhaps after a cool drink and a few dates his head would clear.

Without the PDA to analyze the water for purity and

the dates for poison, Korda knew he was taking a gamble, but the same desperate dryness that had led him to try to drink from the bottle during the sandstorm drove him to drink and then, thirst satisfied, to eat.

The water could not have tasted better if it had been the wine he had envisioned the mysterious bottle holding. He drank thirstily, the beginnings of a thought worrying at the edges of his mind. Nothing more occurred to him, so he picked and ate some of the fruit.

Refreshed, he lay back against a sand dune and contemplated the golden sky. It looked peaceful, like something spun from glass, but he knew if he walked closer the storm would reawaken to its full fury.

Glass? Bottle?

The idea was patently ridiculous, but it would not leave him, even when he tried to push it away.

Could he be in the bottle?

The more Korda weighed the idea, the more it appealed to him. Tico Higgins had told him that magic worked on Aurans—a magic of creatures and things rather than spells. Korda had picked up the bottle and when he opened it he had found himself here. Perhaps instead of the bottle spilling water out, it had sucked Korda in.

Korda sat up suddenly. Jester would be frantic. His own bottled time would run out. He had no leisure to spare lounging in the sand.

He checked the indicator in his shades—he had about six hours left. If he did not figure out a way out of first the bottle and then the storm within those six hours, he would be stranded at best until someone else reactivated the universe of Aurans—at worst, for the rest of his life.

Fortified with another drink from the oasis pool, Korda made a brisk circuit of his newfound refuge—and prison. On the far side of the pond, partially hidden between the swelling of two sand dunes, he spotted a cluster of half a dozen tents.

They were the shades of a tawny rainbow—tan, rust, beige, pale lemon, eggshell white. Some of the door flaps were tied open with broad braided cords, granting the shady interiors fresh air and light. Tightly knotted rugs in oriental patterns were scattered over the sand both inside and outside the tents.

On one of these rugs, a plump, bald man sat softly playing a flute to a snake swaying in a basket. He wore flowing desert robes and sandals; his wrists glinted with bracelets of silver and gold.

He raised his head and lowered his flute as Korda approached. The snake sunk back into its basket. When the man turned his face toward Korda, Korda could see that the flute player's eyes were white, blank, and blind.

Almost as soon as he had registered that fact, Korda realized something even stranger. Even though the universe of Aurans was in stasis, the blind flute player was active.

He stopped, not certain he liked this. In Urbs, those who had bottled time had been the servants of the distinctly hostile Deter. Would Dwistor of Aurans be any more trusting?

"Come closer," the blind man said, his voice deep and slightly gravelly. "Who is it that moves over silenced sands?"

Korda considered retreating, but discarded the notion immediately. He might never find his way out of this bottle without help. Alienating the blind man would be foolish.

Walking closer, he answered. "It's me, Rene Korda, of Old Terra."

"Rene Korda of Old Terra." The blind flute player smiled slightly. "What brings you to Aurans, stranger to our sands?"

"I . . . ," Korda paused, considering how much to say. "I seek to learn why this universe has been put into stasis and to reawaken it once again."

"Admirable," the blind man said, "but how will you achieve this goal trapped within this bottle?"

Korda shrugged, realized that the blind man could not see the gesture, and elaborated.

"I really don't know," he said. "There must be a way out. I'll just have to find it."

"That may take time," the blind man said cryptically, "and time is one thing that you have little of, is it not?"

Reflexively, Korda glanced at the indicator in his shades. Less than five and a half hours remained. If he didn't get out of this bottle and back to the *Jester* within that time . . .

"No," he said. "I do not have as much time as I could wish. However, I may have enough. Tell me, sir, how is it that you were not captured by the stasis?"

The blind man smiled and held up a glowing green unit of bottled time.

"I was prepared for an eventuality such as this," he said, "before I came into the bottle oasis."

"Did you have warning?" Korda asked.

"No." The blind man shook his head. "No, Rene Korda of Old Terra, I did not, but Arabou the Trader has learned to prepare for many eventualities."

"Arabou the Trader," Korda repeated. "Is that your name?"

The blind man bowed, although he did not rise from his seat on the carpet.

"I have been called that. Arabou is the name that I am best known by in the universe of Aurans."

"Do you know other universes?" Korda asked.

"Many—and I have heard your name in some of them," Arabou replied. "That makes me believe your story of why you have come to Aurans. However, you do not have time for me to speak of my travels. Your time is running out even as we speak of such polite inconsequentialities."

"True," Korda said. "Do you know the way out of this bottle?"

Arabou smiled, his blind eyes focusing on nothing.

"I do," he said, "but what will you give me if I tell you how to leave this bottle, to evade the sandstorm, and to go on your way? I am a trader, you understand, and I give nothing for nothing."

Korda frowned. "I don't have much with me, just my bottled time and the tools of my trade. I have food and some goods on my ship, but I'm cut off from that now."

Arabou's smile did not fade; in fact, Korda had the impression that he was vaguely pleased.

"Since you have nothing I want," he said, "would you consider performing a service for me in return for the information you desire?"

Korda hesitated for only a moment. Time was running out.

"If the service does not involve killing someone or gratuitous injury, I would do so," he replied.

Arabou nodded. "The service I wish involves neither. Now sit with me, have some iced wine to drink, some sherbet to eat. According to the customs of our people, if we share a meal we are bound not to injure each other."

"Beats a peace treaty," Korda said, folding his legs under him and accepting the refreshments Arabou brought from one of the tents.

"I agree," Arabou said. "Now let me tell you what I wish from you. My daughter, Miriam, sleeps in one of these tents. I brought her with me to this place for her own protection."

"I wondered what you were doing in a bottle," Korda said, sipping his wine. "It didn't exactly seem like a vacation spot."

"No," Arabou smiled, "but it is isolated and most people on Aurans do not even know of its existence. The northern deserts are known to be dangerous—so dangerous that travelers often do not return. It made a good place to hide my daughter."

"Hide her from what?" Korda asked.

"My daughter is in love with a man of whom I quite approve," Arabou said. "I had given them permission to marry, but before the wedding could occur, he was sent from Aurans on business for his employer. When her fiancé became overdue, my daughter went to ask after his whereabouts. Through mere chance, she was seen by his employer—who immediately desired her for his harem."

"Not good," Korda said.

"No, not good," Arabou agreed. "Miriam fled to me, begging me for my protection. I brought her here and soon after stasis fell on the universe. Twice since, devices I have in one of the tents registered a ship under bottled time entering the universe. The first time, shortly before your arrival, the signature could have been that of my daughter's betrothed's ship. The second time, I believe it was yours."

Korda nodded. "So you want me to find your daughter's fiancé."

"Yes," Arabou said. "I want you to find him and then to arrange for them to be married. Once they are married, she will be safe from any man's harem. Such is the custom of this universe."

"Very well," Korda said. "I will accept this duty. Can

you tell me where I might find your daughter's fiancé?"

Arabou took a map from his tent. "The palace of the Sheikh of Aurans is here. I believe my daughter's fiancé would have returned there. Perhaps his bottled time ran out and he is there, perhaps he is even now searching for us. Still, this would be a good place to begin."

"How will I know this fellow," Korda asked. "Do you have a picture?"

Arabou spread his hands. "I do not, nor can this blind man describe him. I had thought to send my daughter with you. She will know him and this way you can more quickly arrange for a marriage."

Korda swallowed a sigh. Since he needed Arabou's help to escape the bottle he would have to take Miriam with him.

"If that's how it has to be done," Korda said, "then I'll take her with me. Tell me, what's her boyfriend's name?"

"Tico Higgins," Arabou said.

"I should have known! I met Tico on Urbs," Korda explained, "under very odd circumstances. He told me that he was in the employ of Dwistor of Aurans."

"That is correct," Arabou said. "Dwistor of Aurans, the Sheikh of the Universe, is Tico's rival for my daughter's hand."

"Oh, boy," Korda said, a sinking feeling filling his gut. "What have I gotten myself into!"

VIII

Miriam was as slender as a lily stem, as graceful as a gazelle. Her wide eyes and long, thick hair were both as dark as night. When pouting red lips that seemed created for kissing curved in a smile at him, Rene Korda found himself half in love with Arabou's daughter.

"I am Miriam, daughter of Arabou," she said, gracefully offering Korda her hand. "You will ever have my gratitude if you help me find my beloved Tico and save me from the lusts of Dwistor."

Korda found the composure to bow over Miriam's hand. Her slender fingers, he noticed as he did so, were tipped with rounded nails painted a delicate coral. Miriam wore loose trousers gathered at the ankle and a tight half-blouse that showed off a very cute navel.

"I will be honored to serve you, lady," he said, "but I must admit that Tico's gain will be the loss of every man in every universe ever created."

Miriam giggled and Korda found himself liking her as well as admiring her. He wondered what Jester would think of their new guest and dreaded that he already knew.

Arabou had risen from his seat on the carpets to awaken Miriam and now he took her arm.

"Daughter, I will give you a device so that you can wear bottled time like Korda and myself. However, you will have only three hours time with you—unlike Rene, who is equipped with almost twice that. You must listen to him and stay close. If he says to return to his ship, you must do so at once."

Miriam nodded obediently. "Yes, Father. I will do as you say."

Korda wondered at her apparent meekness. He suspected that there was steel in that graceful body—after all, she had the courage to resist the will of the ruler of the universe.

"Now, to your departure," Arabou said. "Among my carpets is one that has the power of flight knotted into its weave. Rene, you and Miriam shall take this carpet and fly to the top of the bottle. Once you are there, force the cork out and then fly directly up. Beware the djinn who maintain the sandstorm, for they will attempt to stop your flight. If they do, there will be no saving you."

Korda pushed inane questions about flying carpets and djinn from his mind. Hadn't he designed universes that contained things at least as far-fetched?

"Very well, Arabou," he said. "There's just one more thing I need to do. I came to the northern deserts to use a device that will enable me to pinpoint the world key for this universe. I'm going to take a gamble that this bottle is where I must use it."

"This bottle?" Arabou sounded astonished. "Why should you think so."

"Well," Korda said, starting to set up the resonance tracer, "it's in about the right place geographically. Secondly, you yourself admit that this section of the desert is known for its dangers. I suspect that the sandstorm and the bottle oasis are both meant to protect Aurans' magnetic north."

Miriam clapped her hands in glee. "Yes, I understand! First, one may not reach the place, then, if one does, one is trapped within a bottle."

"Precisely," Korda said, switching the tracer on. "That way, even if those with ill intent manage to get here, they can't escape with the knowledge they gain. You did say, Arabou, that the stasis occurred soon after your arrival here. The saboteurs must have slipped in and out past your tents while you were inside and out of sight."

"But how did these saboteurs escape?" Arabou said. "Certainly they did not have a flying carpet."

Korda watched as the resonance tracer etched the paths of the planet's magnetic field, then set it to read and record. He could transfer the data to Jester as soon as they were back to the ship.

"No, I doubt they had a flying carpet," Korda answered, "but I suspect they had plenty of time to research Aurans and learned enough to come prepared for both the storm and the bottle."

Arabou frowned and turned his blind gaze on his

daughter.

"You have formidable opponents, Rene Korda," he said. "Perhaps Miriam should remain here where she will be safer now that we know that you will recognize Tico."

Miriam stamped one pretty foot. "I will not stay, Father! Tico could be in danger—if not from these saboteurs then from Dwistor. I could not rest for worrying."

Arabou gave a crooked smile, but he relented.

"Actually, daughter, the stasis would make certain that you rested undreaming, but I respect your determination. Go with Rene, advise him and assist him even when matters do not concern your Tico. He is here as the savior of our universe."

Miriam bowed and embraced her father. Korda, made a bit uncomfortable by the blind man's praise, folded up the resonance tracer.

"I have my reading," he said. "Where's that flying carpet?"

Under Arabou's direction, Miriam found the correct carpet among those scattered on the sands. It was large enough to carry two people easily—three if they didn't mind crowding. Its dominant color was a clear azure, but the arabesques that adorned it were every color in the rainbow.

Korda stared down at this, hoping that he was not about to be the victim of an elaborate practical joke.

"Uh, you drive, Miriam," he said. "I'll sit behind you and keep the djinn away."

"Very well, Rene," she said, embracing her father and

then taking a cross-legged seat at the front of the carpet.

Korda placed a hand on Arabou's shoulder.

"Thank you for your help, Arabou," he said. "I'll try to take good care of your daughter for you. Don't worry."

Arabou smiled his mysterious smile. "I shall not, Rene Korda, for after you depart I shall turn off my bottled time and wait either for your return or for the return of time. Both will tell me of your success—and if neither comes I shall wait undreaming throughout eternity."

Korda shivered slightly at the calm acceptance in the blind man's voice, but he kept his apprehensions to himself as he stepped onto the carpet behind Miriam and took his seat.

"All right, Captain," he said, trying to keep his tones light. "Everything secure for take-off."

"Hold on to the edges of the carpet," Miriam advised. "It will steady you until we level off."

Korda did as she said, although he would have much preferred to put his arms around her slender waist. The thought was so distracting that they were airborne and rising almost before he noticed.

"That was easy!" he exclaimed.

"This is a good carpet," Miriam said. "I have directed it to pick up speed right until we come to the top of the bottle. When you see the cork, get to your feet and be prepared to push it loose."

Korda did as she said, pleased to find that he had not completely lost the reflexes he had developed surfing over half a century before. He wished Miriam would turn and look at him, but the lovely girl kept her attention focused on directing the carpet.

They reached the cork at speeds that Korda guessed were close to fifty miles an hour. He felt a momentary flash of fear that he would break something when his arms hit the cork, but the impact came before he could flinch. One moment the enormous mottled brown cork was looming overhead, the next he felt a faint bump and they were through.

All around them the sandstorm swirled, but under Miriam's skillful piloting they flew safely within the eye of the storm. Above, a round blue patch of clear sky grew larger and larger.

"We will be out soon!" Miriam shouted over the howling of the wind. "Watch for the djinn!"

"Aye, Captain!" Korda shouted back.

They burst through a thin curtain of sand at the top of the storm and into the clear sky. Korda did not have time to cheer, for he was immediately aware that what he had taken for looming mountains in the distance were towering djinn right up close.

There were three of them—broad-chested, muscular men clad only in flowing trousers, turbans, and brass armbands. The skin of their bare chests was painted with the emblem for the universe of Aurans—a double crest over a rising sun.

Miriam attempted to steer the carpet over and between two of the djinn, but the carpet was already pushed to its limit. They would pass within arm's reach of the nearest djinni.

Aware of how foolhardy his action was, Korda leaned out as far as he could over the side of the carpet. He felt firm hands balancing him, but he hardly registered that they were Miriam's. His goal was the turban of the nearest djinni.

Snagging the fabric with the tips of his fingers, Korda pushed the turban free. Outraged, the djinni forgot to reach for the carpet. It grabbed its turban and clamped it back on its head.

Korda fell back onto the carpet and—incidentally— into Miriam's arms. The girl's blush only made her more beautiful. He was trying to apologize and free himself from her unintentional embrace when a shrill voice sounded beneath his ear.

"Sugar Pop! Here I've been worrying myself sick about you and I find you rolling around with some hussy! I—"

Transmission cut off suddenly and the PDA, which had been hovering forgotten at his shoulder since the last contact with his ship, rose indignantly into the air and sped off in the direction of the *Jester*.

Miriam stared at him, embarrassment forgotten. Korda managed to pull himself upright. He couldn't help but notice that Miriam looked no less lovely with her hair all tousled by the wind.

"Rene! Are you a sorcerer?" the desert girl asked.

"A sorcerer?" Korda shook his head. "No, I'm not, Miriam. I'm just a universe creator who is going to have to deal with a very, very upset AI."

"AI?" Miriam looked puzzled.

"Artificial Intelligence," Korda explained. "My starship has a computer that is as intelligent as a person—and as temperamental. It—she—is sort of protective of me."

"Protective?" Miriam smiled, her dark eyes twinkling. "Is that what you call it? Very well. I will accept your words."

Korda flushed. "Can you take us to my ship? It's right down there. Hopefully, Jester will let us aboard before our bottled time runs out."

Miriam nodded and they swooped down to park alongside the *Jester*. Korda had to beg and apologize, but Jester relented before he had to start unbolting manual access ports. Still, when he came aboard, the computer refused to talk to him except in response to direct commands and no perky hologram manifested to keep him company.

Even as he settled Miriam into a guest cabin, Korda felt obscurely lonely.

He fought the feeling while he set the navigation program to seek out the palace that Arabou had mentioned. Even though it was a long shot, he set a secondary scanning program to look for the *Whirlwind*, Tico Higgins' ship.

On one level of his mind, he knew that Jester, as his ship's computer, was aware of everything he was doing and had, in fact, probably made deductions based on that information. On a second level, Jester was his friend—

a somewhat touchy person, an almost girlfriend, a . . . That second level made no sense, but that second level was what made him speak hesitantly to the air.

"Jes?"

No answer. Well, he hadn't really expected one.

"Jes, the young lady who is our passenger is the daughter of a man named Arabou the Trader. Arabou gave me the means to get out of the center of the sandstorm, but there was a price."

He paused, hoping that Jester would ask what. The silence continued unbroken.

"The price was that I take his daughter Miriam with me, reunite her with her beloved, and arrange for their marriage. There is some need for haste in this, for Miriam has awakened the lusts of a powerful man and if she is not safely married to her promised husband this man may kidnap her for his harem."

Korda listened. Was that a faint sound—perhaps a gasp of indrawn breath?

"Jes, I had to make the deal in any case. I couldn't stay in a bottle at the heart of a sandstorm until my bottled time ran out. I'll be honest with you, though. Miriam's problem touched me—I know I wouldn't want to be forced into captivity, not when my heart was given."

He bit his lip. Had he overdone it with the flowery language? Usually Jester was a sucker for such touches. He ran a hand through his hair.

"The big shock came when I learned who Miriam's beloved is. I bet you'll never guess."

Again he paused. Would Jester take the bait? He was opening his mouth to continue when Jester's hologram flickered into sight on the holopad.

"I can guess, Boss," Jester said, her voice full of perky impudence. "Tico Higgins, right?"

Korda grinned and sketched the hologram a salute. "You got it, Jes. How did you figure it out?"

Jester grinned back at him. She still wore her Arabian Nights costume but, perhaps in imitation of Miriam, she now wore cascades of bracelets and long earrings.

"I guessed when I heard the girl sobbing in her cabin, praying to Allah that she find Tico and be saved from her terrible fate."

Korda kept himself from bolting to check on Miriam. After going to all this trouble to reassure Jester that his only interest in Miriam was that of a rescuer, it would not do to show too much concern. Instead, he turned to Jester.

"Could you go and speak to Miriam, girl-to-girl, and reassure her that we will do our best for her? I hate to think of her alone in there, but I may not be the best comfort."

Jester nodded happily. "The navigation program has found a desert city called Palace Gate, but the palace itself may be shielded. Do you want me to ask Miriam where we should start?"

"If you would, Jester," Korda said, leaning back in his command chair. "I'll go take a shower and change. That storm drove sand into every crevice of my clothes and right into the tips of my boots."

Jester drew her veil modestly across her face. "I'll report audio only then, Boss."

Korda could only shake his head in response, but he was whistling as he headed off to the showers.

IX

M y father did not mean to mislead you," Miriam explained some time later, as they conferred in the *Jester*'s lounge, "but the palace that most believe that they are seeing is a mirage. Explaining to one who has been blind from birth the idea of something that is seen but does not exist at that place is difficult. Tico and I never tried."

Korda nodded. "I understand why. So this mirage explains why maps of Aurans locate Dwistor's palace on the fringes of Palace Gate, but my sensors find nothing there. Is it elsewhere in the universe?"

Miriam shrugged gracefully. "I do not know where the palace actually rests. As far as I know, the palace cannot be reached by normal means. Only Dwistor's trusted counselors know how to defeat the mirage."

"Was Tico one of those counselors? Did he tell you the secret?" Jester asked.

"He was and he did." Miriam's mysterious smile reminded Korda of her father. "However, we may not need that knowledge. Tico had a house in Palace Gate. Perhaps he is there or has left a message for me."

"Wouldn't he have left a message for you at your father's house?" Korda asked.

"Father did not have a permanent address," Miriam said. "As a trader, he preferred to wander. He trusted the murmurs of the marketplace to bring his news to him."

Korda straightened. "Well, we cannot waken everyone in the marketplace from stasis to find if Tico left a message for you. Let's start with Tico's house and, if we don't find anything there, you can tell us the secret to reaching Dwistor's palace."

Korda left the *Jester* hidden in the desert outside of Palace Gate. With Miriam as guide and Jester's PDA at his shoulder, he entered the city. As they walked, he pulled out the direction finder.

"What is that?" Miriam asked.

"It's a device keyed to the readings I took at magnetic north right before we left the bottle," he explained. "I thought that since we were here I would check to see if it gave me any sign of where the Aurans world key is concealed."

He looked in the direction the flashing arrows pointed, then frowned.

"What is wrong, Rene?" Miriam asked.

Korda tucked the direction finder back into his belt stealthily before answering.

"It seems to be indicating the palace," he said, "but

that seems unlikely since you told me that the palace is not there."

Miriam touched his arm lightly. "Actually, what I told you was that the palace is concealed by a mirage. I do not know where it actually is."

"That seems to be straining at gnats," Korda said.

Miriam wrinkled her pretty nose in disgust. "That is a terrible image, Rene, but I understand its sense. All I ask you to remember is that in Aurans magic is as real as sand and sun."

"But not nearly as omnipresent," Korda said. "My boots are full of sand already."

"You can empty them when we get to Tico's house," Miriam said, "or perhaps you can buy a pair of sandals. The fastest route to Tico's is to cut across the bazaar."

"All the merchants will be in stasis," Korda reminded her.

"Yes, I know," Miriam said. "How could I forget when all around us the city is silent and unmoving? My ears ache from straining to hear the cry of the street runners, the plaints of the camels, the wailing songs of people at prayer."

"Yeah, Boss," Jester said. "How could she?"

"I apologize," Korda said. "If this bazaar is as crowded as it looked on my viewscreen our passage may create a momentary ripple in the stasis."

Miriam trembled slightly. "We will seem like ghosts drifting through the sleepers' dreams."

"Perhaps," Korda said, "but more likely they will forget we have ever been there. As Arabou so aptly put it, the sleep of stasis is dreamless."

Even with this reminder, their passage through the bazaar was eerie. Korda told Miriam and the PDA to stay within his area of effect in order to minimize the radius of the bottled time. Even so, as they walked, all around them the merchants returned to their business for a few moments.

"Pots mended! Pots made! Clay or glass or tin!"

"Sweet honeyed dates to tease your mouth! Melons so ripe—every one a pearl beyond price!"

"Cool water! Iced wine! Sherbets!"

"Sir, buy a bangle for the lovely lady?"

"Fortunes told! Futures rendered! Why take a risk when you can know!"

A few of the merchants—those who remained within the effect of the bottled time the longest or those who were most observant—noticed the uncanny silence that cloaked all but their area of the bazaar. Some, seeing Korda's outlander clothing or recognizing Miriam, called out.

Korda gave no answer, nor did he permit Miriam to stop and talk. Even a few people within his radius could delay them and he did not desire to awaken a riot.

So they hurried along past booths where vases and platters of polished bronze and copper gave the sun back its light, past shadowed tents in which cut gemstones glittered in the torchlight and the scents of heavy incense teased them to linger.

Passing one merchant's display at the edge of the bazaar, Miriam bent and scooped up a pair of broad-strapped black sandals. She tossed a silver coin embossed with a man's face into the sand in their place.

"Ali does good work," she explained, "and these look about your size. If you are not careful, those boots will give you blisters."

Korda smiled his thanks. "I'll put them on when we get to Tico's."

"We are almost there," said Miriam, pointing to a solid adobe house.

The few exterior windows of Tico's house were key-hole arches, latticed with carved wooden screens patterned with strange beasts and stranger people. Flowering shrubs blossomed in a multicolored border along the path that ran up to the door and continued along the front of the tile-trimmed wall.

Miriam broke into a run and hurried up the walk. Seizing a doorknocker shaped like a dragon, she rapped sharply. There was no answer.

"Why do not the servants at least come?" she fretted, rapping again.

Jester brought the smiling face of her PDA between Miriam's hand and the door when the girl would have knocked a third time.

"Don't panic, Miriam," the computer reassured her. "The servants are in stasis, just like the rest of Aurans. Even if Tico came back, he would not have had enough bottled time to keep them active. We had to fit the

Whirlwind with a unit so that it could leave Urbs. I doubt that he had a lot to spare."

Miriam let her hand fall from the dragon's tail. Then she blushed, the rosy color doing marvelous things to her cheeks.

"I have been a child," she said. "I was so certain that Tico would be here that I did not think."

The PDA tapped her lightly on the cheek.

"Don't let it worry you. Humans don't think all the time. I could tell you stories about the Boss . . . ."

Korda decided it was time to interrupt.

"Miriam, do you know if Tico has a key or a passcard hidden somewhere? We could use it to go inside and see if he left any messages."

Miriam nodded. "Yes, he kept a key hidden," she said then inexplicably blushed again. "He told me where in case . . . I mean—"

"So that you could get into his house in case of emergency," Korda said, keeping his face straight with effort. Unlike many "girls" he met on Earth, Miriam was clearly as young as she appeared.

"That's right," she said, relieved. "It's under a tile at the edge of the path."

Miriam dropped to her knees, her fingers questing beneath the fragrant shrubs.

"It should be right about—"

A shriek interrupted her sentence. Korda caught a glimpse of something furry and golden blond lurching from under cover of the shrubs toward Miriam. As it emerged, he saw multifaceted eyes, eight strong jointed legs, and the wide, flat body of a tarantula the size of a large dog.

With an audible crunch, the golden tarantula bit Miriam. A second scream faded as Miriam collapsed into an unconscious heap on the tiled walkway.

Then, while Korda gaped in astonishment, the tarantula started dragging the unconscious girl away toward the bazaar. The nimbus of her bottled time surrounded them both so that, ironically, Miriam was unwittingly assisting her assailant.

Korda ran after them. Jester's PDA darted ahead to slow the spider by diving at its eyes.

"Hurry, Boss! Hurry!" Jester cried. "Ugly eight-legs is way too big for me to stop and if it gets in that maze of tents there will be no way for us to stop it without awakening most of the bazaar!"

Korda didn't waste breath answering. The tarantula might be preternaturally strong and swift, but Miriam's inert body was slowing it considerably.

Pushing off from the sandy road, Korda leaped out in a flying tackle. He missed the spider, but grabbed Miriam in his arms. After a brief tussle, he pulled her away from the monster. With a spitting, hissing wail, the spider dashed under the edge of a tent and was gone.

"Don't go after it, Jes," he called to the PDA. "All we would do would be to provide it with bottled time to flee in and—if it ran through the bazaar—start a riot."

"Good thinking, Sugar Pop," Jester said.

Sitting up in the middle of the street, Korda held Miriam. A quick check reassured him that she was still breathing, although each breath was dragged unwillingly from the heart of the deepest sleep Korda had ever observed.

Beneath her eyelids, Miriam's eyes rolled restlessly. Her sleep might be deep, but it was far from dreamless. Korda frowned.

"You just can't keep your hands off of her, can you, Sugar Pop?" Jester said, interrupting his thought.

Korda looked up to see the PDA hovering at eye level.

"Jes—" he began, but the computer interrupted him.

"Hey, just joking, Sugar Pop! Boy, you're too grim! How's the lady? If that spider killed her, I'm gonna—"

Korda shook his head to dispel Jester's fear. "Miriam is alive but the spider's poison put her under. Can you do anything?"

"Not here," Jester replied. "On the ship, probably. Do you want to head back?"

"Miriam doesn't seem in any immediate danger," Korda said, getting to his feet and adjusting his grip on Miriam. "We're awfully close to Tico Higgins's house. I'd hate to leave without seeing if he's there. Buzz on over there, my friend, and see if you can unlock the door."

"Gotcha, Boss!"

The PDA swirled once around his head, paused near Miriam's face, and then went to hover in front of the door. Korda followed more slowly, carrying Miriam. As he arrived, the PDA was opening its grinning mouth and extruding a delicate probe.

"I can pick this one," Jester said. "It's a good lock—you might be interested in knowing that the maker is an Urbs company—but it isn't better than me."

"Ah, modest as ever, Jester," Korda said.

"I'm modest, Boss," Jester said, retracting her probe and bobbing up to smile in his face. "It's just that I'm honest, too. Give the door a shove with your toe. It should come open now."

Korda did as directed. The door swung silently open into a tiled foyer at least ten degrees cooler than the desert heat outside. Rich oriental carpets, piled with artistic disarray on top of each other, cushioned his feet as he walked.

Keyhole arches led into rooms on the right and left. A spacious corridor to the back and a stairway leading up gave some sense of the size of Tico's house. Clearly Dwistor's trade minister was not wanting for material comforts.

Glancing into the room on the right and seeing that it was furnished as a parlor, Korda carried Miriam in. He set the unconscious girl on a sofa and arranged her comfortably. Her eyelids still showed active dream patterns quite at odds with the depth of her sleep.

The PDA watched as Korda crossed to Miriam and turned off her bottled time.

"Why did you do that, Boss?"

"If the poison from the spider bite could harm her, stasis will stop its spread. If it would work its way out naturally, then I have delayed her recovery but not halted it—and she won't feel the difference."

Korda glanced around the room. "Also, with her time stopped, she is safe here. The spider could carry her away because she had time. If she hadn't accidentally awakened it when she was searching for the door key, it would never have harmed her."

"Good, thinking, Boss." The PDA sped to the doorway. "Let's go talk to Tico."

Considering his options, Korda turned to the waiting PDA.

"Jes, I want you to scout out the house. See if Tico Higgins is here or if he left any evidence that he has been here since his return from Urbs. Remember what Miriam said about servants and do your best not to awaken any of them."

The PDA bobbed once, as if nodding, "Gotcha, Sugar Pop! Don't get fresh with Miriam while I'm gone."

Korda sighed. "I won't. The thought never occurred to me. What I was planning to do was empty the sand out of my boots, put on my sandals, then see if that carafe on the side table holds anything cool to drink."

"Just checking!" Jester said. "Be back in a flash."

She returned just as Korda finished pouring himself a goblet of imported wine, a Falernian he was certain, brought from a universe called Roma that he had crafted when he was barely a hundred and fifty and thought that he knew everything.

He sipped the wine and listened to his computer's report.

"There are an old man and woman in the kitchen sitting at the table," Jester said. "I think they were having a light lunch—soft goat cheese and flat bread, good olives, a pale green melon cut on the sideboard for dessert."

Korda heard his stomach rumble. Ignoring it, he gave Jester a nod to continue.

"They were the only people on the ground floor," she said, "so I went upstairs and, guess what?"

"You found Tico Higgins," Korda said, taking a sip of his wine. "He ran out of time while doing something here?"

The PDA bobbed gleefully. "That's right! He's sitting at a writing table with a half-finished letter in front of him. I used my zoom lens so that I could read it without awakening him from stasis. He was writing to tell Miriam that he had returned from his trip to find Aurans in stasis. Since he hadn't been able to find her, guess what he was going to do?"

Korda hid a grin. "He was going to leave Aurans and find us, then he was going to bring us back to get Aurans out of stasis."

If the PDA had been capable of expression, Korda was certain that it would have been bug-eyed with surprise.

"How did you know!" Jester said. "Did you sneak upstairs while I was in the kitchen?"

Korda shook his head. "No, I've been right here. I just guessed that Tico would have done the same thing I would in a similar circumstance. I'm delighted to see we think alike. Show me where he is. We can bring him out of stasis and up-to-date."

"Do you want me to go up and then bring him down here?" Jester asked, deferential for once.

"No," Korda said decisively. "If Tico feels as strongly about Miriam as she does about him, then the sight of her unconscious will drive all coherent thought from his head. Let's tell him about her predicament last. We only have a few hours worth of bottled time here—we can't waste too much on lover's hysterics."

"Right, Sugar Pop."

When they awakened Tico, he was startled to find them there, but not completely taken aback. As his unfinished letter had shown, he had considered the possibility that Korda might be interested in the problems of Aurans.

Sketching a bow that included both the PDA and Korda, he reached for a tray containing bread and cheese that rested on his desk.

"You have twice been my saviors," he said solemnly, "and I would formally offer you bread and salt. According to the customs of Aurans, this binds me to you as an ally—and, if you wish, it makes us friends."

Korda bowed in return. "I would be honored, Mr. Higgins."

"Tico!" the diplomat said with his bright smile. "Tico, it must be if you accept my offering."

Putting out his hand, Korda took the piece of bread

and cheese—to which Tico had added a tiny pinch of salt.

"Tico it is then," he said, "but you must call me Rene."

"And me Jester," the PDA said.

Taking a bite from his own bread and cheese, Tico nodded happily. "Now, I can guess that whatever has put Aurans into stasis has brought you here, friend Rene. Tell me what you have seen since your coming."

Briefing Tico went smoothly until the dark-bearded diplomat learned about Miriam's presence and injury, then nothing would do but for him to hurry down the stairs and . . .

"Boss, Tico's smart but he is kind of impulsive, isn't he?"

Korda looked at Tico stranded in stasis a step outside the radius of Korda's bottled time. The diplomat's desert robes were flared in air stirred by his passage and then frozen in time.

"Perhaps Tico isn't as impulsive when Miriam isn't involved," Korda said, trying to be fair, "but where her safety is concerned common sense does seem to go out the window. How much bottled time do we have left?"

"About four hours, Boss, for you. Maybe one for Miriam, even with you switching her unit off."

"We'll need to head back to the ship eventually, but I think we can finish our conversation here." Korda stepped forward and placed a hand on Tico's arm.

"Slow down, Higgins. You just carried yourself out of the range of my bottled time. We haven't recharged the unit you let run down earlier."

Tico Higgins tugged embarrassedly at his beard. "Oh, dear, I did, didn't I? I can't get accustomed to the idea that time has been switched off."

"Remember it, bud!" Jester said. "You keep running out of time in your hurry to save time!"

She giggled and after a moment Tico joined her. The trio progressed to the lower floor at a more dignified pace.

Tico paused in the doorway to stare longingly at his beloved, who slept like a princess in a fairy tale.

"She is so lovely," he murmured. "So strong, so wise, so gentle! And her courage! She could have let you find me without endangering herself, but she is a lioness among women, my Miriam."

"I think I'm going to be sick," the PDA muttered in Korda's ear.

"Hush," Korda said. "Tico, if you come over by Miriam with me, you can sit within her bottled time after I reactivate her unit. That is, if you can bear sitting that close to her while she is still under the poison's effects."

Tico looked shocked.

"Bear to sit near her! I shall be the trellis on which my flower of the desert will lean. Not only will I be her support, I will be her spreading shade against the sun, her—"

Korda raised a hand. "Tico, before I reactivate her unit, tell me one thing. Do you know anything about the effects of the bite of the blond tarantula?"

The innocent question drained the blood from Tico's face. He leaned against a wall, stared blankly at Korda.

"The blond tarantula?" he whispered. "You said she had been made ill by a spider bite! You did not say that it was the bite of the blond tarantula!"

Korda looked at him. "This, then, is a significant oversight on my part?"

"Slyve!" Tico hissed in reply. "Slyve! The blond tarantula, the servant of Sheikh Dwistor, he who rules the universe of Aurans."

"This doesn't sound good, Boss," Jester commented.

Tico continued speaking as if he had not heard the PDA's words. "The first bite from Slyve causes sleep, deep and filled with dreams of the torments suffered by sinners in the afterlife. The second bite! The second bite, for all but a very few, brings death and those few who live suffer insanity!"

"How do you know all this?" Korda said. "Could it just be conjecture? Rumor?"

Tico shook his head. "Slyve was a gift to Sheikh Dwistor from mad Merriwind Tatchet, the ruler of the universe of Verdry. In Verdry what is insane is normal, all that is normal becomes insane. I do not know why Merriwind Tatchet made this gift to Dwistor, but I do know most truly the effects of the blond tarantula's bite."

Korda stared at him, dreading the answer that he knew must come. "How do you know this, Tico?"

"I am a close servant of Sheikh Dwistor," Tico said softly. "There is a hierarchy among those who serve our all-powerful lord and ruler. The average citizens of Aurans do their jobs and live their lives below the burning glow of the twin suns. For them, life is much as it is elsewhere, although there is more of magic and order, and for many that is enough to make even a servant's tasks things of beauty.

"Those who further the will of Dwistor himself are ranked by what secrets they share—and no secret is more precious to Dwistor than the secret of the palace mirage. Those who know this are given the most important titles, the greatest wealth, the most fascinating duties, but Dwistor does not trust even these. If you are invited to enter the innermost circle of Dwistor's servants, you must seal your pact . . . "

He stopped as if the words choked him. Korda finished for him.

"You must accept being bitten by the spider, Slyve. If you do so, then he has a hold over you, for a second bite means death or insanity." Korda's voice dropped. "What a horrid thing!"

"Yes," Tico said. "The experience is more terrible than my poor eloquence can express. Now, I learn that my darling, my desert flower, my sweet rescuing angel, is caught within those mad, mad dreams! And why?"

"We told you that Dwistor coveted her for his harem," Korda said sternly. "Apparently when Dwistor could not find her, he set Slyve to watch for her coming here. When the stasis fell, it trapped the spider but Miriam accidentally awakened it."

Tico stood straight, self-pity falling from him in response to the challenge in Korda's voice.

"You are correct, Korda, as far as you speak, but you do not know the worst of it. Stories say that Slyve and Dwistor can communicate telepathically. If, in those moments when he was active, Slyve contacted Dwistor, then Dwistor is warned of your presence here. Dwistor may not know of your talents, but he trusts outsiders as little as Deter of Urbs does. You must decide whether you will speak to Dwistor before you continue your job here and reawaken Aurans."

Korda considered. "I think that my first job is to get you and Miriam back to the *Jester*. Once we're there, we can recharge your bottled time unit and Jester can see if she can whip up an antidote for Miriam. Then we can talk further about my goals."

"And plan a wedding!" Jester piped up. "Remember, Boss! You promised Arabou that when you found Tico you'd arrange to get him and Miriam hitched!"

Korda rubbed his eyes with the heels of his hands. "Thanks, Jes. I just might have forgotten in all the other excitement. Very well, you find a way to awaken Sleeping Beauty and I'll see what I can do about marrying her to her handsome prince."

X

It was quite possibly the strangest wedding that Korda had attended in all his centuries. Had there ever been another wedding where the father of the bride had to be pulled—literally—out of a bottle? Or where the maid of honor was a ship's computer and the best man also the celebrant? Oddities aside, it worked beautifully.

Jester used the ship's medical libraries to come up with an antidote for Slyve's poison.

"It isn't perfect, Sugar Pop," she confessed, "but it will enable Miriam to recover without having to suffer all of those nightmares. She's still going to be at risk from a second bite—maybe not as much as Tico will be, but the chance that the second bite would be fatal is pretty high."

Korda looked down at Miriam. She was sleeping peacefully now, her features just a bit flushed.

"I'm certain that she'll avoid being bitten at all costs," he said. "I can't imagine that nightmare is a situation that one invites."

When Tico was certain that Miriam was out of danger, he donned a freshly charged harness of bottled time and rode the flying carpet in to bring out Arabou.

The blind trader's face was streaked with tears of relief when he was reunited with his daughter and her fiancé. Not knowing how Dwistor would react to his prize being taken away from him, Tico and Miriam decided to be wed by the laws of the Old Terran Regional Government. In this way, they would not bring Dwistor's wrath down on any unwitting religious authority or justice of the peace.

Korda brought the *Jester* just outside the pocket universe and then, in his capacity as captain of the ship, performed the wedding service. The bride and groom decided to forgo their honeymoon until Korda was done with his work and Aurans was out of stasis. Instead, they pledged their assistance to Korda.

Although a part of him wanted to have any civilians out of the way, Korda could not deny that he needed their help. He set course to refuel the *Jester*, then—after the wedding breakfast had been cleared away—he poured a final cup of coffee and put his mind to work.

"Tell me what you can about Sheikh Dwistor," he said to his three Auransan allies. "Anything at all, no matter how insignificant, may help me to deduce the manner in which he would have a world key hidden."

"Why does that matter?" Jester asked. For the wedding she had appeared in an even more elaborate version of her Arabian Nights costume, complete with a gold ring in her navel and a band of polished coins across her forehead. For this conference she had reverted back to her standard jester's garb. "Didn't Nizzim Rochtar do the hiding of the world key, the way Charlie Bell did on Urbs?"

Korda nodded approvingly. "The answer is yes and no. Yes, Nizzim Rochtar would have done the mechanics, but I suspect that on Aurans, as on Urbs, some of the details of the design would have been dictated by the purchaser —in this case, by Dwistor."

Silence fell as each of those present mulled over Korda's request. Arabou broke the silence first.

"I was not born on Aurans. The universe was first opened to emigrants when I was a man in my twenties. A new universe is a good market for a merchant. I liked the idea of being able to work in a place where the rules had yet to be fixed, so I came to Aurans.

"At that time, the planet open for habitation was Aurans itself. Haring, although more earthlike in its range of climates and temperate zones, was not offered as an option. This made many turn away, but I was fascinated by what I learned of Aurans' deserts, beasts, and magics. I came looking for a job, I found a home."

Arabou paused and felt around the table for his juice glass. With silent courtesy, Miriam put it in his hand and closed his fingers around it. After he had drunk, the blind man continued.

"In those early days, Dwistor himself was still interviewing those who would colonize his universe. I was struck by his strange, untouchable charisma. This was a man who could lead armies—who most certainly had led troops of some sort—but those who followed his banner might never know why they followed him with such devotion.

"I was granted my entry visa, told the rules of trade, and permitted to bring in trade goods from Universe Prime. I was even invited to attend a biannual trade conference to help shape how Aurans would develop. I did so—and at those meetings I learned something about Sheikh Dwistor that I found frightening."

The old trader's voice fell as if, even outside the universe of Aurans, Dwistor might hear his words. Around the table, the others leaned forward.

"There is no pity in Dwistor. A blind man learns to recognize pity and its kinder sister, compassion. Dwistor feels pity for no one at all, not even for himself. And without pity, he cannot grant mercy, nor give compassion, nor love, either—he cannot understand the need to assist those in need. He understands law and limits and even something of loyalty, but he does not feel pity."

Korda shuddered. Aurans, despite its blazing twin suns, suddenly seemed like a very cold universe. Across the table, Tico slipped his hand around Miriam's shoulders and hugged her close.

She touched her husband's beard gently with her fingertips, a tiny, private embrace. Then she spoke.

"My memories of Sheikh Dwistor are not as old as those of my father," the newlywed bride said in hushed tones, "yet I was born beneath the sister suns and something of the pulse of Dwistor's universe is knotted into my blood and bone. Before my mother died a few years ago, she was the center of a circle of weaver women who met at our house to knot both carpets and stories."

On the holopad, Jester raised a hand for attention. "Wait a second. I thought that you said that you didn't have a house."

Miriam's pretty face became tinted with sorrow. "Father and I sold the house after Mother's death. It was too haunted by her presence. We preferred to wander from bazaar to bazaar."

"Right." Jester fidgeted a little uncomfortably.

"There is no need to feel awkward or sad, little electronic imp," Tico said. "Now Miriam and her father both have a home with me."

Jester beamed at him. "You *are* a nice man, Tico. Even if you are impulsive!"

Tico blushed. "Let my dear lady tell on, Jester."

Miriam picked up the thread of her story. "Always, the weavers' gossip would turn to matters of the heart—marriages, divorces, betrothals. One piece of news would always stir the weavers into great debate and this was the news that Sheikh Dwistor had chosen to take another woman into his harem.

"The weavers were greatly divided as to whether this was an unparalleled honor or a tragedy. Often whether the girl had given her heart elsewhere would decide the question, but others were certain that even an unattached girl could have no more horrid fate than entering Dwistor's harem."

Miriam wove a lattice out of her fingers. "Some said that the harem women were given the finest medical care, including drugs that preserved their youth and beauty.

They had no other work than tending to Sheikh Dwistor and, as he seemed indifferent to the rivalries and favoritism of the harem, this was not a difficult task. Some friends of my mother, those who had worked hard beneath the suns all their lives and had seen their beauty shrivel in the heat, thought that the harem girls had a fine life.

"Others argued, however, that the harem women had empty lives. They were not permitted to bear children, for Dwistor wants no rivals to his power. Their entertainments were the simplest and the most frivolous, so their minds ceased to grow.

"One woman—a friend of my aunt—told us how her sister had been taken into Dwistor's harem. Twice a year the sister was permitted to visit her family. With each year that passed, although she stayed young and beautiful, the sister became more and more vacuous until the family felt as if a ghost with their kinswoman's face visited them. When she failed to visit them for over a year, no one noticed, and when at last they inquired after her from a representative of the palace they were told that she had slipped in a bath and drowned."

"Gee!" Jester said when Miriam fell silent. "I'm awfully glad that we rescued you from that."

Miriam smiled, something of her vivacity returning as she hugged Tico. "So am I, Jester! So am I!"

Korda made a few thoughtful notes on a notebook with a light pencil. What he was learning had convinced him that access to the world key would be hidden within the palace. An untrusting man like Dwistor would not put the key to his universe in any less secure place.

Tico waited until Korda finished writing before offering his own anecdote.

"As a member of Dwistor's inner circle, I learned many things about our supreme ruler that others might only suspect. Dwistor is a strange man. Sometimes he is so aloof that one could suspect that, as Arabou said, he feels nothing for anyone."

Arabou raised a finger in protest. "I said that he felt no pity and that I thought he could not feel any of the caring emotions without that insight into another's need."

"I am not contradicting you, father-in-law," Tico said, "I only bring up your point to show the contrast to another facet of Dwistor's personality."

"Speak on, son," Arabou said.

"Sheikh Dwistor would often leave the palace and his comforts to go out among his people in the guise of one of them," Tico said. "His chamberlain told me that Dwistor's favorite costume was that of a desert nomad. In those robes, he would join one of their caravans, claiming to be from another tribe. He would stay with them, listening to their talk, hunting the fierce ketter beasts, and then vanishing again."

"Was he spying?" Jester asked.

Tico spread his hands wide in an eloquent gesture of puzzlement.

"I do not know, impling," he said. "For a time, I believed this was the case and made a study of the nomads. My research taught me that they live in a culture of their own. They view the cities as useful places to buy manufactured goods, but they do not pay attention to politics or causes. In many ways, they are like the gypsies of Old Terra—a people within a people—exclusive to themselves."

Miriam stirred from her listening silence. "So, Sheikh Dwistor could not learn much from them, could he?"

"Not unless he set them to find specific information for him," Tico said. "I began to believe that Sheikh Dwistor used his time with the desert nomads as a vacation, a time when no one knew him and nothing was expected of him that he could not earn with his own personal strengths."

Korda made a note, then turned to Tico. "Did Sheikh Dwistor ever leave the universe of Aurans?"

Tico nodded. "Yes, he had several trips he made each standard year. Once a year he went to the pocket universe of Fortuna to enter his racing camels in the Camel Derby. Aurans has several large prize races each year, all for the purpose of helping Dwistor select those camels he would take with him to Fortuna. It is a great honor to be selected and a winning breeder or trainer becomes an Auransan hero."

"Camel races," Jester muttered. "That's really weird."

Miriam shook her head. "Not at all, Jester. The racing camel is a beautiful sight and since the races incorporate endurance trials as well as speed, they are fine and vital beasts."

Korda wrote "Racing camels. Fortuna." Then an idea occurred to him.

"Jester, check the notes we had from the Terran Regional Representative. If I remember correctly, both Fortuna and the place Tico mentioned earlier—Verdry— are among the universes commissioned by God's Pockets."

Jester made a show of checking in a vast file cabinet, although, of course, the information had been ready since Korda framed his question.

"You got it, Sugar Pop," she said, slamming a file drawer shut. "It seems that the owners of these universes and the mysterious financiers of God's Pockets might be one and the same."

The three Auransan guests looked puzzled, but they were too courteous to pry. Rubbing his hands together, Korda turned to Tico.

"As one of Sheikh Dwistor's ministers of trade, would you happen to know other places where Aurans did business?"

Tico scratched one eyebrow. "Urbs and Universe Prime, of course. Some with Fortuna, almost all export; Fortuna manufactures little but opportunities for games. We are also members in a central trade nexus for pocket universes. The nexus is something of a clearinghouse that allows representatives of pocket universes to meet and do business without giving away the locations of their home universes. That is all I can think of from the official end."

"Arabou?" Korda said. "Is there anything that your murmurs in the bazaar have hinted?"

"Last Cybersoul," Arabou said, "I heard something. Give me a moment to remember the details. Is there any more of this excellent mango nectar?"

"Plenty," Jester assured him. "I'll have the dispenser fill you a glass. Ice?"

"Please," Arabou said.

He sat in meditation for several minutes, sipping his juice. At last he spoke a single cryptic phrase.

"Silicon chips and electronic hardware." The blind man pushed his juice glass from him. "Are you all familiar with the holiday of Cybersoul?"

"You bet I am," Jester said. For once her hologram's cute features wore a serious expression. "It's a celebration recognizing the unique spiritual nature of intelligent machines. I celebrate it every standard year—and the Boss gives me flowers."

Korda shrugged, almost embarrassed. "Well, she *is* a lady—or she thinks she is, which is good enough for me."

"On Aurans," Arabou said, "we also celebrate Cybersoul. Along with Eallsfaith, it is one of our two most important spiritual observances. Last Cybersoul, I went to a party held by Cho Redi, the very talented android accountant who handles my records. As might be expected, given the holiday and the host, the majority of the guests were not flesh and blood people. There were many androids and computers, as well as cyborgs and 'normal' people like myself.

"My blindness became a topic of conversation. Many of the guests could not believe that with cyborg enhancements available, I choose to remain without sight. The debate was fascinating, with some arguing that artificial sight could not be anything like 'real' sight and others, especially some computers, arguing heatedly that as the analogs were identical there would be no difference. A few of the cyborgs, who had experienced both, got embroiled in a heated argument, with some holding that their enhanced sight was better and others not.

"I may seem to stray from the topic, but as this argument threatened to become more than verbal, Cho Redi said, 'It really is a moot point at this moment. Even if Arabou wanted to try artificial sight, there has been such a run on parts that I doubt he could get eyes.'"

Korda made a note. "That is very interesting. Do continue, Arabou."

Arabou cleared his throat. "Many of those attending Cho's Cybersoul party were in trade. They told story after story about peculiarities of the current electronics business. Those in manufacturing recounted how their entire production lines had been purchased by mysterious agents they had never met before. Those in sales told of having their entire line bought out and then being unable to purchase more because the manufacturers were working full speed on another order.

"After the party, I did some quiet research and learned that the stories were true, but I had no luck finding out who the purchaser was. Then, about two months after it had started, the rush ended. A few businesses were ruined; a few more profited. That was that."

Miriam stretched and then rose to refill her father's glass with mango nectar. When she returned to the table, she looked at the serious faces of the three men.

"You all think that Sheikh Dwistor was the mysterious purchaser, don't you?" she asked. "Why does that trouble you so much? Isn't one of the reasons for having a private universe to be able to get whatever you want and not answer questions?"

"Precisely!" Tico said. "My love is as brilliant as she is beautiful. Truly Allah has blessed me. Only Dwistor could have made those purchases without official comment, but Dwistor would not have needed to make them in secret. The charter that every immigrant signs on taking up residency and every born citizen signs on achieving adulthood acknowledges that we are here on Dwistor's sufferance. He could have commandeered what he wanted. Why didn't he?"

Arabou rubbed his temples. "I don't know, my son, and not knowing makes my head ache. Dwistor has commandeered the fruits of private enterprise in the past. Twice, to my knowledge, he has 'borrowed' starships— once merely to transport racing camels to Fortuna. I know stories of his taking other, less obvious things that have caught his fancy."

"Like women for his harem?" Jester said innocently.

Arabou did not rise to the bait, but continued rubbing his temples. Korda glanced over his notes.

"From what I see here, the only reason for Sheikh Dwistor to hide the acquisition of large quantities of electronic parts is that he did not want it known what he was doing. The only reasons I can see for that are either that he wanted the stuff for some secret project or that he was afraid someone would learn he was stockpiling electronics and that the knowledge would in some way hurt him."

Jester twirled on her holopad. "Boss, I'm not sure I followed that."

Korda grinned. "It was convoluted. Fine, let's take it a step at a time. Has there been any construction that you know of, anywhere within the universe of Aurans, that would justify Dwistor needing so many raw electronic parts."

Two heads shook and Tico said, "No, not that I have heard—and the Minister for Internal Development is one of my closest friends. She and I play poker once a week and trade inside stories. I'm certain she would have said something."

"Then," Korda said, "either the construction is so secret that even the Minister for Internal Development knows nothing of it—"

"I think that's unlikely," Tico interrupted. "She's a cyborg and a hacker. She makes it her business to know even what she's not supposed to know."

"Or," Korda continued with an appreciative nod, "Dwistor was acquiring those electronic parts for someone else, someone he does not want anyone to know he is associated with, possibly someone of whom he is afraid."

"Afraid? Sheikh Dwistor?" Miriam's laughter pealed like bells. "I may not have wanted to be in his harem, but I will defend him on this. The man wrestles ketter beasts for fun, duels with experts—and wins. His courage is beyond question."

Tico patted her hand. "I agree, my pretty whirlwind, that in normal things Sheikh Dwistor's courage is beyond question, beyond even comment. We of Aurans accept his courage as we do sand and sunlight."

"As omnipresent annoyances?" Jester quipped.

Tico smiled briefly. "Yet, there was a day when I was at the palace that I would swear that I saw Sheikh Dwistor as cowed as a gerbil faced by a cobra."

Tico paused, filled his glass with ice water, and then, since there were no questions, he went on.

"I was attending a meeting of the senior ministers of Aurans. Sheikh Dwistor was attending the meeting, listening, commenting, but not presiding. This was his habit. Partway through the meeting, a message was brought to him. Sheikh Dwistor paled beneath his tan. Even the whites of his eyes seemed to become whiter—"

"Tico . . . You're exaggerating . . . ," Miriam chided softly.

"Perhaps a small amount," Tico said, pressing his fingers together to show how slight the exaggeration was. "I have never seen a man so cowed. Dwistor rose without comment, left the room, and did not return. When next I saw him, he seemed normal, but for days I watched the heavens expecting some nameless catastrophe of cosmic proportions, for I had come to believe that only that would make Sheikh Dwistor afraid."

Korda glanced at his notes. "Tico, do you recall who brought the message? It could have been a clue about the saboteur. If I could speak to the messenger—"

"Yes, I understand," Tico said. "Let me think. It was not one of the usual runners. It was Slyve!"

"Slyve?" Korda said. "The tarantula?"

"Yes," Tico answered. "I am sure of that because the sight of that monster always made me uneasy and I wondered why it had come into our meeting."

"Why didn't Slyve just telepathically contact Dwistor if it wanted him?" Jester asked.

"The message was hard-copy," Tico said. "A small glass disk, as for a reader. I doubt the spider can read."

"How long ago was this?" Korda asked.

"Quite a while ago," Tico said, "At least three-quarters of a standard year."

"Right before," Arabou said thoughtfully, "the run began on electronic equipment. How very, very interesting."

Korda glanced back over his notes. "We've strayed quite a way from the question of how Sheikh Dwistor might hide his world key, but I think we've got some interesting stuff here. Dwistor seems to be dealing with at least three other God's Pockets universes: Urbs, Fortuna, and Verdry.

"Although usually fearless—even cold—there is someone or something Dwistor fears enough that he pales when a message arrives—even before he has a chance to read the message. This person or thing may have enough leverage over him to force him to secretly disrupt his own economy."

Miriam spread her hands. "But is the person he fears the same who shut off the universe or someone else? What could an absolute ruler of a universe fear?"

Korda turned off his notebook. "I don't know. To be honest, I'm not certain I want to find out, but I have a terrible suspicion that I just might before all this is over."

XI

The *Jester* reentered the pocket universe of Aurans a few hours later. Nothing appeared to have changed. The worlds still sat unmoving in their orbits, the suns hung frozen in their dance.

"Fuel efficiency has improved, Boss," the computer reported. "Looks like your alterations are working fine."

"Thanks," Korda said. "Tico, you tell Jester where to take us."

Following Tico's instructions, the *Jester* landed in a section of desert that from above resembled a fragmented jigsaw puzzle. Jagged interruptions of black rock shot with mica glittered like a demon's wedding band in the sunlight. Cliffs and mesas interrupted the smooth golden sand.

"Rene, I don't suppose you remember what I said about the name of my private starship, do you?" Tico began with his usual indirect approach.

"I remember that you had named it the *Whirlwind*," Korda said, "and that whirlwinds were means of transportation on Aurans."

"Allah has blessed you with a sharp memory, friend,"

Tico said with a smile. "Whirlwinds are indeed a method of transportation on this planet. As I understand it, Sheikh Dwistor wanted some of the conveniences of modern transportation without ruining the planet's Arabian Nights motif. Therefore, we have flying carpets, winged camels, and whirlwinds."

Miriam made a swirling gesture with her index finger. "Special whirlwinds travel designated routes—usually between cities or major oases. Using one, travelers reach their goal within minutes rather than hours."

"Do you just walk into the wind?" Korda asked, remembering his own unpleasant experience with the sandstorm on magnetic north.

"Yes and no," Tico said. "At the start of your journey, you purchase a ticket. Then you are given an amulet that protects you from the force of the wind. Without such an amulet—as many a would-be fare-jumper has found—the wind will batter you, sometimes even to death."

"I bet I've guessed what this has to do with the world key," Jester said smugly.

Tico grinned at her. "I am certain that you have, imp of electricity, but your thought processes are as swift and sure as the legs of a running gazelle."

"Gee!" Jester said. "Boss, why don't you say such nice things?"

"I might," Korda said, "especially if you stopped calling me 'Sugar Pop.'"

"That's blackmail!" Jester protested.

"Enough, Jes," Korda said sternly. "Let Tico finish his story."

"As Jester has guessed," Tico said, "the only way to the palace is to ride a specific whirlwind—and to ride this whirlwind you need a special amulet. I have one, but we will need two more."

"Two?" Arabou said.

"I'm going with them, Father," Miriam said firmly, "but you must remain. Dwistor's palace is a dangerous place."

"And I am no longer young," Arabou finished sadly, "and blind in addition."

"I am certain that your blindness would not be a limitation," Korda said honestly. "Miriam tells me that you have traveled all through Aurans and to other universes as well. However, I would like Tico's help and Miriam insists that she will not let him go without her."

"Allah save us from a stubborn woman," Tico said with a fond glance at his wife.

Miriam blushed, but did not budge from her position that she must go with them.

"I have a touch of the second sight," she said, "and I believe that you will need me."

Arabou turned his blind gaze on his daughter. "I will remain, for I do not see how I could be of much assistance. I have never been within the palace, nor have I any knowledge of universe design."

"You will not be as useless as you seem to believe," Korda said. "Thanks to the supplies in my ship, we will be able to carry about eight hours of bottled time apiece.

That should be enough—but if it isn't, we may not be able to return in time to recharge. You will be able to track us through Jester's PDA. If we fall into stasis, you must take the *Jester* and report for me to the Terran Regional Representative."

Arabou nodded. "And Jester will listen to my commands, even if I must tell her to abandon you?"

"She will," Korda said, aware that from the holopad Jester was glaring at him.

Tico pushed a light pad into the center of the table and began to sketch a rough map.

"I learned from my friend the Minister for Internal Affairs that the extra amulets for the palace whirlwind are stored in the caverns within these cliffs. In addition to ignorance, they have several protections."

He pointed to his map. "The first is the maze of the caverns itself. Dwistor has an enchantment set on them so that their appearance changes. Only after many visits can one learn the pattern. I have put what I remember on this map. We should each carry a copy."

"I can make them," Jester offered.

Tico continued. "The second defense is the ketter beasts that prowl the maze. The third is the siren crystals."

"Siren crystals?" Korda asked.

"Singing crystals that make a music so sweet that the listener stands entranced, unaware of anything else," Tico explained. "I heard one once, when I came to investigate the caverns. The sound was nearly as lovely as

Miriam's voice."

Miriam giggled. "Tico, sometimes you are over-ful-some in your praise."

"Not at all, my desert flower," he said, clasping her hand. "I mean every word I say. Were it not that your voice is the sweetest sound in any universe to me, I should have been trapped. Sheikh Dwistor would have been very angry with me when I was discovered in his secret place."

Korda tapped his chin thoughtfully. "If we're careful to keep from awakening the crystals with our bottled time, we should be safe from their lure. Like everything else on Aurans, they should be under stasis."

"Ketter beasts are ferocious but stupid," Miriam said. "They are also always hungry."

"I'll synthesize you some beastie biscuits," Jester said, "along with the maps. How soon will you need them?"

"As soon as possible," Korda said, rising from his seat. "I'll go put on my sandals and hit the 'fresher."

They entered the caverns through a narrow crack between two leaning rocks, which the wind had carved with mournful faces. Jester led the way, the mouth of her PDA open and a beam of clear light shining forth.

The humans edged in after her. Scraping slightly against the rough edges of the stone, they came into the first chamber. Korda switched on his powerful flashlight so they could see the area and immediately took a step back.

"Watch it!" he warned. "There's a drop-off here. We're safe enough on this ledge, but this is no place for a wrong step."

"I see what you mean, Boss," Jester said, sending her PDA out to look into the cavern.

The cavern had been beautifully designed to look as though sometime in Aurans' built-in geological past a river had cut its way through the glittering limestone. What it had left was a fissure in the heart of the rock that soared above into blackness and below into echoing depths.

Assorted hunks of rock, small in the titanic vastness of the chamber but each several meters across, interrupted the void—islands of stone whose roots were buried in the darkness below. From the ledge on which they stood, the trio could see that strung between the stone islands were thick cables of spiderweb. They glistened with a viscous fluid that occasionally released a pearlescent tear to drop into the darkness.

"This cavern is somewhat changed from my last visit," Tico said, shining his own light about. "Then the webs were not here and there was a narrow ledge around the edge. If you knew it was there, you could creep along it to the tunnels on the other side."

Jester's PDA darted along the edges. "I don't see anything at all, Tico. My personal radar agrees with the visual check. If there was a ledge, it has been removed."

"The spider webs bode ill," Miriam said. "Perhaps they were woven by some ordinary giant spider, but what if

Sheikh Dwistor has sent Slyve here before us?"

Korda decided he really didn't want to know about other types of giant spiders. Instead he knelt and gently touched a strand of the web.

"Sticky," he said, "and I don't think it's strong enough to carry us—even if I wanted to trust myself to it."

He twanged the web more decisively then shone his light around the cavern.

"A spider would have come to see what was caught in its web, wouldn't it?" he asked Tico and Miriam.

Tico tugged at his beard. "Perhaps, but not necessarily. Aurans has its share of magical beasts. A giant spider might be clever enough to watch from concealment."

"Slyve would be," Miriam agreed with a shudder. "Still, we do not wish to turn back. Are there any other ways in, Tico?"

"Not that I know of," he admitted.

"Then we must find a way from what we have with us or waste time returning to the ship."

A playful grin lit stars in her beautiful dark eyes and she removed the pack she carried and drew a roll of fabric from within.

"I have accompanied my father on many trade missions and have learned to prepare." She shook out the fabric and laid the flying carpet on the stone. "Your vehicle awaits, my friends. Tico, please sit behind me. Rene, you sit behind him."

"Did I not say that Miriam is as wise as she is lovely!" Tico exclaimed, taking his place on the carpet.

"You did indeed," Korda agreed with a small chuckle. "Lady, we await."

"I'll take the high guard and let you know if any spiders are going to jump you," Jester said cheerfully.

"My joy," Korda said softly as the carpet rose, "knows no bounds."

"Thanks, Sugar Pop!" Jester said. "I appreciate you, too."

Miriam steered the carpet over the webs and beneath the jagged ceiling. Although her passengers watched the shadows above and below with tense shoulders, nothing dropped to attack.

"I'd almost feel better if something had attacked us," Tico said, as Miriam landed the carpet on a ledge on the other side. "Now I have reason to suspect that Slyve has indeed been sent to guard this place against us."

"But how would it move in the stasis?" Jester said.

"The same way we do," Korda said, waiting for Miriam to finish stowing the carpet. In a small corner of his mind he admired how the tightly knotted weaving stowed away as if it had little more bulk than a beach towel. "Sheikh Dwistor—or someone else—has outfitted it with bottled time."

Tico held out a hand to Miriam. "Then we proceed with even more care than we planned. Perhaps it will run out of time before we do."

"Seven and a half hours left," the PDA reported, anticipating Korda's request, "and counting."

Korda shone his light in front of him. Two tunnels,

each dark, each unmarked, interrupted the smooth rock wall.

"Which do we take, Tico?"

Tico frowned. "Left, I think. Left for the heart, since the love of my life stands at my side."

"Is there no better reason to choose, my husband?" Miriam asked, smiling in spite of herself.

"No better," Tico admitted. "If the caverns are as they were before, both tunnels will lead into the labyrinth. Neither is more direct than the other. We may as well choose our omens."

Korda stepped through the left entrance and motioned for the others to follow.

"Jes," he said, "you take point, but don't get too far ahead. Remember that your bottled time will awaken anything, even on the fringes of its effect, so don't get too curious."

"Right, Boss," she said.

They walked for about fifteen minutes in watchful silence. Paths branched off periodically, but Jester probed ahead. Her radar would reach only as far as the limits of her bottled time but she spared them taking many dead ends.

"Boss," she reported, "I've located a purplish glow leaking around the next bend. Any thoughts?"

"That is the light of one of the siren crystals," Tico said. "They lure the unwary near with their light and beauty then sing them to their doom."

"Cover your ears, folks," Korda said. "Jester, turn off

your audio receptors, then go and see if there will be room for us to get around the crystal without taking it out of stasis."

Her report marched across the inside of his shades: "YOU CAN GET AROUND THIS ONE, BOSS, IF YOU HUG THE RIGHT SIDE OF THE PATH. I'VE CHECKED AND THERE ARE NO SPIDERS OR OTHER NASTIES IN THE ROCKS."

Korda shared the information. Tico nodded and Miriam burrowed in her pack again and came out with a handful of earplugs.

"I had Jester fabricate these," she said, "as soon as Tico mentioned the crystals. She said that they may not block all of the effects, since she didn't know how to block magical music, but they may help."

Korda rubbed his forehead. "I can't believe I overlooked such an obvious precaution. Thank you, ladies."

The PDA bobbed over to grin in his face. "Don't worry about it, Boss. Miriam and I couldn't let you fellows get hurt. Who would we have to pick on?"

Tico grinned and began another paean to Miriam's beauty and wisdom. Sighing, Korda stuffed the plugs in his ears, interrupting comparisons to Cleopatra and the queen of Sheba.

The siren crystal stood about five feet high and was faceted much like a quartz crystal. Captivating violet light glowed from within, all the more striking against the darkness of the tunnel. Even knowing the danger, Korda found himself tempted to break off a chunk. It would make an elegant jewel to dangle from a woman's ear.

He sighed, glad no one could hear him. Who did he have to give jewelry to? His one marriage had ended centuries ago. He didn't even know if his ex-wife was alive. The PDA would look even sillier with an earring and Tico, not him, should be thinking about hanging jewels from Miriam's shapely lobes to set soft fires within the ebon darkness of her flowing hair.

Korda hurried his steps, wondering if some small part of the siren crystal effect was reaching him despite their precautions. Perhaps over time a faint aura of its magic had penetrated the crystal's surroundings. Not wanting to explain, he did not ask Tico and Miriam what, if anything, they had felt. Hopefully, it would not matter.

About fifteen minutes later, after skirting several more siren crystals, the path they were following took them into another cavern. The ceiling and floor were lower than in the tunnels and interrupted by stalagmites and stalactites. A faint scent of dampness and musk permeated the still air.

Tico rubbed his hands together happily. "We are on the right track now. On the other side of this chamber we should find the mystic Lake of Transport. Dwistor stores his amulets within the waters for they help to preserve and strengthen the magic."

"Boss!" Jester interrupted suddenly. "Movement from inside the cavern. Several somethings. Big! There's a bottled time glow with them."

Korda set his light down on wide beam to free his

hands. He heard Miriam give a small shriek of terror.

"Ketter beasts!"

Tico cursed. "I feared this when we did not meet any in the maze. Someone has brought them here to wait for us."

Korda knelt and began rifling through his pack to find the "beastie biscuits" Jester had made for them. Then he saw the first ketter beast and his hands fell still.

His immediate impression was of a toadfish crossed with a *Tyrannosaurus rex*. The ketter beast was at least nine feet in height, but it was so blocky that it gave the impression of being massive rather than tall. It was bipedal, balanced by a heavy tail. A huge head made up at least a third of its length. The head was dominated by a wide mouth full of teeth. Tiny eyes stared out of folds of mottled brown skin.

Despite its bulk, it moved with a linebacker's solid grace. Korda felt certain that the only reason that it had not sprung on them before Jester could give warning was that the stalagmites and stalactites impeded its progress slightly.

"Jester, how many of them are there?" Tico yelled.

"I see four," the PDA replied. "Ugly in the front, Uglier and Uglier coming around the sides, and Ugliest waiting by the exit into the next cavern. If it's any comfort, I think old Ugliest is chained in place."

Korda rose, his handful of biscuits seeming rather small and insubstantial. He would need to make certain the creature's mouth was open when he tossed them—

he couldn't risk that it would ignore the offering. From the corner of his eye, he could see that Miriam and Tico were similarly prepared.

"Maybe we should just shoot them," he said, half in question.

Tico shook his head. "Unless you have a complete disintegration beam, it will do you little good. The vital organs are well protected within the body mass. Sheikh Dwistor is one of the few hunters I know who can hit the vitals on a regular basis. Almost everyone else wounds the beast and makes it so insane with pain that it goes berserk."

"Oh," Korda said.

Hoping that his arm remembered the reflexes he had honed while pitching Little League over thirty decades ago in Tennessee, he feinted toward the lead ketter beast.

"Hey, Ugly!" he yelled.

As he had hoped it would, it opened its mouth to roar at him. He pitched and his aim was true. Five beastie biscuits soared into the ketter beast's gaping maw. Two vanished down its gullet. The slimy tongue rippled as if tasting the others.

Tico was readying himself to deal with the ketter beast approaching on the left. Miriam stood with her biscuits in hand, but she seemed less than certain.

Korda readied another handful of biscuits. "Jes, what did you put in these?"

"Dehydrated meat, meat juices, salt, parmesan cheese, and a solid dose of soporific," the PDA answered.

"Sounds good," Korda said. He tossed again, this time not aiming for the beast's mouth, but for the ground in front of it. He wanted it to slow down enough to let the soporific have a chance to knock it out.

On his left, Tico was doing well enough with his ketter beast, Korda was turning to check Miriam when Jester's voice came through his private audio link.

"Boss! Miriam has frozen up and the beast's closing!"

Hoping that his beast would at least pause for its cookies, Korda spun and pitched the remainder of his available biscuits at the ketter beast on the right. Most of his pitch went wild, but one biscuit hit it solidly in a tiny eye.

The beast paused to claw at its injury and Korda dove in front of Miriam. The desert girl stood pale and terrified, her hands shaking and a whimper escaping her pretty lips as she stared at the lumbering monstrosity.

Hoping Tico would not be distracted from his own battle, Korda pulled Miriam's supply of biscuits from her limp fingers and, as if throwing a fastball, coiled up and bulleted them at the ketter beast.

This time his aim was good. The biscuits hit the opening mouth at something like thirty miles per hour. The ketter beast grunted, squinted shut its good eye, and swallowed. Korda tossed another biscuit in front of the slowing beast and watched as it squatted to scoop it from the ground with its scrawny arms and stuff it into its mouth.

Korda dared glance at his first opponent. The ketter beast had turned to follow him, but its lumbering progress had slowed. As Korda watched, it teetered to a halt and with a tiny, pathetic keen fell onto its side.

Taking Miriam into his arms, Korda carried the terrified girl back to the tunnel entry. She did not protest, but cuddled into his arms as if afraid even to look. Behind him to the left, Korda heard a thud as Tico's beast went down. Then another to the right.

"Allah be praised!" Tico cried. "Allah and Jester, both! We have defeated them!"

Korda turned to see and realized that he still held trembling Miriam. His face reddened and he started to explain. Tico saved him the need, by giving a sweeping bow and taking his wife into his own arms.

"My thanks, friend," he said huskily. "I saw you save my angel when fear transformed my tigress into a poor, trembling rabbit. We will be forever grateful."

Korda smiled, hoping that Tico never knew just how desirable Korda found Miriam. He looked over at the three sleeping ketter beasts.

"You see if you can get Miriam to come out of that," he said. "I'm going to remove the bottled time from the beasts before they come around again."

Tico nodded agreement. Each beast wore only a single flask, good for about an hour. When Jester tested them, she reported that they still held at least a half hour.

"Well, we have something of a reserve," Tico said, "but I dislike what this bodes."

Korda snapped one of the extra units into his harness. "I know. Someone activated these monsters about the time we penetrated the maze. I don't doubt that their supply would have been recharged if necessary."

As Miriam accepted her extra unit, Korda noticed that she was no longer trembling. Her voice when she spoke was as dulcet and strong as ever.

"Then we are being waited for," she said. "This means that we do not dare wait for time to run out on the last beast. Do we have any biscuits left?"

"Plenty," Korda assured her, digging into his pack. He decided not to tell her how close he had come to running out of his available supply when he had been defending her. "I had no idea how many of the beasts we would meet. Let me go ahead of you two and get rid of the guardian. You can be backup."

The chained ketter beast was easy enough to convince to eat its biscuits, but it fell partially blocking the tunnel entrance. Although her initial fear had been soothed somewhat by Tico, Miriam refused to climb over the beast. As it was too heavy to push, they solved the problem by having her lie down flat on the carpet and glide under the lintel. Korda and Tico clambered over the beast. The PDA, of course, flew.

They walked down a narrow passage and emerged in a cavern lit by the glow of siren crystals. A huge, tranquil lake dominated the room; its waters were a dark purple blue.

"Is this it?" Korda asked.

Tico nodded. "Yes, before us lies the Lake of Transport. Allah willing, we should gather the amulets swiftly."

A husky, whispery voice sounded within each of their heads. They looked almost as one to where a huge blond tarantula was lowering itself from the shadowy recesses of the ceiling.

"Allah may be willing," said Slyve, "but Dwistor is not, and therefore I am not. Come forward at your peril, for I will be your deaths!"

XII

S tay back!" Korda put out his arm to block Tico when the other man would have confronted the hated spider. "You've already been bitten once. We can't risk you."

Tico hesitated, but before he could argue, Korda had left him behind. He walked across the sandy cavern floor, the crunching of his sandals the loudest sound in that windless place. As he approached, he addressed Jester through his throat-mike.

"*Jes, see if you can find a way to cut that creature's line. If we can drop it into the drink, that should short out its bottled time.*"

"RIGHT, SUGAR POP!" she wrote across the readline.

The blond tarantula swung slightly as it dropped a few feet lower. Korda could see its bottled time glowing green in a harness slung around its midsection.

"You think that you are the only clever one, human?" it hissed, the words, as before, coming directly into Korda's mind. "I see your little bee. I will sting it, but first a gift for you and the other humans."

Slyve made a tossing gesture with one of its forelimbs. Instinctively, Korda leapt back, expecting a coil of sticky web. Instead, a chunk of violet crystal landed at his feet. A sweet song rang forth, filling Korda's ears.

Immediately, he ceased to worry about Slyve's presence. The blond tarantula seemed no more a danger than a bauble hung on an Eallsfaith harp would be.

In the periphery of his vision, he saw that Tico and Miriam were embracing, dancing slowly and with careful steps to the music of the crystal. Idly he wondered if Slyve had given them a crystal of their own or if they had been close enough to share the sound of his.

Korda smiled at their happiness, nothing of loneliness or longing in the feeling. The singing of the crystal was so pretty. He hummed a few bars of the music.

His hands rose to conduct the orchestra. There was applause. He was doing brilliantly and he had never conducted before. With the slightest motion of his little finger, he gestured for the violins to soften. It was almost time for the glifnod solo; he must shift the tempo to accommodate its more jazzy tones.

A-one and a-two and a-three . . .

"Sugar Pop!"

What was that noise? Korda batted at the air around his ears. The glifnod solo was coming. It would not do for him to be distracted.

"Sugar Pop! Listen to me!"

How annoying! Korda motioned for the timpani to give a thunder roll. That effectively drowned out the noise and prepared the way elegantly for the glifnod solo. Here came the first notes—saxy and cool. They made him want to tap his feet.

"RENE KORDA, PAY ATTENTION TO ME, DAMN IT! THE SPIDER IS WALKING ACROSS THE SAND AND WILL BITE YOU IF YOU DON'T DO SOMETHING RIGHT AWAY! DON'T EXPECT ME TO DO ANYTHING. I CUT ITS THREAD BUT IT SNARED ME IN SOME SILK AND I CAN'T MOVE."

Korda looked at the words with incomprehension. Then, like a lighting flash through his cerebral cortex, he understood their import. He forced his eyes open (when had he shut them?) and saw that Slyve was inches away from his leg and rearing back to bite.

It took all of Korda's available attention to stumble back a few steps, but he succeeded in reeling far enough that the spider's bite struck the bare sand. While it spit out sand and gravel, Korda shook his head to clear it. The siren crystal was still within his bottled time, luring him back to conduct its imaginary orchestra. Hurriedly, he moved far enough to leave it singing to absent time.

Slyve was pursuing him again. Korda suspected that he could not outrun the spider for long. When it grew weary of playing tag, all it needed to do was climb back to the ceiling and web him from there.

Korda pretended to stumble and when Slyve (laughing nastily within Korda's mind) hurried up to sink his fangs into a temptingly exposed calf, Korda scooped up a double handful of sand and hit the spider in the face. While the blond tarantula was temporarily blinded, Korda reached over and snapped loose the harness holding its bottled time.

He rolled, then, so that Slyve would no longer be within his own sphere, but he was not quite fast enough. The tarantula's fangs sank into his leg. Korda felt a burning sensation that spread from the wound and flowed through his veins and arteries along with his blood. With his last bit of focused strength, he kicked out and sent Slyve flying.

As soon as it left his bottled time, the spider hung suspended in the air. Afterward, Korda was never completely certain if he had indeed seen a chisel-featured, thin, rather British blond man dressed as an Arab sheikh appear and pluck Slyve out of midair. It might have been the first of the hallucinations, for they came on hard and fast as Slyve's poison took possession of him.

He was falling—or was it that he was he rising? Each muscle in his body ached as they became separate entities, each agitating to pull away from the whole. With an effort that nearly finished him, Korda gathered the warring body into a whole. His head pounded but his vision was clear enough that he could see the castle on the horizon.

When Korda landed on the foam rubber doorstep, the thud jolted his bones, turning the marrow into peach jam. Some of it leaked out of his nose and he wiped it away carefully. He had to look his best because the doorman (who looked like an extraordinarily fat wombat in a formal kimono lapped to the right) was coming to take him before Almighty God to be judged for the events of his life.

Korda suspected that Almighty God wasn't going to be very happy with him. Hadn't he felt like a god when he created pocket universes and terraformed worlds? God most certainly wouldn't approve of such presumption. What might come next—Korda trying to use God's credit card or sleep in his bed?

Almighty God's audience hall resembled an English pub. God was playing pool on a table covered in black velvet. When Korda got close enough to the table to see the balls he discovered that they were suns and planets. The pockets were universes. Korda wondered if he had made any of them and if God approved of his artistry.

Almighty God looked rather like Charlie Bell, floppy mustache and all. His nose, however, was pointed, and long whiskers curled up from the sides (the mustache hung down). God wore many hats—a silk top hat, a straw sombrero, a baseball cap turned backward, a tall fur Russian hat. A green eyeshade was pulled low on his forehead.

When he looked at Korda, Korda saw that God had orange eyes and that they flared like suns going nova.

"Einstein said that God doesn't play dice with the universe," Almighty God said to Korda in a remarkably conversational tone, "so I don't anymore. I mean, who argues with Einstein? Pool isn't a much gentler game, but one cannot disappoint the fans. I guess you're here for judgment, aren't you?"

Korda blinked. "I think that I am."

"As you wish," Almighty God said, "but I'd rather play pool. It gets rather boring playing by myself. I mean, I'm perfect, why should I practice?"

Korda nodded rather weakly. A swarm of bees had appeared from somewhere and were stinging him. God did not appear to notice. He handed Korda a pool cue and a cube of chalk. The cue appeared to be a stiffened boa constrictor, but the chalk was just blue chalk.

Almighty God was racking the balls in a triune godhead. Korda recognized Old Terra, Mars, and Jupiter among the planets. There were the twin suns of Aurans and a couple of heavenly bodies he didn't recognize, including a planet shaped and painted like an Easter egg and another that looked like a faceted ruby.

"I'll let you break and go first," Almighty God said generously. "If I went first, you'd never get a shot. I'm perfect, you know."

"I know," Korda said, lining up the cue ball (which looked just like Jester's PDA) for what he hoped would be a good break.

As he drew back his arm to shoot, Almighty God said casually, "Why, then, did you feel a need to improve on my creation, Rene Korda? Didn't I do a good enough job the first time around?"

Korda was trying to find an answer when the cue ball rose from the table and Jester's PDA floated in front of his face.

"Jester," he hissed. "Get back there! I can't keep God

waiting!"

"Sugar Pop?" Jester said. "Are you hallucinating?"

"Jester," Korda said sternly, "get back on the table!"

The PDA continued to float in front of him. From just out of sight, God spoke softly.

"I'm still waiting for your answer, Rene Korda. Why did you improve on my perfect creation?"

Korda snagged the PDA from the air and lined up his shot.

"Because it was there?" he offered and then he made the break and planets and suns spun across the table and the pocket universes loomed from the corners and sides of the table. One rose larger than all the rest and Korda realized that it was going to swallow him.

He saw sand and rocks. "It's Aurans!" he muttered in surprise. Then he felt hands shaking him and cool water splashing across his brow.

"SUGAR POP! AM I REACHING YOU?" marched the words across the readline in his glasses.

"Jester?" he said, trying to sit up and realizing that his head was pillowed in Miriam's lap. "I was playing pool with God. How did I get here?"

The PDA laughed. "Boss, you were right here all along. Slyve bit you but I gave you the antidote. Are you feeling better?"

"I feel . . . strange," Korda answered, reluctantly removing his head from its soft rest. "Very."

Tico handed him a canteen of water. "The poison may still have some effect on you for twenty-four hours. Do you want to retreat to the *Jester* until it can wear off? We have about six hours of bottled time left, as it stands."

Korda shook his head, regretted the gesture as it made him dizzy, but got to his feet despite his spinning head.

"No, we need to keep going. For some reason, Dwistor is not helping us, even though we are trying to help Aurans. We need to keep moving before he can set up more obstacles."

"Sheikh Dwistor," Tico said, "is not a very trusting man. He probably dislikes all we have learned about the workings of his universe and fears that we will learn more."

"Is he likely to forgive us what we know?" Korda asked.

"No," Tico answered.

"Then we must continue onward," Korda said. "Perhaps if we reactivate Aurans he will understand that we don't mean either him or his universe harm."

"Perhaps," Miriam said, rising and shaking the sand off of the folds of her trousers in what Korda found a distracting fashion, "but no matter what Dwistor fears, we owe the people who live here time. They are too vulnerable to looters or vandals equipped with bottled time if we leave them in stasis."

Tico pointed to the purple Lake of Transport.

"I have already drawn forth amulets for you and Miriam, Rene, but the Lake may do us another service."

He poured the remaining water from his canteen into a cup and gave it to Korda, then he carried the empty canteen to the lake and filled it.

"The waters of the Lake of Transport," Tico explained, "when drunk, give the power of teleportation. The drinker concentrates on where he—or she—wishes to go and then if the wish is strong enough, is carried there with the speed of thought."

Korda frowned. "Why do people use whirlwinds, winged camels, and all the rest to travel, then? This seems much more efficient."

Tico rose and sealed the canteen. "Because, good Rene, the wish must be both strong and precise. Many have been lost after drinking this water. Others have appeared in the wrong place. A few failed to appear at all. Sheikh Dwistor ruled in the dim past that the water should only be used for amulets and emergencies."

Reflecting that the "dim past" of Aurans couldn't be much more than fifty or sixty years, Korda nodded. Sometimes universes were designed with historical events as well as terrain features. Aurans was apparently one of these.

"Well, this is certainly an emergency," Korda said. "Let's hope that if we need it, the water works in stasis."

"Let us hope," Miriam said, clinging to Tico's hand, "that we do not need it at all."

"Time's a-wasting!" Jester reminded them. "Let's find the whirlwind and get to the palace!"

❖ ❖ ❖

Leaving the maze was simple, as Jester had recorded the correct route. Since Korda was still weak, they rode the flying carpet, keeping low and dismounting only to work around the larger clumps of siren crystals.

Once they were outside, Tico instructed them to rub their amulets vigorously between thumb and forefinger.

"This will summon the whirlwind," he explained. "I believe it was also a small lesson in self-discipline from Sheikh Dwistor to his advisors. We were required to wear the amulets on a chain around our necks and keep them with us at all times so that they could not be stolen. Of course, there were those who could not keep from toying with something that close to hand—"

"There must have been some rather startling incidents," Korda said chuckling.

"There were indeed," Tico said. "Fortunately, I was not the source of any of them."

The PDA rose in the air. "Boss! Look, due west, something's coming!"

They all looked and Tico said, "That is the whirlwind. Jester, I suggest you tuck your floating manifestation within one of Rene's pockets. Otherwise, you may be blown away or smashed."

In wide loops, rather reminiscent of the approaching wind, the PDA descended. Korda undid the flaps on his tunic pocket.

"This should be safe," he said, motioning to her.

"Oh, Sugar Pop," Jester cooed softly. "You're hiding me close to your heart!"

Unaccountably, Korda felt himself blushing. He covered his reaction by concentrating on getting to his feet. The medication Jester had given him had nearly countered the poison, but he still felt a bit woozy.

The whirlwind that arrived was neatly self-contained compared to the sandstorm at magnetic north. Its purposeful approach left no doubt that this was what Tico had summoned, but Korda found himself surreptitiously wiping sweaty palms on his trouser legs.

"How . . . How does it work?" he asked. "I don't see any seats."

Miriam answered him. "If this is anything like the more usual whirlwinds, we simply walk into the spiral. It picks us up and catches us within its currents. We are driven into the eye of the storm where, as with the sandstorm at magnetic north, the air is still and breathing is possible. Then it carries us to our destination."

"Where is the palace, anyway?" Korda asked. "I've been meaning to ask ever since I used my direction finder in the area and found that it kept pointing directly to the mirage."

"Your direction finder was not as wrong as it might have seemed," Tico said. He was flailing his arms as he spoke, guiding in the whirlwind. "Dwistor's palace is within a mile or so of the mirage. He felt that no one would look for it where it was not. The enchantments of Aurans are such that weapons of destruction like bombs will not function here—the physics do not permit it. Therefore, the palace was safest hidden in plain sight."

"Sheikh Dwistor," Korda said, watching as the whirl-wind—twirling like a dancer on one toe—spun to a halt in front of them, "is a very clever man. I wonder what he is afraid of?"

"Let us hope," Tico said, as he gestured for them to follow him into the whirlwind, "that we do not find out—if we do, I suspect that we will not live lest we share that information."

"The wind waits," Miriam said, wrapping all of her face but for her lustrous eyes in a silk scarf. "Let us go."

Using a handkerchief, Korda imitated her and was glad that he had. The whirlwind was less punishing than the sandstorm had been, but he was glad for the protection. He followed Miriam's gently swaying form into the eye of the storm and found that the centrifugal force held him comfortably in place.

"This reminds me of an amusement park ride I went on when I was a teenager," he commented, reflecting that when he had been a teenager, not only had Tico and Miriam been unborn, but Aurans itself, for all its apparent age, had not yet been even design notes.

Tico, who was holding Miriam's hand as they spun, smiled at Korda. "I believe that you will find that, unlike an amusement park ride, this will not even leave you dizzy. There are enchantments against it. Sheikh Dwistor could not have his counselors reeling like drunken fools whenever they arrived in his court."

"I'm glad for that," Korda said. "Almighty God is still showing a disconcerting tendency to play pool in my brain. I don't think I could handle dizziness."

The whirlwind came to a halt in a tiled courtyard. It spun in place for a moment, but when Korda would have begun to push his way out, Tico made a restraining gesture.

"Wait, Rene."

Korda leaned back into the spinning sand and watched as the spiral began shedding its mass layer by layer. The process neatly lowered their feet even with the courtyard and when the final veil of sand dissipated, they were standing on a small dune.

"When we depart the arrival area," Tico explained, "the whirlwind will reform and go to join the others in the desert near the palace. There it will become a hazard to those who would invade Dwistor's privacy while it awaits another summons."

Korda brushed sand from his hair with his fingertips. "It would if there were time in Aurans, but I fear that when we take our bottled time away, it will simply remain an inert pile of sand."

"FIVE HOURS AND FORTY-FIVE MINUTES OF BOTTLED TIME LEFT," marched words across the readline of his glasses, "AND MAY I PLEASE COME OUT OF YOUR POCKET? THE PROXIMITY OF YOUR BEATING HEART IS A THRILL, BUT REALLY I'M NOT MUCH HELP HERE."

Korda quickly unbuttoned his tunic, glad that Jester had not shared that last bit for public consumption. She was clearly picking up Tico's fondness for the well-turned flowery phrase. He wasn't certain how much of that he could take. The blushing alone was certain to raise his blood pressure.

"Welcome to the palace of Sheikh Dwistor!" Tico said, guiding them through a beautiful wrought iron gate worked with elegant arabesques. "You see before you a place that few on Aurans have visited. Indeed, generations of families live and die without even one of their number walking these hallowed halls."

Miriam sniffed disdainfully. "It is beautiful indeed, Tico, but I prefer your taste in decoration. I should not have approved of this place if Dwistor had brought me here."

"My desert rose . . . ," Tico murmured.

Politely ignoring the flow of endearments between Tico and his bride, Korda walked a few steps ahead. He could not agree with Miriam's assessment of Sheikh Dwistor's taste. If he was to set himself up as a desert sheikh, this would be about how he would decorate. He suspected that Miriam's hatred for what Sheikh Dwistor would have done to her made her unable to appreciate the beauty around her.

From the arrival courtyard, they entered a broad plaza. It was unadorned except for the beauty of the flagstones themselves. These were rough-textured diamonds cut just enough to glitter slightly in the light from the twin suns. Looming ahead was the onion-domed glory of the palace itself, covered all in beaten gold except for delicate hints of color in the enameled tiles that bordered the arched windows and doors.

Nothing troubled them as they crossed the open space and, when they arrived before the main gate, it swung open in front of them. The outer environs of the palace were a series of courtyards set up as a classic Eastern bazaar. Here, unlike the hurly-burly of the bazaar of Palace Gate, the wares were all fit for a king.

Frozen in stasis, a nomad chieftain held a string of racing camels. One, white as snow, bedecked with a tasseled harness of scarlet satin, was so beautiful that Korda longed to stroke it. To one side of the camel seller, a woman hawked silver trays holding crystalline fruit. Another vendor sold short, fat pottery bowls that might have seemed pedestrian except for the elegant floral designs with which they were painted. A third had no obvious wares spread on his blanket, but his robes were embroidered with mystic symbols and the stasis had caught him with his arms spread wide as he made a speech to a small group of men in palace livery.

"If we are careful," Korda said, dragging his gaze from the colorful scene with some difficulty, "we should be able to cross the bazaar without awakening any of the others from stasis. This is not nearly as crowded as the public bazaar in Palace Gate."

"Nor should it be," Tico said. "This bazaar is almost more for show than for function. Sheikh Dwistor liked the noise of genteel commerce, so this is arranged almost as a drama for his amusement. Some vendors, like the nomad chieftain with the camels, are probably new-comers. Others, like the magician to the side, belong to the palace staff."

They threaded their way through the bazaar with Jester's PDA in the lead, measuring tight spaces and advising them how best to get through. A few times, their bottled time awoke a hawker from sleep for a moment and a cry would break the stillness.

"Cool water! Iced drinks in crystal cups!"

"Fortunes and futures! Destiny described!"

"Tico! What a pleasure to see you, my lord! May I offer you the choice of my jewels for the doe-eyed beauty at your side?"

Tico looked tempted by the jewelry seller's offer, but Miriam dragged him along.

"I only wished to give you something fitting your love-liness!" he protested.

"Later, Tico," Miriam laughed. "I promise you, I shall not always be so selfless, but we have a task before us."

Korda grinned. Despite his envy of Tico for having won Miriam even before Korda could have entered the race, he was warmed by their honest love for each other. Jester seemed to feel the same way, for he heard the softest of sighs from the PDA.

"They're just so sweet!" she murmured, and for once he was not certain if the computer meant him to hear the words.

Leaving the bazaar courtyards, they came into the palace proper. The entryway was a vast central foyer from which three corridors radiated. After the open bazaar, its roofed area seemed momentarily dark, but as his eyes adjusted, Korda could see that here Sheikh Dwistor had chosen to display his wealth as well as his power.

The tiled floors were polished to a shine as brilliant as any mirror. The walls were hung with shimmering rugs, any of which made their flying carpet seem coarse by comparison. Fluted columns supported the domed ceilings and delineated niches in which elegant sculptures and petal-thin pottery waited for admiration.

Here also, for the first time, they saw guards. One stood before each corridor. They could have been identical triplets—and perhaps they were. Each was a burly man over six feet tall. They were clad in indigo blue trousers and turbans. Their matching vests were adorned with gold piping. They held their arms crossed at ease over their muscular chests, but each carried a scimitar unsheathed at his waist.

"Well, Boss?" Jester asked. "Which way do we go?"

Korda shrugged and looked at Tico. "Any suggestions?"

Tico shook his head. "I know little of the interior of the Palace, but I will share what I do know. The corridor to the left leads to the areas in which Sheikh Dwistor meets with his advisors. There is a bath there, several conference rooms, a banquet hall, and assorted gardens.

"I have heard that the central corridor leads to Sheikh Dwistor's private chambers. The right corridor, I am fairly certain from seeing the Minister for Finance use it, leads to the treasury and supply areas. I, however, have never been there."

Korda took out his direction finder. "Perhaps this will be some help."

He turned it on and the glowing arrow immediately pointed down the central corridor. Korda shifted his own position several times, just to make certain, but the arrow always reoriented on the central corridor.

"That helps," he said. "Tico, what do you know about the guards?"

"That they are impossible to defeat in battle," Tico said ruefully. "They are the natural-born triplet sons of a great sorcerer. The stories of their birth alone are near miraculous. Their father was the seventh son of a seventh son, their mother the twelfth daughter of a twelfth daughter—"

"A dozenth dozenth daughter," Jester muttered. "Oh, boy!"

"The triplets themselves were conceived under the moon of the third month in the third year of their parents' marriage," Tico continued. "They were born in the third hour of labor."

Tico's voice grew soft. "It is said that so that no one son would be born before another, the sorcerer cut open his wife's belly and delivered them all together. Their cords were cut in one stroke. Thus, they all share in potent birth magic, which has been channeled since they could crawl into making them warriors."

Korda frowned. "I've designed enough magic for pocket universes to know I don't want to challenge these boys.

Jester, can we fly the carpet over their heads?"

The PDA rose and took measurements. "Too tight, Boss. Even if you rode flat on your belly the radius of the bottled time would still reach the guard."

Tico raised a hand for attention. "We might be able to get past the leftmost guard. Our amulets mark us as invited guests and the left corridor is the one for which I have clearance. Although I have never seen one, perhaps there are cross corridors between the segments of the palace."

"That makes sense," Korda said. "After all, Sheikh Dwistor would not want to make a public appearance every time he went to another area. Given what you have said about his distrust, secret passages seem a given. I only hope he doesn't just use sorcery to get around."

Tico shook his head. "I doubt that he does. Magic can be diverted. I am certain he would not want to rely on it exclusively. Now, stand behind me and follow my lead."

Striding forward, Tico waited until his bottled time had awakened the guard. The guard bowed from the waist, and did not reach for his sword. Korda figured that was a good start.

"Hassan," Tico said, his tones firm and authoritative, "I am here with visitors for an audience requested by Sheikh Dwistor."

Hassan now drew his sword. "I must see their amulets of transport."

Aristocratically, Tico gestured for them to pull out their amulets. Wordlessly, as if cowed by the grandeur of the palace (and to be honest, Korda was rather overwhelmed by the subtle aura of menace the guard radiated), they pulled out their amulets.

After examining the amulets closely, Hassan studied both Korda and Miriam as if memorizing every feature before he let them pass.

"Remember," he said as he watched them walk by him, "my sword is sharper than shaving steel and my blows as solid as the kick of a camel. If any of you betray my lord, I shall winnow you like grain and leave your blood to water the sand."

Miriam shuddered and hurried her steps. Tico stood protectively between Hassan and his allies until they were safely down the corridor.

"I will remember your words," Tico promised. He let Hassan retake his guard post and then hastened away so that the stasis would reclaim the fearsome warrior.

Korda and Jester took point as they headed down the corridor. The PDA scanned the walls, searching for an echo that would betray the presence of a secret passage.

The first room they came to Tico called a conference room, but it was unlike the practical rooms Korda was accustomed to in Universe Prime. Huge cushions were scattered on the carpeted floor. Low tables held not only pen and paper, but beaten brass carafes for coffee or tea and blown glass hookahs. The air was scented with incense from discreetly hidden burners.

"I see that Sheikh Dwistor did not believe that meetings need to be uncomfortable and boring," Korda said, sniffing the contents of one hookah.

"Uncomfortable, no," Tico said with his white-toothed smile, "but most meetings contain an element of boredom. I believe it is part of their role in the divine plan."

The PDA sped over to Korda. "Nothing here, Boss."

The next room was a bath. Potted palm trees shaded an enormous square pool of heated water. The mosaic at the bottom of the pool bore Dwistor's face. He looked so much like Lawrence of Arabia that Korda wondered if he had submitted to plastic surgery to gain the resemblance. Possibly he had always looked that way and his appearance had been the root of his obsession. Korda doubted he would ever know.

He was still musing over the implications of appearance on personality when Jester gave a squeal of satisfaction.

"Found something, Jes?"

"It's good news and bad news, Boss," she reported. "There is a passage here, but I think it's the drain tunnel for the pool rather than a secret entry. Still, it might do in a pinch—it seems to be wide enough for you three."

"Map it," Korda ordered, "and we'll keep looking."

The next several rooms offered nothing more. In the banquet hall, they grabbed bread and cheese to eat while they searched.

"The direction finder still says that the world key is toward the center of the palace," Korda said. "Center and possibly subterranean."

"I know of no underground rooms," Tico said. "If they

exist they were not common knowledge."

In a courtyard off of the banquet hall, Jester located another passage.

"This one goes in the right direction," she reported. "It's taller, too, like it was made for humans to walk upright in. There's just one problem."

"What?" Korda said sharply.

"I detect several large life-forms. I can't be absolutely certain, but I think they are probably ketter beasts. My suspicion is that the corridor opens out enough to give them room to move, but not enough that anyone could get by without dealing with them."

Korda checked his supplies. "I still have some of your beastie biscuits. I think this is the route to take. Tico? Miriam?"

"We're with you," Tico said.

Miriam had paled somewhat, but she nodded bravely. Clearly, she was not happy about facing the monsters again, but she was not going to back off either.

"We have less than three hours," Korda reported, checking the readout inside his shades. "Jester, how do we open the secret corridor?"

The PDA flew to hover in front of a wall tile painted with a winged camel. "Press this, then the one to the right, the one to the left, and back to this again. The door will slide open."

"Go first with your flashlight on so my hands will be free," Korda ordered. "I'll follow with the beastie biscuits."

"Aye-aye, Captain!" Jester said, flicking her light on.

Korda pressed the tiles as he had been directed. The wall slid back and he was facing a dark corridor. The air smelled strongly of ketter beast and, at the fringes of Jester's light, he could see lumbering motion.

Miriam called softly. "Be careful, Rene."

He nodded, but for once his attention could not be distracted by the lovely woman. Hefting a handful of Jester's beastie biscuits, he strode to confront the ketter beast.

"THEY'VE BEEN OUTFITTED WITH BOTTLED TIME, BOSS," came the words across his readline. "I CAN SEE THE GLOW."

"*Thanks for the warning, Jes,*" he murmured into his throat mike.

He progressed steadily, knowing that he must have a clear shot at least for the first beast. After that, the scent of the biscuits might raise some hunger reaction in the others. He already suspected that Sheikh Dwistor did not feed his pets well.

When he could see the white of the first beast's teeth, he tossed the biscuits and then jumped back. As before, the beast swallowed and then eagerly searched out and devoured the biscuits that Korda tossed onto the floor. Five other ketter beasts were dispatched in this manner and when the last had fallen asleep the entire supply of biscuits carried by the three had been exhausted.

Miriam was suppressing her fear of the beasts well this time. She helped Tico remove the bottled time and dole it out.

"These will give us each another hour," she said.

"That's good," Jester responded, "because even with them we're down to under three hours. Searching the palace took time we really didn't have to spare."

Korda, meanwhile, had been probing the end of the tunnel. Ladder rungs had been built directly into the stone. Testing them, he climbed to the top, where the wall held a flat panel.

"Jes, come and take a look at this," he called. "I think this is another combination lock. Can you figure it out?"

The PDA bobbed up next to him and pinged her radar over the works.

"I've got it, Boss," she said. "Slide the tiles until you assemble a representation of the Aurans symbol. It will come open then."

Korda set to work. "Any idea what's on the other side?"

The PDA probed again. "A large room with life-forms."

"Ketter beasts?" Miriam asked hesitantly.

"No, I don't think so," Jester answered. "They seem about human mass—small human. If I were a guessing type of computer, I'd guess that we're below the harem."

Korda had the door puzzle about solved now.

"The harem, eh?" he grinned at the PDA. "Now Miriam can get a glimpse of the lifestyle she gave up when she decided to marry Tico."

Tico laughed. "She can look, but she cannot change her mind, because she is my wife now!"

"I wouldn't change my mind, Tico," Miriam murmured, "not for anything in all the universes."

Korda shoved open the trapdoor and found himself looking out of a round doorway concealed in the wall mosaic. Shoving a few enormous overstuffed pillows to one side, he took a better look at the room.

It was long and roughly rectangular. The main items of furniture seemed to be pillows and carpets, but here and there were low tables. The latticed windows held caged birds, their songs frozen by stasis as their freedom had been taken to amuse Dwistor's women.

The women lounged on the pillows, all scantily clad in halter tops and semi-transparent harem pants. Most stared blankly with bored expressions on their pretty faces or were sound asleep. Two were playing backgammon at one of the low tables. Another was standing bent over, combing long, fiery red hair that tumbled to the floor. A small group was studying a computer catalog that, as far as Korda could tell, displayed various jewelry fashions.

"Boy!" Jester said. "If we didn't know this room was in stasis, I'm not sure you could tell the difference!"

Absently, Korda hushed her. In the far corner of the room he had seen a door opening and then shutting again.

"Jester, go take a look—"

"No need, no need," hissed a familiar voice within his head. "It is I, Slyve, and I escort my master—whom you have made very angry with your presumptuous behavior."

"Sheikh Dwistor!" Tico cried.

"Yes, that is right," replied the slim blond man who

had now stepped into view at the center of the room. A few of the women had awakened as his bottled time touched them, but at the sight of the expression on his face, they had frozen in terrified silence.

Sheikh Dwistor stood before them, clad as Korda had seen Lawrence of Arabia clad in many famous photographs. He wore a white Arab headdress, its spotless linen bound with a braided cord. His robes were also spotless white, and at his waist he wore a curved scimitar in a discreetly jeweled sheath. One hand gripped the hilt of the scimitar and Korda did not doubt that the ruler of Aurans meant to use it.

"Tico Higgins," Sheikh Dwistor said. His voice was cold, his accents neat, upper-class British. "You have defied me and come to places where you are not welcome. You have defied me in other ways as well. You were told that I meant to have the woman at your side—the woman you have taken to wife."

Tico growled something low and angry in his throat, but the diplomat did not rise to the taunts. Korda admired his forbearance, for the covetous, lustful gaze that Dwistor was now directing at Miriam made his own blood run hot in his veins.

"And you, Miriam, daughter of blind Arabou," Sheikh Dwistor continued, his voice somehow becoming a lewd caress, "you are a foolish girl to defy me. Fortunately for you, I do not require intelligence in my women. Come to me now and I shall spare you for my harem, otherwise, I shall slay you with the others."

Miriam's only answer was to grip Tico's hand more firmly and spit, "Never!"

Before Dwistor could address either Miriam or Tico further, Korda stepped forward.

"Sheikh Dwistor, you have opposed me through every step of my progress across your world. I ask you, why? You must know that I am here to help you, to restore time to your universe; why do you not let me do so?"

Dwistor's pale blue eyes narrowed as he gazed at Korda. Despite their prosaic humanity, there was something of the serpent sizing up the rabbit in that gaze.

"Rene Korda of Old Terra and elsewhere," he said. "Yes, I know why you have come. However, I prefer not to be a supplicant to any power or person."

"How could you be a supplicant if you didn't ask me to come here?" Korda asked. "I am the supplicant, for now I am begging you to let me do what I can to return time to the universe of Aurans."

"No," Sheikh Dwistor said. "I do not grant your request. You are nothing to me."

"Then let me do my job for the sake of the peoples of Aurans," Korda said. "Until time is returned, they are at the mercy of any bandit with bottled time."

"No," Dwistor said. "They are mine to dispose of as I will and I do not will to let them have time at this juncture."

Korda bent knee, though kneeling to this cruel man with the handsome face was one of the hardest things he had ever done.

"Sheikh Dwistor, please let me help!"

Dwistor sneered down at him, his hand restless on his scimitar.

"I think not, for if I accept your help, then I am still indebted to you."

He studied them one by one. "Instead, I shall slay you all and be done with this intrusion. I believe that Miriam shall die last and in her widowhood she shall have a faint taste of the joys she might have had if she had not defied me. Then I will give her to Slyve and she will die in nightmare's embrace."

"I would have already felt nightmare's embrace!" Miriam cried angrily. "Nothing in your poison spider's bite could be worse than your touch!"

Korda's mind raced. In moments, events would be beyond his ability to help. The three of them might be able to defeat Dwistor and Slyve, but the sheikh could have means to bring the sorcerer-born warrior triplets to assist him. There must be something. . .

"Sheikh Dwistor!" he shouted, rising to his feet. "As the one who married this couple, I must defend their marriage. Since you plan to kill me anyway, will you grant me the privilege of a duel?"

"Why?" Dwistor drawled. "Even if you win, your executions are a matter of certainty."

"Because I will die with my honor intact," Korda said. "Certainly, you understand the demands of honor!"

"Honor is only an issue between equals," Sheikh Dwistor said, "and not a one of you is my equal—"

Jester made a rude noise. "Ah, he's just scared that you'll beat him, Rene. He won't give you a chance. Old Dwistor's just a bully—he doesn't like it when he has to fight someone who's as tough as he is."

Dwistor grew pale and still. With a single graceful movement, he unsheathed his scimitar. For a moment, Korda thought that the desert sheikh might simply slash his throat. Then Dwistor nodded once, curtly.

"I will grant this duel. Women, clear us a space. Deadman, what is your weapon?"

Korda knew that his best weapon was arrogance. He shrugged and smiled, hoping that his sneer was at least as good as Dwistor's.

"I'll fight with just what I have here," he said. "I don't think I need more to clean your clock."

Dwistor snarled. In his mind, Korda could hear the echoes of Slyve's humorless laughter.

"Very well," Sheikh Dwistor said, licking his lips with the tip of his tongue. "The rest of you, stand back. I will slay this arrogant human quickly. It will whet my appetite for the game to follow."

Korda set his backpack on the floor and flexed his muscles. He could hear Tico and Miriam speaking to him, but he stilled his mind until everything was inconsequential except the man in front of him. Then came a single word.

"Begin."

XIII

Dwistor was angry that Korda dodged the scimitar's first swipe easily. The second wasn't as easy, but he managed to subvocalize a message to Jester.

"Hey, Jes."

"HAVE YOU FLIPPED, SUGAR POP?" the readline asked.

"No, I said I'd fight him with 'just what I have here,'" Korda said. He tucked and rolled, coming up against a squealing harem girl. *"That includes a certain very clever PDA."*

"I'M WITH YOU," Jester said. "WHERE WOULD YOU BE IF I WASN'T?"

Korda didn't spare the breath to answer. He knew he was far better in hand-to-hand combat than Dwistor had expected, but then many underestimated a three-hundred-year-old universe creator. If they knew his age, they assumed that he had lost interest in physical skills. If they did not, they only saw his casual manner, the glasses, and the PDA, and dismissed him as a threat.

Both impressions worked to Korda's advantage and he made a point of not advertising his abilities unless it was precisely necessary.

Time to start showing off and let Jester do her thing.

First he launched into a flying kick. Dwistor was good enough that Korda failed to disarm him, but the sheikh's arm was temporarily numbed. Korda retreated in a series of back flips that set those harem girls who were not in stasis into cheers.

Dwistor was infuriated. He tossed his scimitar into his free hand. His next series of attacks sliced a thin, bloody cut across Korda's abdomen and proved that the sheikh was effectively ambidextrous.

Korda heard Miriam scream and Tico grab her to keep her from running to his rescue.

"This is a duel, desert flower," the diplomat said, his voice grating with suppressed emotion. "We dare not interfere lest we break the terms."

Hooking his foot behind Dwistor's ankle, Korda set his opponent off balance. Unfortunately, he also took a nick to the side of his neck. The blood ran warm and free, soaking his collar.

"Sugar Pop!" Jester cried.

"*I'm okay,*" he muttered. From the faint crackle of static, he could tell that Dwistor had come close to severing his throat mike. There was no time for further reflection. Dwistor was coming at him, cool and collected now that he believed he had the win in hand. Korda felt himself being backed into the wall.

Ducking, he scooped up an overstuffed pillow and flung it in Dwistor's face. As the desert sheikh dodged, Korda bent down, grasped the edge of one of the small oriental rugs that littered the harem floor, and tugged. Dwistor fell.

"*Jester, any time now would be fine with me,*" he gasped, wiping his face and feeling his sleeve soak up blood. Dwistor must have tagged him again.

"HAVE TO FIND THE FREQUENCY, SUGAR POP," she answered. "WOULDN'T WANT TO SWITCH YOU OFF, NOW, WOULD I?"

Korda didn't waste time shaking his head. Dwistor had regained his footing and was coming at him. The silver of the scimitar's blade was washed with the red of Korda's blood. Korda himself was just about out of tricks.

Dwistor was avoiding the pillows and had kicked most of the rugs to the side. His numbed arm had regained its sensation and he stood poised, tossing his scimitar from hand to hand, waiting for Korda to come to him.

Weaving with an exhaustion that he wished was completely feigned, Korda stood looking for an opening. It really had been a hell of a day. Almighty God was clicking pool balls in his hand. His voice resonated with thunder.

"WHAT WAS WRONG WITH THE UNIVERSE I DESIGNED?" Almighty God asked cordially. "YOU NEVER REALLY ANSWERED MY QUESTION."

"Come to me, Rene Korda," Dwistor said. "You asked for this duel. Do you concede?"

Korda shook his head. "No."

"PUNCH HIM ONE AND THEN DROP BACK," the PDA ordered. "IF YOU DON'T, YOUR BOTTLED TIME WILL KEEP DWISTOR ACTIVE AND NOTHING I DO WILL MAKE A DIFFERENCE."

"ANSWER MY QUESTION, RENE!" Almighty God bellowed.

Korda struck a kata, then moved on Dwistor. His eyes were on the blade, on the alert pale face below the Arab headdress. He feinted and Dwistor swung, slashing Korda's thigh.

Then Korda grabbed Dwistor's braided headband and pulled down. At the same time he brought his knee up—hard. Gasping, Dwistor doubled over.

Korda reeled back, lightheaded from blood loss.

"Because your universe was so full of jerks," he said to the waiting God. "I thought I could do better."

"DID YOU?"

"Not really," Korda said, trying to stand. "But I had to try."

Pawing his headdress from his eyes, Dwistor pushed himself to his feet using his scimitar as a cane. The desert sheikh's blue eyes were full of Korda's death and Korda realized that he would not be able to move in time to stop him.

Then time stopped for Dwistor.

"None too soon, huh, Sugar Pop?" Jester said cheerfully.

Korda wanted to answer her, but the noise of the pool

balls clacking was too loud. He slid down the rough stucco of the ornamental wall into a heap of pillows.

"YOU BROKE LAST TIME," Almighty God said. "STILL, I'LL GIVE YOU FIRST SHOT."

When Dwistor was seized by stasis and Rene Korda collapsed in a faint, Miriam started to cheer. Then she saw Slyve lowering itself from the ceiling on a thick strand of cable and the joyful shout died in her throat.

"Tico," she cried, pointing, "if that spider gets within range of Dwistor—"

"Its bottled time will reactivate him," Tico finished, already running to block Slyve. "Jester, can't you do anything?"

The PDA hung in the air. Its reply was flat and mechanical, an indication that it was diverting a great deal of computing power to finding a solution.

"Working. Solutions that do not create stasis for all involved complicate computations."

Slyve was retreating to the ceiling now, clearly aware that it would be able to reach Dwistor more easily without ground-level impediments.

Hollering an inarticulate battle cry, Tico hurled one of the smaller pillows at the spider's web. His bulky missile succeeded in breaking the drop line. Slyve fell to the floor—unhurt, but unable to reset a line on the ceiling without making itself vulnerable to attack.

It reared on its back four legs, its front legs and mandibles moving menacingly. More slowly, it moved toward the wall.

"Stay, stay away," it hissed into their minds. "Slyve am I and Death am I to you who have felt my poison once. Stay back and live."

"For what?" Miriam said. Her voice was steady, but there was a wildness in her dark eyes that made them flash like ebon diamonds. "So that your master can kill and torture us?"

"Miriam!" Tico shouted. He reached for her, but was too late.

The slender desert girl flung herself directly at where Slyve's bottled time glowed at the joint of its abdomen. There was a crinkling noise as she wrenched it free, but now her own bottled time kept the blond spider activated.

As it had outside of Tico's house, Slyve wrapped its legs around Miriam. With a solid crunch the deadly mandibles delivered their poison into her arm. She fell limp.

Slyve dropped her, but stood over her like an aggressive dog, waving its forelimbs in challenge to Tico.

"Come, bridegroom, come and join your bride in the halls of insanity," it hissed seductively. "Perhaps if you hasten, you will walk with her."

Face streaked with tears, Tico lumbered like a sleepwalker toward the blond tarantula and his dying bride. His sobs nearly drowned out the words of the hovering PDA.

"Parameters shifted. Solution found."

And time stopped for Tico. Beneath Slyve, Miriam's bottled time went dormant. The spider froze.

From the vantage of her PDA, Jester surveyed the room. A few of the harem girls within her area of effect and a few close to Korda were active. Most of their faces were slack with terror and incomprehension. Others were looking at their stasis-bound master with an emotion approaching hatred.

One, the redhead who had been brushing her hair when the stasis came, set down her comb. She tilted her head to make eye contact with the PDA.

"Your master bleeds," she said in a clear soprano, "and you lack hands. Would you have me bind his wounds?"

The PDA lowered to face her. "If you hurt him, I'll make certain that anything Dwistor would do to you would seem like a holiday."

"I am Ruth," the redhead answered, "and I have no love for Dwistor. Let me help Rene Korda, he bleeds and as he bleeds Slyve's poison regains its hold on him."

"Right, Ruth," Jester said. "Take Rene's pack. There's a first aid kit in it. I'll tell you what to do."

Ruth picked up the pack. "I may know something of what to do. Before I was taken into the harem, I was training to be a veterinarian. Dwistor saw me when he was inspecting some racing camels that were in my care, and he coveted me. I was given no choice but to come here."

The PDA had turned to watch the other active harem girls. "All of you trot over against that wall. The stasis will take you, but, as you already know, it won't hurt."

Perhaps it was some measure of how successfully Dwistor had broken their will, but all the girls obeyed the little sphere without question.

"Gee, that was easier than I thought it would be," Jester commented to Ruth.

After administering a soporific to Korda, Ruth had soaked a wad of gauze in antiseptic and had begun cleaning Korda's cuts. She glanced up at the PDA.

"They all have learned to obey," she said. "I protested at being brought here and was told that if I did not obey, my family would be killed. To prove that he was serious, Dwistor tortured my mother. I stopped fighting at once."

"That's horrid!" Jester said. "I guess if it hadn't been for the threat of Slyve's poison you would have killed Dwistor."

"The threat to myself would not have stopped me," Ruth said calmly, "but Dwistor warned each of us that upon the event of his death at the hand on any one of us, all of us and all of our families would be tortured to death. Such a threat makes one meek indeed."

"Indeed," Jester replied. "I guess we'd better get you out of here when we go."

Ruth frowned. "Can your ship carry all of us and all of our families?"

"Uh, no," Jester said. "We don't even have the digital storage capacity."

"Then we must remain and hope that Dwistor places

the blame solely on Rene Korda," Ruth said. "I believe that he will, and since you have made certain the rest of the harem is in stasis, there will be no witnesses to our conversation."

The PDA bobbed, but not even the vast computer brain could find a better answer. Even if she slew Dwistor, his final commands would remain. She could not kill every one of his servants—she didn't even know who would have been given his murderous final orders.

Ruth did not seem to feel any useless pity for herself or her circumstances. Her slim fingers moved deftly as she checked each of the wounds for poison or infection. Veterinary studies had clearly included use of a sonic skin knitter, for she deftly stitched closed the worst of Korda's wounds.

Korda tossed some as she worked, but the sleeping drugs and blood loss held him. Occasionally he muttered something about side pockets and balls. Once, quite clearly, he asked for the chalk.

"He will recover quickly now," Ruth said, giving him a final shot. "The drug I gave him will stimulate blood replacement and the new blood will dilute the remaining poison in his system. How much time do you have left?"

Jester checked the reading. "Wow! Rene and I have less than an hour apiece. The others have more. Since I turned off their units, they haven't used any."

"Korda will need about an hour to regain his strength," Ruth said. "I suggest to you that the others return to your vessel and you take their time."

The PDA would have frowned if it could.

"Perhaps we should all go back," Jester said. "Rene could heal and, well, if Miriam . . . Tico's going to be in bad shape."

"Normally, I would agree," Ruth said, "but there is one thing I have not told you. Sheikh Dwistor received a message about a day before your arrival—I cannot be certain how long as our universe was already in stasis. He, however, had reactivated the harem to amuse him while he considered what to do, so I witnessed its arrival.

"It came on a message missile, equipped with bottled time and sent to home in on Dwistor himself. I believe that someone is coming to Aurans—and any ally of Dwistor would most certainly not be a friend of yours."

Jester agreed. Leaving Korda to begin recovering, she took a length of rope in her mouth and, carefully judging the limits, she touched Tico with her own bottled time. When the diplomat came active, she drew him clear of Miriam and Slyve.

"Nothing is going to happen there that hasn't happened already," she explained patiently. "The only thing that might happen is that you start things moving again and ruin any chance that Miriam has. Now, are you ready to listen?"

Tico wiped the tears from his face, took a shuddering breath, and nodded.

"I listen, electronic imp," he said with a poor imitation of his usual eloquence.

"Good. First of all, do you still have that transportation water?"

"I do," Tico said, tapping the canteen at his waist.

The PDA's tones brooked no argument. "Then this is what you are going to do. We're going to pull Miriam out from under Slyve. If we move fast enough, we should be able to do so without fully reactivating the spider.

"Next, I'm going to dose her with my antidote. The poison barely had a chance to get into her system this time before she went into stasis. Hopefully, the antidote will slow it further.

"You're going to leave all but one unit of bottled time here, drink that water, and take Miriam back to the *Jester*. My facilities there may be able to help you. If not, I can direct you how to put her into digital storage. I think that once we're outside Aurans, Slyve's poison will lose some of its potency—it has to be dependent on the physics of this universe for some of its effectiveness. Got it?"

Tico nodded, his astonishment evident. Like Korda himself, Jester was easy to underestimate. Her teasing playfulness usually made people forget that she was, after all, a computer powerful enough to run a starship.

"I understand and I will obey," he said. "I have only one question. You speak of helping me to treat Miriam. Certainly, you do not plan on abandoning Rene?"

The PDA giggled. "I can be more than one place at once, Tico. For most of this jaunt, I've been playing sekhet with Arabou back on the ship as well. I won't abandon the Boss. If things get too heavy here, I'll just tune you folks out and concentrate on helping him."

"Then I agree to your plan," Tico said. "I pray to Allah that we will indeed be able to preserve my love's life."

The retrieval went according to plan and, although Miriam was clearly suffering nightmares, she was also still alive. Tico vanished with her back to the *Jester* just as Korda began coming out from under the effects of the soporific that Ruth had given him.

He sipped water while Jester introduced him to Ruth and brought him up-to-the-minute on events. When the computer finished, he sighed and propped himself up on one elbow.

"Then the only thing that remains is to find the world key and reactivate the universe of Aurans," Korda said.

"I saved enough of the transport water that we should be able to return to the *Jester* when the job is done," the PDA said. "That way, we shouldn't need to tackle Dwistor again."

"Good," Korda said. "I'm at a loss as to where to find the world key, though. The direction finder says it's here, but I don't see it. Does your radar find anything underground?"

"Not really, Boss," Jester replied. "I scanned while we were waiting for you to come around."

Ruth cleared her throat. "I have been thinking, ever since Jester told me of your need. I believe I may have your answer—or at least part of it. There was something that I once heard Dwistor recite. It was so odd that I committed it to memory."

"Yes?" Korda said.

Ruth smiled. "How are you at riddles, Rene Korda?"

"Riddles?" Korda said. "Fair. Let's hear this one."

Ruth folded her hands, lowered her eyes, and recited:

> *Born in a bathtub,*
> *Giver of wishes,*
> *Scented with juniper,*
> *Sealed by Solomon,*
> *Tell me who I am.*

"Now," Ruth said with a sad smile, "I will retreat into stasis with my harem sisters. It would not do for me to hear the unraveling of this riddle."

"Are you certain we can't help you?" Jester asked, her tones pleading.

"Free our universe from stasis," Ruth said, "and perhaps someday we will free ourselves from the tyranny of Dwistor. Farewell and good luck."

Taking her hand, Korda pressed her fingers to his lips. "My thanks for your help. We will do our best for you."

"Thank you," Ruth said, then she walked away from them and out of the grasp of time.

Jester sighed. "That's one brave and noble lady. We've got to help her."

Korda frowned. "We do indeed. Jester, start a scan for anything that might link these lines."

"Boss!" she exclaimed. "That's cheating!"

"When the fate of a universe and all its people rests on my guessing a riddle," Korda said, aware that he sounded hopelessly pompous, "then I cheat."

While Jester processed, Korda paced, checking the limits of his strength. Perhaps it was the lingering effect of Slyve's poison encouraging him to think in a nonlinear fashion, but he made an immediate connection.

"Jes, what was Solomon's Seal used to close?"

"A genie bottle," she answered promptly.

"Genies give wishes," Korda said, "so that fits. Anything in your records linking bathtubs with any of this or with juniper?"

Again the answer came quickly. "Juniper is an evergreen. Its scent is associated with the alcoholic beverage, gin. Gin, of course, was distilled in bathtubs during the period known as Prohibition."

Korda interrupted her. "Gin—spelled slightly differently—with a 'd' and an extra 'n' is another word for 'genies.'"

He addressed his words to the room at large. "So that's what you are—djinn or genies!"

Around them, the room shimmered. Korda felt a slight, uncomfortable sensation, as if he was being turned inside-out. Then he stood before the complex panels of the Aurans world key.

"SENSORS REGISTERED ANOMALIES CONSISTENT WITH THE USE OF MAGIC WHEN THE ROOM WAS EXPOSED," Jester reported. "BOSS, WE COULD HAVE DUG TO THE PLANET'S CORE AND WE WOULDN'T HAVE FOUND THIS PLACE."

Korda flexed his fingers, feeling—as always when standing before a world key—a bit like a maestro confronted with the largest piano in creation.

"How is Miriam?" he asked, starting to work.

"Tico and Arabou are working with her. They think she's out of physical danger, but there is the question of damage to her sanity."

"Two doses of Slyve's poison could do that," Korda agreed, thinking of his encounters with pool-playing Almighty God. "Whoever did the shutdown was a professional. This is a tidy job. I wonder . . . ."

"What, Boss?"

"If I know whoever it is who did this," he said. "Some of the little quirks seem familiar."

"Quirks?"

"There are lots of ways to work a world key," Korda explained as he did so. "I'm fairly conservative. I tend to set up all the safety features before I work. Whoever did this job left a few steps out."

"Maybe whoever it was was in a hurry," Jester said.

"I'm sure that was part of it," Korda agreed, "but it still speaks of a reckless style. I'm willing to guess that whoever did this job didn't finish the entire course of training at the Academy. I know I got a lot more careful after I finished the course and learned firsthand all the effort that goes into making a universe."

"Maybe we could check the Academy files," Jester suggested.

"We could," Korda said, "and we should, but that will probably give us more dead ends than not. Lots of people drop out. Universe creation isn't learned overnight."

"I'd still advise checking," Jester said primly.

"Oh, I agree," Korda said. "I'm just haunted by the sense of familiarity here. When you cross-check, see how many of the dropouts were students of mine. We'll run the search on those first."

"Gotcha, Boss," Jester promised. "I can't start until we're back in Universe Prime, but when I get there I'll run the charges through the Terran Regional Rep's office."

"Good," Korda said absently, distracted by the increasingly fine manipulations the world key demanded of him.

He worked for about ten more minutes checking sequencing and assuring himself that Aurans was now up and running.

"Done!" he announced. "Let's drink that water and get out of here. Time's running for everyone now—and that includes some people who are pretty angry with us."

He downed a swig from the canteen Tico had left. The water was slightly effervescent and stung his mouth pleasantly. He concentrated on the bridge of the *Jester*, his comfortable chair.

"Remember, Boss," Jester said, snuggling her PDA into his hand. "There's no place like home."

As soon as they were back on the *Jester*, Korda ordered the departure sequence started, then he hurried to where Tico and Arabou were watching over Miriam.

"At Jester's advisement, we started a blood transfusion from your stores," Tico said. "We've also been talking to her steadily in case our voices can penetrate the hallucinations and comfort her."

Korda nodded, his attention on Miriam. Her breathing was slow and steady, but there was a bruised look to the skin around her eyes. Tico didn't look much better.

"We'll be leaving the universe of Aurans in three minutes," Jester reported, her hologram popping into sight on the nearest holopad. "Boss, I detected a ship under bottled time on the far reaches of the planet Haring just before stasis was broken. Do we want to check it out?"

"No!" Korda said, the word coming out more forcefully than he had intended. "We've done what we came for. Let Dwistor deal with his own visitors—they may even be welcome."

When the *Jester* departed the universe of Aurans, within five minutes two things happened.

"Miriam shows marked change," Jester said, her hologram dancing from foot to foot. "My medical sensors report that REM sleep is drifting into a more restful cycle. Her heart rate and breathing are rising toward normal levels."

Tico did not release his grip on Miriam's hand, but his dark eyes brightened.

"Then she is recovering?" he asked.

"Seems like it, Tico," Jester said. "Looks like the Boss was right when he said that the physics of Aurans had something to do with the effectiveness of the poison.

Lucky guess, huh?"

Korda felt too good to rise to the bait. Arabou beamed, two tears trickling from his blind eyes down his face. Removing his flute from his breast pocket, he began to pipe a haunting but happy melody.

"BOSS, I DON'T WANT TO INTERRUPT THE CELEBRATION," Korda's readline said, "BUT I HAVE A MESSAGE FOR YOU FROM THE TERRAN REGIONAL REPRESENTATIVE."

"I'll take it on the bridge," Korda said and he slipped away from the music and the glow of the relieved father and husband.

"Mr. Korda," Conchita Devenu said, her recorded smile a bit tight, "we have information that the saboteur responsible for the stasis on Aurans and Urbs may now be in the universe of Fortuna. If you are interested in continuing this job, have Jester contact my office directly. We will send you the coordinates.

"The owner of Fortuna is named Alachra. He has agreed to your coming, but otherwise does not seem very worried about the possible threat. The information regarding the saboteur and your assistance was relayed to him through intermediaries, so as far as I know, he does not know of the involvement of the Terran Regional Government. I would prefer that it remain so.

"If you accept, I thank you in advance. If you do not,

I appreciate your working with us thus far. Good luck."

Korda stretched. "Get those coordinates, Jes, then pull the file on Fortuna. I'll head down and ask our passengers if they'd like to come along. Tico and Miriam certainly deserve a honeymoon after everything they've been through—and I've heard Fortuna has some of the best luxury resorts around."

"Right, Sugar Pop!"

Korda grinned. Let Jester have her fun. They were closing on the saboteur and he'd have his own fun soon enough.

Interlude 2

Deter brought the *Endgame* out of close orbit around the planet Haring. The disembodied brain had spent a very instructive wait observing the construction planetside. Dwistor was apparently replicating various sites related to what Old Terra still called World War II.

One did not need to have Deter's encyclopedic knowledge of military conflict to be aware that most of the sites being reconstructed related to major events in the career of Lawrence of Arabia. Deter wondered if—when Dwistor grew tired of playing Arabian Nights on Aurans—he planned to step into the history of T.E. Lawrence.

Perhaps Dwistor would invite Deter over to play. The disembodied brain chuckled to himself. He would rather enjoy playing the Turks and Nazis.

However, such diversions would need to wait until the current . . . difficulty was resolved. Deter waited until Aurans was out of stasis and the *Jester* had departed before moving to contact Dwistor. He had found Rene Korda disquieting and wanted nothing more to do with the universe creator.

Deter landed the *Endgame* on a sandy field near Palace Gate and signaled Dwistor in a code that very few other people—six, to be precise—knew. Dwistor answered immediately.

"Deter?" The desert sheikh, Deter noted, looked rather the worse for wear. "What brings you here?"

"I believe I sent you a message regarding my coming," Deter said. "Perhaps the blows you have evidently taken to your head have removed the knowledge."

An angry red flooded Dwistor's pale countenance. He glowered at Deter.

"Perhaps I had more important things on my mind than your message, Deter," he replied. "I have located your ship. Stay there and I will join you shortly."

Deter had no intention of doing otherwise. His mechanical augmentations had a disquieting tendency to malfunction when he visited Aurans, especially if he strayed more than a quarter mile from his ship. He suspected, although without evidence, that Dwistor had used the magic of Aurans to set a permanent defensive curse on Deter's equipment. Deter would have done the same to Dwistor had the physics of Urbs permitted it.

The whirlwind that deposited Dwistor near the *Endgame* sparkled with fragments of mica. They rained around Dwistor—newly garbed in fresh snowy robes— as the whirlwind dispersed. The overall effect was to give the desert sheikh a halo.

As usual, Dwistor was accompanied by Slyve. The

blond tarantula hated Deter, largely because it could not find a way to bite the disembodied brain. Deter—who, like Slyve, was somewhat telepathic—was well aware of this, and exploited it whenever possible.

Dwistor carried a small rolled carpet tucked under his right arm. He shook it out and a small pavilion, complete with a table of refreshments, manifested. Permitting himself a small grin from the corner of his mouth, Dwistor seated himself cross-legged in the shade.

Not permitting himself to express his surprise, Deter brought the conversation directly to the matter at hand.

"Both your universe and mine have been put into stasis," he said bluntly. "Were it not for Rene Korda's intervention, they would still be so."

"Yours might be," Dwistor said, "but I know the secrets to reactivating mine. I simply chose not to do so."

Deter waved a waldo. "I, too, know how to reactivate my universe. That is not the point. Had it not been for Korda, I would have left Urbs in stasis and waited to see if the criminal returned. Korda's intervention made this difficult to do. He forced me—as he forced you—to reveal your activity."

Lifting a crystal carafe and admiring the play of light through its facets, Dwistor poured himself a small glass of date wine. Pointedly, he did not offer any to Deter.

The disembodied brain did not eat or drink in a conventional fashion, but it might have requested some other form of hospitality. Dwistor would have been put in an awkward social position. Deter knew quite well that

Dwistor observed the antiquated hospitality rules of the Arab peoples. These rules granted protection to anyone to whom you gave water, bread, or salt—a rule later extended to encompass any form of food or drink.

Dwistor really did not know if these rules would include crude oil or diesel fuel, but he did not care to discuss such semantics with Deter. Let their alliance stand as it had these fifty or so standard years and leave it at that.

"So Rene Korda forced us to act other than we might have wished," Dwistor said. "For this he will, of course, have to die, but I do not need to confer with you, my metal-bound ally, to know this. Come to the point."

Deter drew what looked like a circuit diagram in the sand with the tip of one of his waldo extensors.

"Do we warn Alachra of what has occurred?" he said, his tones shrill. "Is this within the bounds of our mutual nonaggression and protection compact?"

"I believe we should warn him," Dwistor said, "although not precisely for those reasons. Rene Korda was sent both here and to Urbs by some outside agency. If we do not warn Alachra, he may be warned by this outside agency, then he will wonder why we did not warn him. If we do warn him, then we are taking friendly initiative. Alachra may feel a debt and, whatever else I think of him, Alachra scrupulously honors his debts."

"It will be as you have said, then," Deter replied. "A message missile is being drafted even as we speak. Perhaps it will arrive before Rene Korda, perhaps not. Perhaps Rene Korda does not head to Fortuna, but analysis of his departure trajectory from the vicinity of the Aurans entry point leads me to believe that Fortuna is his destination."

Dwistor finished his palm wine and rolled up his rug. The pavilion vanished. He stood tall, slim, and as deadly as the scimitar at his side.

"I, for one, shall take the *Lawrence* and pursue Rene Korda," he announced, not quite phrasing his announcement as a question, but something in his tone making it so.

Deter twittered. "And I, too. Perhaps we should sail in company."

Dwistor nodded. "Yes, that will be wise. Two ships can attack with more finesse than one."

"And then the *Jester* will be laughing smoke and fire," Deter concluded, with a rare leap into metaphor, "and soon she will not be laughing at all . . . ."

XIV

Entry into the universe of Fortuna will be achieved in about forty minutes," Jester announced. "I've sent your message ahead to the relay beacon and we are indeed expected."

With a conspiratorial wink she shifted to her readline, "AND I'VE ARRANGED FOR THE HONEYMOON SUITE AT THE OCEANIC CASINO FOR TICO AND MIRIAM. ARABOU HAS REQUESTED A ROOM IN A REGION CALLED THE OLD WEST—HE WANTS TO SEE AN OLD FRIEND WHO WORKS THERE. OUR ROOMS WILL BE IN THE BLACK PYRAMID."

"Our rooms?" Korda said, arching an eyebrow at her.

The image on the holopad giggled. "Why, Sugar Pop! I never knew you liked me that much! Of course I'll stay in your room."

Korda sighed, realizing what he had walked into. So much for romantic dalliance in *this* universe. Jester would get sulky and, with the saboteur still at large, he needed her full cooperation.

"Tell us about Fortuna," Miriam said, when he left the

bridge and joined the others in the galley. "I know the entire universe is devoted to gambling, but I hardly know what to expect."

Arabou hastened to clarify her question for Korda. Perhaps he thought the universe creator would think Aurans was uncosmopolitan.

"We do have gambling in Aurans—especially on camel races—and on feats of skill. Card games are also popular, but dice have never been so. Magic makes nudging a falling cube a bit too easy."

Korda rubbed his chin, trying to summarize what he had read in both the Terran Regional Representative's notes and in Fortuna's own promotional brochures.

"Fortuna's an odd place," he began. "As with the other God's Pockets universes, it was created about fifty years ago. Unlike the others, most of which I had not heard of until I took this job, it is open to the public.

"Fortuna's economy is based on gambling and nothing else. There is a planet called Tracks devoted exclusively to racing. Aqua is a water world used for water sports and big-game hunting. Fortuna proper is covered with casinos. Basically, if there is a game that people can take a risk on, Fortuna has facilities for it."

Some of the cynicism that Korda was learning underlay Tico's cheerful exterior surfaced now.

"Seems like people would stop coming to a place like Fortuna," he said. "A closed shop doesn't exactly give the best odds."

Korda slid a notescreen containing various of Fortuna's

official brochures across the table to him.

"Look at this, Tico," he said. "Fortuna actually posts the starting odds on various races well in advance. The pay-off odds for the slot machines shift regularly but they are posted as well. Whenever possible, odds are posted for any contest. It's the Fortuna equivalent of a stock market report."

Miriam studied the readout.

"How strange," she commented. "I thought that the way gamblers get hooked is by believing the odds are better than they are. Anyone who reads a posting would acquire a very realistic idea of what the chances of a big win are."

Korda chuckled. "That shows that you aren't much of a gambler—except on your bearded swain there—"

Tico gripped Miriam's hand. "I am no gamble! I am as reliable as the two suns, as constant as—"

"Time?" Jester quipped.

Tico laughed. "You are too quick for me, imp."

Korda continued his lecture. "Miriam, gamblers don't gamble because they believe the odds are with them— they gamble because they believe that *luck* is with them. On Fortuna, the usual greeting is 'Good Fortune to you' or some variation on that theme. Lady Luck is their goddess."

"Allah protect us!" Tico said.

Korda keyed a new screen on the reader. "I'm certain that Allah will, Tico, but it will help if all of us remember the basic rules of Fortuna. There are two premises and the rest of the legal code is extrapolated from them.

"The first," Miriam read aloud, "is 'A bet is a bet and to be honored as such.' That sounds obvious."

Arabou gave one of his mysterious smiles. "It does so indeed, my daughter, but I recall an event that occurred during one of my visits to Fortuna. That first rule means that one must watch one's language with great care.

"There was an Auransan wine importer who made a deal to deliver a cargo of rare vintages in time for the camel races. In the course of sealing the contract, his Fortunan customer asked him if the wines would arrive in time. The foolish merchant replied, 'I would bet my life on it.' When the wines did not arrive in time, his life was forfeit."

Miriam steepled her fingers and bowed to her father. "I will remember your wisdom, father. I wouldn't want to make a bet I would not care to keep."

"You bet!" Jester giggled.

Korda sighed and shook his head before reciting the second rule. "On Fortuna, cheating is not wrong unless the cheater is caught."

"That's strange," Tico said. "Why should they put such emphasis on posting the odds on their games and then permit cheating?"

"As I understand it," Korda said, "cheating is viewed as another form of gambling—one that is less structured than many. However, the penalties can be severe. Sometimes a dealer will simply exact a fine; other times the penalty is a fine combined with exile from Fortuna. Death is not an uncommon penalty and is always enacted in the case of a repeat offense."

Tico slipped his arm around Miriam's waist and pulled her close. "And I am taking my sweet new wife to this murderous place for our honeymoon?"

"Don't worry, Tico," Jester assured him. "She's got to like it better than she liked ketter beasts."

Miriam stuck her tongue out at the hologram and Jester wiggled happily. The computer had never had so many friends to interact with. Korda suspected that she would never again be as content with his solitary retirement. With a sudden flash of intuition, he wondered if he would be.

That, however, was a question for when the job was done. Entry to Fortuna was drawing near.

"Don't worry, Tico," Korda assured his friend. "There is much to do in Fortuna that doesn't involve gambling. The casinos are architectural marvels. Musicians from throughout the known universes come to perform in the nightclubs. The sports facilities are open to amateurs as well as professionals—as long as you don't mind people on the sidelines betting on things as silly as whether or not you will hit the ball or stay up on your water skis."

"And when the games get dull, you *do* have a new wife," Jester winked.

Both Tico and Miriam blushed.

Almost as if he could see the young couple's response, Arabou chuckled. "And, if all of that fails to amuse, we can all help you to capture this mysterious saboteur."

Korda bit his lip. "Yes. Yes and no. I don't want to put you at risk, but—given the population of Fortuna—extra eyes and ears would be useful to me. Unlike Urbs and Aurans, this universe is going to be active."

"Won't Alachra let you simply wait in the world key?" Miriam asked. "Or is that a stupid hope?"

"No hope is ever stupid," Korda reassured her, "but I do not think Alachra will let me into his universe's control center. That would be a tremendous risk for him to take—I'm not certain he'll like the odds."

"Odds?" Arabou asked.

"Yep," Korda said. "The odds that I won't betray him, that an enemy (and anyone rich enough to own a pocket universe has enemies) won't capture me and get the information from me, or any number of other possibilities."

Tico frowned. "Yes, especially after working for Sheikh Dwistor, I can understand this worry about internal security. Still, Alachra must want the saboteur caught!"

"I'm certain that he does," Korda said, "but not at the expense of making things easy for potential future saboteurs. Honestly, we may not be able to catch up with the saboteur until he has done his job. Then the odds will be more in our favor because only a limited number of people will have bottled time."

"You'll let us have some, won't you?" Miriam asked.

Korda laughed. "Of course. It will restrict your choice of attire some, but I suggest that you each carry a full eight-hour harness with you at all times. Hang it on the bedpost at night. I'll give you a comm link with the *Jester* so if we're apart and stasis falls we'll be able to stay in touch."

"The other people you expect to have time," Arabou said, "would be members of Alachra's own staff, correct?"

"That's right," said Korda, nodding. "I'll try and get an idea of how many when I see Alachra. So it will be us and them against the saboteur."

"I notice that you have started using the singular," Tico said. "When did you become convinced that we have one opponent?"

Korda shrugged. "When I looked around the world key in Aurans. I had a sense that this was the work of one person—quite likely a person I know. However, I could be wrong. It could be a team or it could be one universe designer with a mess of mercenary bodyguards, so stay alert."

Jester waved her hand for attention. "Excuse me folks, but we're about to enter Fortuna. I'll need the Boss to deal with people stuff and all that."

Korda rose and headed to the bridge. "Does Fortuna still read active, Jes?"

"It does," the computer answered. "We've been cleared through customs. After you deal with some standard entry treaties, you have been 'requested' to attend a brief meeting with Alachra."

"Very good," Korda said, seating himself in his command chair. "Take us on in."

"You bet, Sugar Pop!"

The computer giggled at her own joke, but her electronic hand on the helm was firm and steady as she took them through the solar system.

"Outer system traffic is heavy," Jester reported. "I'd give odds that there is a major event planned."

"No takers," Korda said, with a grin.

The forms he needed to fill out were handled quickly. He messaged them off and checked his gear. This time the variable setting on the universal tool was a probability driver—a device that could be used to alter the odds in a situation. Recalling Fortuna's attitude toward cheating, Korda hoped he wouldn't need to use it. Due to Tico and Miriam's help on Aurans he hadn't needed the universal tool there. Maybe he would be as lucky here.

Korda glanced at the navigation screen as they passed the blue and white globe of Aqua, the varicolored surface of Tracks, and then homed in on Fortuna, which looked almost prosaic by comparison.

Descending through the Earth-normal atmosphere, the Jester homed in on a landing beacon and zipped lower and lower over the urban sea of Fortuna's neon-outlined buildings. When they were directly overhead, the top of the Black Pyramid opened and a landing platform rose.

The Jester touched down, cutting off external engines and growing silent as the platform lowered, the sides of the pyramid folded closed, and the building swallowed them.

❖ ❖ ❖

Korda was rather surprised to learn that his meeting with Alachra was to take place in the office of the Fortuna transportation director. Somehow he'd imagined a more glitzy setting, someplace like a booth in a darkened nightclub or an office filled with tasteless curios and pictures of Alachra with various celebrities.

He certainly hadn't expected this barren, utilitarian compartment directly off one of the main hangars, but it was here that the transportation director had brought him.

"Call me 'Irish,'" the freckled redhead said in a brogue that was explanation enough for the nickname. "Alachra said you should be waiting for him here, now. Himself is off to Tracks for the Solar Regatta, but he'll give you a moment or two of his time before he goes."

"I'm grateful that he will," Korda said. "Do you know anything about the situation?"

Irish winked at him. "Well, now, I haven't been told anything more than I should know, but I'll wager that you're here to deal with the fellow whose ship we have under guard in Transport Bay Four. Nice ship, she is, sleek and mean-looking. I'd bet she's built for more than speed."

"I'd like to have a look at it after I speak with Alachra," Korda said.

"If Alachra doesn't have a problem with your looking at the ship, I certainly don't." Irish's chuckle made a riddle of his words. "But I suspect the ship might want to be given a word or two first."

Korda might have asked more, but there was a sound

in the hangar outside—a sound remarkably like the collected trot of a well-trained dressage horse. Then a towering shadow blocked the doorway.

It was a woman at least seven feet tall and rippling with muscle. Her brown hair was skinned back in a severe fashion that emphasized the bones of her face. She wore a skintight black jumpsuit trimmed at throat and wrists with white. A natty bow tie and a businesslike handgun completed the ensemble.

"Hands on the bulkhead," she snapped by way of greeting, "and spread your legs. And keep that PDA out of my face or I shoot it down."

Blinking to keep from revealing his astonishment, Korda did as he had been commanded. After he had submitted to the most thorough, although utterly professional, patting down of his long career, he was permitted to take his hands from the wall.

"He's clean, Alachra," the woman called into the corridor. "He's carrying bottled time and some other tools, but no weapons."

"EXCEPT FOR YOUR HANDS AND FEET, RIGHT, BOSS?" an indignant Jester printed across his readline.

Korda didn't bother replying, but he gave the PDA a small smile that made him feel more confident than this peculiar greeting had left him. He needed all the confidence he could garner when Alachra entered Irish's office.

Nothing in the Terran Regional Representative's documents had prepared him for what stood before him. Perhaps her office had not known, perhaps they had merely thought it unimportant. Fortuna publicity photos had only shown Alachra from the waist up—perhaps because the rest would not fit well in a standard frame.

Alachra was a centaur. He stood at least a foot taller than his bodyguard, his human portion that of a muscular man in his mid-thirties. His horse body was brown, adorned with a silvery white tail like a palomino. The hair on Alachra's head was shaved except for a trailing mohawk that was a matching silver streaked with fluorescent pink.

Clothing did not seem to be Alachra's style, but this did not mean that he didn't care for body ornamentation. His arms and sections of his torso were tattooed with designs that Korda suspected were lucky charms. Multiple fine gold rings pierced his earlobes; a larger one adorned his navel. The entire effect was completed by a large cigar held firmly between teeth that would have done credit to a horse.

"Wow!" Jester whispered, tucking her PDA under Korda's ear. For once, it seemed that the computer was intimidated—an odd thing, Korda realized, since her own "body" massed far larger than Alachra's.

"Rene Korda?" Alachra said, removing his cigar as he spoke. "Good Fortune to you. I hope you will enjoy your stay on Fortuna."

"Fortune follow you," Korda answered politely. "I suspect that I will enjoy my visit. Thank you for letting me continue my investigation in your universe."

"Not a problem," Alachra said. "I'm not really worried. My security is on the lookout for the intruder. Still, if the Terries want to send a few more to join the chase, it only adds to the fun."

Korda took a deep breath and immediately regretted it. Alachra's cigar smelled putrid. "Alachra, how do you know that this intruder is my target?"

Poking his cigar back into his mouth, Alachra spoke around it.

"Give him the dope, West."

The bodyguard looked down at Korda. "The usual procedure for guests on arrival in Fortuna is to submit their ships to deep radar probes. This ship—the *Shrike*—was probed as standard procedure. Initial analysis showed nothing out of the ordinary and the *Shrike* was given its berth. Its single passenger, a male human who gave his name as Montgomery Cristo, was permitted entry into the universe.

"When the tape was submitted to standard review, a glitch appeared that troubled South, the intelligence officer on duty. She ran the tape again and became convinced that the *Shrike* was equipped with a device that automatically jammed any probe and inserted false information into its data stream. Had South not detected the splice, we would not have been able to narrow down suspects when the agent for the Terran Regional Representative contacted Alachra with her warning."

When West stopped speaking, Korda asked, "Has this Montgomery Cristo been located or his ship searched?"

West shook her head. "No to both questions. He has

apparently vanished and his ship is guarded by a high-powered security system. We are pursuing the matter, but with so many visitors in the universe for the Solar Regatta, our resources are stretched."

"Do you have any pictures of him?" Korda asked. "It may help me to recognize him."

Wordlessly, West keyed a notescreen and extended it to Korda. Displayed on it was a short video of a young man with light brown hair and extraordinarily average appearance. Neither plain nor handsome, he could vanish in a crowd of two.

Korda frowned. "I believe we can guess where Cristo will be heading. I request permission to wait for him there."

As expected, Alachra shook his head in an eloquent negative. Removing his cigar, he stabbed the air to punctuate his points.

"Sorry. Can't risk it. He may not find it or he may track your activity and find it more easily. I suggest you nose around for as long as you wish. Treat your stay here as a vacation. If time goes out, then go to work; if not, we wait until the Regatta is over and then we quietly check everyone in the universe."

"Why not before or during the Regatta?" Korda asked, though he suspected that his suggestions would fall on deaf ears.

Alachra looked astonished that Korda would even suggest a change in his plan.

"This is the *Regatta*," he said, "the Solar Regatta, the

single most important sporting event in Fortuna. It's fast becoming one of the top ten most watched events in Universe Prime! I don't want news of a manhunt made public and beamed out with the sports news to every planet and pocket universe."

He loomed over Korda. "I don't want to take the risk, Korda. Relax. Have a good visit. You'll find a line of credit has already been opened for your party. Play some games while you ask around—the best way to be obvious here is to not play the games."

"I see the wisdom in your course of action," Korda said. "I will do as you request."

"Good." Alachra smiled and stuck out an enormous hand to shake Korda's. "Now, I'm on my way to the pre-race events and to limber up my ship. I'm flying the *Jolly Roger*—and, much as I want the win, the odds aren't in my favor. Solar sailing isn't my only hobby, like it is for so many of these people. Still, I don't want to make a fool of myself."

"Fortune sail with you," Korda said, shaking Alachra's hand in return. "And thank you for your briefing, West."

"It was a pleasure," West said, but her face showed no real emotion. "I will be with Alachra, but other members of the security staff will be here to help you. Please remember that you do not have legal immunity here, even if you are working with us. The laws of Fortuna bind you—and your friends—as they do any visitors."

"I will remember," Korda promised.

When Alachra and West had left, Irish turned to

Korda. "Quite a woman, West, eh? Well, they're all like that—we call 'em the Cardinal Points. They're all alike but all distinct. Clones, you see, perfect for their job and as devoted to Alachra as they can be. Now, how about taking a look at another intimidating lady?"

"I don't understand," Korda said.

"The *Shrike*," Irish said, laughing. "The spaceship. Ships are ladies, are they not? And the *Shrike* is an imposing lady, indeed."

"I bet she's not as smart as I am," Jester said in Korda's ear. She hadn't brought her PDA out of concealment. "Right, Boss?"

"I'm not certain that anyone is as smart as you, Jester," Korda said, "at least not as smart-mouthed."

"Boss! You're just plain mean!"

Irish was listening to the exchange with amusement. "Why now, isn't that a cute little PDA! I don't think I've ever seen the like. You call her 'Jester,' do you?"

"Same as my ship," Korda said. "Jester, meet Irish, the transportation director for Fortuna."

"Hi, Irish," Jester answered, bobbing her PDA out to flirt with the transportation director.

"Oh, you are a fine, sweet lass," he chortled. "Lovely design."

"Gee . . ." Jester managed to seem coy. "You say the nicest things, Irish."

Korda sighed and let Jester prattle on until they came to where the *Shrike* stood on a locked landing platform. Cristo's ship was indeed sleek and lean. It was also well-armed. Korda noted over a dozen weapon placements, including a contingent of missile tubes.

"*Shrike* has a nice security system," Irish said. "Discriminating, too, or we would have fried several Cardinal Points before we gave up. Let me show you."

He walked toward the ship, but before he was within five feet a flat, vaguely female voice said, "Warning! Password needed for further access."

Irish walked back to Korda and shrugged. "She's like that—won't chat like your Jester. Just says those six words. If you close within four feet, she fires a shot at your feet. Next shot is to kill. We would have lost North, but that those jumpsuits the Points wear have reflec in the weave. As is, she was pretty badly burnt."

"*Anything in your scan?*" Korda subvocalized to Jester.

"NADA, SUGAR POP," Jester answered on his readline. "DID YOU NOTICE THAT THE *SHRIKE* HAS ALMOST NO CARGO CAPACITY? SHE HAS ENOUGH FOR STANDARD GEAR AND FOR HER MISSILES, BUT NOT ENOUGH TO MAKE LOOTING WORTHWHILE. IF MONTGOMERY CRISTO IS OUR MAN, THEN HE EITHER HAS OTHER SHIPS TO CARRY HIS JUNK OR LOOT ISN'T WHAT HE'S AFTER."

Korda grunted his agreement and continued to study the *Shrike*. He didn't plan to amuse Irish by shouting guesses at the *Shrike's* security system—hell, there might be a "three strikes and you're out" rule in effect and he didn't plan to go out that way.

"We're going to need to do some further investigating

before we try that security system," he said aloud. "Jester, start a library search on the word 'shrike' and the name 'Montgomery Cristo.' They may contain some clue."

"Right, Boss," she said.

Korda shrugged. "I guess the best we can do is follow Alachra's instructions. Let's go check into our room here in the casino and make certain that the others have had no problems with theirs. Irish, thank you for your help."

The freckled redhead grinned. "This is more excitement than my department has seen in ages. I'm pleased to be in on it. Give a call if you need more help. I'm certain that the Cardinal Points will know where to reach you if I have any news."

"They probably will," Korda said, vaguely depressed at the thought of seven-foot amazons watching his every move. "They probably will."

Later that "night"—although, true to the tradition of casinos everywhere, Fortuna did not make a point of dividing night from day—Korda and Jester met with Tico, Miriam, and Arabou in the Café Oceana for a meal and discussion.

"We found that Alachra is covering all our expenses during the visit and has given us a credit line," Miriam said as soon as drinks had been ordered. "This is quite a change from how Dwistor treated us on Aurans."

"It is cooler, too," Korda said, looking around the restaurant appreciatively.

It was decorated like an enormous coral reef. Curving transparent walls held back the water, but everything, even their table and the benches for their booth, was part of the aquarium. Little fish swam away from bigger fish; sharks glided sinuously around barriers invisible to anyone except themselves. All around the diners, the game of predator and prey was played out in elegant silence.

Korda thought the aquarium was a pretty good metaphor for Fortuna at large.

The three desert dwellers were delighted with the experience. Miriam peppered her father with descriptions of what she was seeing and Arabou laughed, caught up in her enthusiasm. He claimed to be able to feel some of the vibrations of the creatures swimming in the aquarium—in one instance so skillfully locating a particularly vigorous moray eel that Miriam gaped at him in awe.

Korda didn't know whether to believe Arabou or not, but the Auransans were so generous in sharing their pleasure at the new experiences that he felt much as he had the first time he had seen something of the sort. He realized that he had forgotten what a tonic the presence of younger people could be and found himself wondering what other vital details of enjoying life he had let slip over the decades.

The menu was fresh seafood, some taken from the aquariums, others brought in from lakes on Fortuna or the vast ocean of Aqua. Korda ordered a shrimp scampi, heavy on the garlic. Arabou had a salmon fillet in a tarragon and dill cream sauce, while the honeymooners split an enormous sampler of broiled and fried delicacies.

Jester, of course, could eat nothing, but Miriam insisted on pouring a ceremonial thimble-sized cup of wine for the PDA.

"To do else would be less than mannerly," she said, "for you were my maid of honor and should take part in our celebration."

Bringing her PDA to dip over the cup, rather like a bee over a flower, Jester "sampled" the wine.

"A fine bouquet," she announced sententiously, "authoritative without being overwhelming, piquant with a faint undertone of raspberry, an excellent accompaniment for the meal."

Tico grinned and saluted the PDA with his own goblet. "A fine analysis, Jester. I could have used you during my brief, disastrous tenure as a purchaser of gourmet food and wines for the palace on Aurans."

He went on to tell a series of quick anecdotes, all of which made quite clear that he was a far better diplomat than gourmet. Arabou, in particular, was greatly amused and contributed tales of his own. Korda listened cheerfully, the business at hand put aside once he reminded Jester to stay alert for attempts to monitor their conversation.

"IT WOULDN'T BE EASY TO BUG THIS PLACE," she replied on his readline (given the danger that stasis could fall at any moment, Korda had carried along most of his tools, though he had given up his practical jumpsuit for evening dress). "THE AQUARIUMS BLOCK ANYTHING DIRECTIONAL. THERE IS A MIKE SET IN THE TABLE, BUT IT'S CURRENTLY NOT ACTIVATED. IF YOU SET YOUR GLASS JUST TO THE RIGHT UPPER QUADRANT OF YOUR PLATE, YOU'LL SET UP A DISTORTION SO THAT EVEN IF IT IS ACTIVATED ALL THEY'LL GET IS FRAGMENTS OF WHAT YOU'RE SAYING."

Korda did as Jester advised and until dinner was over and desert was served, he deliberately avoided any attempts to turn the conversation to business. Only when the server (a goldfish-shaped robot with limited anti-grav who delivered their orders on a scallop shell cart) had left a carafe of coffee and another of tea, did he permit Tico to lure him into discussing how they might go after the saboteur.

"Come now, friend," Tico said, "we have watched your determination as you worked to undo the saboteur's work on Aurans. We insist that you let us help you here. You cannot convince us that you plan to let him work unopposed on Fortuna while you play gambling games and eat fine food."

"He's got you there, Sugar Pop," Jester said. "Tell 'em what's up."

Shaking his head in mock despair, Korda studied the newlyweds.

"I bring the two of you to the finest resort universe

in existence, give you the opportunity for a honeymoon to tell your grandchildren about, and you ask me to put you to work."

"Do not forget me," Arabou said. "This blind old man has learned that blindness can help one to discover secrets, for people often forget that the blind can hear quite well indeed."

"I hadn't forgotten you, Arabou," Korda said, resting his hand for a moment on the man's arm. "Very well, let me start with some background. Right now, it's not much help, but it may give some insight later on."

Miriam nodded. "Just as you knew that Dwistor would find challenge to a duel hard to resist and so saved me, so some small piece of knowledge may save one of us later."

"Or not," Korda shrugged, "but here's what I have. Jester did some research for me and learned what a shrike is. Jes?"

"There are several meanings for the word," Jester said in a pompous, professorial voice. "However, most can easily be discarded. The one that drew itself to Rene and my attention was the following: 'a carnivorous bird, also called a butcher bird from its peculiar habit of hanging its kills on thorns, thus creating a larder.'"

Korda tapped the tabletop, drawing the attention of a curious angelfish. "We have not been able to get access to the *Shrike* itself and, since we suspect that it is set to self-destruct if entered by any but acceptable channels, we don't plan on forcing our way in."

"Self-destruct!" Tico said. "Isn't that rather drastic? Our saboteur would strand himself in that case."

"I don't think that would worry him," Korda said. "His actions demonstrate supreme self-confidence, verging on arrogance. I suspect if the *Shrike* blew itself up, he would just pirate another ship."

Arabou sipped his thick, dark coffee and set down the cup. "That sounds like someone with a confirmed criminal mentality."

"Maybe," Korda said. "Certainly the shutting down of privately owned universes is hardly the action of a law-abiding person. However, our saboteur may believe that he transcends the law. Jes, tell them your deductions about the name Montgomery Cristo."

"Right, Boss." The PDA continued in her professor voice. "In France during the first Age of the Fat Novel as determined by the current literary calendar, an author named Alexander Dumas published a book entitled *The Count of Monte Cristo*."

"Oh!" Miriam said, clapping her hands. "I've read that. It's the story of a young man who was arrested for a political crime of which he was completely innocent. His enemies arranged for him to be imprisoned for life and then one stole his job while another married his fiancée."

Jester bobbed, her professorial guise dropped in enthusiasm for the story. "Edmond Dantes, that was the man's name, escaped the prison and, after becoming a wealthy and powerful man, returned to his homeland to take vengeance on those who had wronged him."

Miriam picked up the thread again, speaking more slowly as the implications became clear. "Dantes believed himself beyond the laws of either God or man and in his arrogance was responsible not only for the deaths of his enemies, but for the deaths of some who were innocent as well. In the end, he leaves a letter to the son and daughter of his enemies apologizing for his arrogance."

"I wonder," Arabou said, "if our 'Montgomery Cristo' remembers all of the story or only the stirring tale of vengeance that precedes Edmond Dantes' final words?"

Korda shook his head. "I don't know, but I think his pseudonym may provide an interesting insight into his mind."

"I wonder who he believes wronged him?" Tico said. "He has struck at three universes. Does he want the owners or the creators?"

"I suspect the owners," Korda said. "The universes were created by at least three different universe designers. As far as I know, none of their other works have been damaged. These universes, however, all belong to the God's Pockets consortium. My belief is that the saboteur holds something against them."

"Did you speak with the designers?" Arabou asked.

"Yes, I did," Korda said. "One was an old friend—one of my former teachers—and the other two extended me professional courtesy. Well, one did, the other . . . the other had died under somewhat suspicious circumstances."

"Oh!" Miriam exclaimed, while the men looked grave.

"Yes," Korda continued, "a fire that not only killed her, but also destroyed her records. Jester, remind me to send messages to Nizzim Rochtar and Charlie Bell telling them of Clia T'rifit's death. If we word it right, it will serve as a warning as well."

"Good idea, Boss," Jester said. "You know, if the saboteur knows who the owners of God's Pockets are, he's one up on us. We have no idea of their real identities. I've run checks on Deter, Dwistor, and Alachra and not one of them appear to have any history before taking up residence in their universes."

"So I saw in your report," Korda said, "and Universe Prime is too large and varied a place for us to try and trace each of them. I doubt any of the owners look much like they did when they started."

"Y'know, Boss," Jester said. "I've been wondering about Alachra's use of the word 'Terry' when he was talking to us before."

"'Terry'?" Tico repeated.

"Yeah," Jester explained. "It's criminal slang—specifically spacefaring—for the Terran authorities. Each planet and pocket universe has its own government for local crime, but the Terran Regional Government has jurisdiction over the spaces in between. Smugglers and pirates in particular have a lot to fear from them, since many worlds and some universes extend automatic permission to pursue to the Terran investigators."

"I take it," Arabou said, "that the God's Pockets universes did not have such a permission on record?"

"No," Korda said. "Had Alachra not extended his invitation, I could not have come here to do this job so openly. Urbs and Aurans were in stasis, so the legal ramifications were a bit grayer."

Tico rubbed his beard with the palms of his hands. "So, you wonder if Alachra, and by extension Deter and Dwistor, might be criminals. If only the universe was not so vast! But I doubt that even fair Jester could answer that for us before the saboteur next strikes."

"I'm only as good as the information in my databanks," Jester agreed. "I can try, but if I'm helping the boss and monitoring my usual jobs, then it's going to have tertiary priority."

Korda patted the PDA. "Don't worry about it, Jes. I am going to need you with me."

He frowned. "I found another thing odd. The Terran Regional Representative told me she informed Alachra indirectly about the threat to Fortuna, but he made it quite obvious that he knew who was behind the message."

"That seems to suggest that he has a rather elaborate spy system in place," Tico said thoughtfully.

"And routinely uses it," Arabou added, "an action quite at odds with his bluff, hearty exterior."

"What is your plan, Rene?" Miriam asked.

"I intend to locate the world key," Korda said. "Alachra may not want to give me the location, but if I find it on my own, I can be waiting for our saboteur. I also stand a better chance of finding him if I'm pursuing the same goal."

"Brilliant!" Tico said. "And what shall we do?"

"Stand by and be ready to help," Korda said. "Listen for rumors of interesting strangers, odd crimes, security alerts. Any of these could help us pin down the location of Mr. Cristo."

"It doesn't sound like much," Miriam said doubtfully.

Korda smiled. "It may be more than you know. Are any of you particularly good with a hand weapon?"

"I am," Tico said. "On Urbs you are not respected unless you are a master of one or more weapons. I chose hand energy weapons because they were small and comparatively easy to learn."

Miriam studied him. "Did that earn you much respect?"

Laughing, Tico hugged her. "No, not really, but it earned me enough that I could perform trade negotiations. What would you have me shoot, Rene?"

"Nothing and no one, if we can help it," Korda said. "But it occurs to me that as soon as stasis falls the saboteur may head for his ship. If you were to get there before him and slow his access, we might be able to catch him."

Tico nodded sharply. "I know my post, then."

"Don't take it too seriously," Korda said. "I hope to prevent him, in which case your skill will not be needed."

Arabou lifted the coffee pot, found it empty, and set it down again.

"Do you want me to order more, Arabou?" Jester asked solicitously.

"No," Arabou replied. "I think not. I shall return to

my hotel and sleep. My friend Sam has invited me to lunch tomorrow. I would not wish to be too groggy to enjoy the meeting."

"Let us take you back to the Old West," Tico said. "After that dinner I could use a stretch."

Arabou looked as if he would protest, then he smiled.

"You are a good son, Tico. Yes, walk with me. I think you and Miriam will enjoy the train."

Miriam turned to Korda. "Will you join us, Rene?"

Korda shook his head. "No, I'm going to crash for a few hours and then get to work."

They parted outside the Oceanic Casino. Korda walked briskly toward the Black Pyramid.

"Jester, where did you say magnetic north is located?"

"Actually, Boss, it's out near the end of the rail line, near the Old West where Arabou is staying."

Korda looked after the others. They were still in sight.

"Hey!" he yelled. "Wait up! I've changed my mind."

The Auransans stopped and Korda ran to join them. Jester's PDA flew near his ear.

"Boss, aren't you going to get some sleep?"

Korda subvocalized his reply. *"I only said that to reassure the others. I want them to enjoy their vacation, but realistically, I don't know how much time we have before the saboteur makes his move."*

He slowed and the companions resumed their walk toward the rail station. Even as he joked with the others, Korda couldn't get rid of a sneaking suspicion that time—bottled or not—was once again running out.

XV

The rail ride proved to be amusing and confirmed Korda's feeling that Clia T'rifit had been a universe designer who would have been ranked with the best if she had lived.

They got aboard a sleek bullet train that shot them out of the port area. Once they were away from the major casinos, the landscape around them flattened. In the darkness, they could see tall saguaro cactus and the rounder forms of sagebrush, juniper, and chamisa.

As the train crossed into the desert, the sound of its passage changed. Its almost silent progress was replaced by a rhythmic thumping. An eerie whistle pierced the air.

Startled, Korda looked away from the windows to see if the others had noticed the new sounds. He realized that the compartment had changed as well. The modern plastic and foam seats had metamorphosed into carved wood and velvet with gilt trim.

Arabou laughed. "Chug-a-chug-a, Chug-a-chug-a. Choo! Choo! Am I right in my guessing, daughter? Has this conveyance become an old-fashioned steam train?"

Miriam reached to squeeze his hand. "It has indeed, father. Was it like this when you were here before?"

"I suspect that it was," Arabou confirmed, "but I never rode on it. I stayed mostly in the trade centers. Today when I went to my hotel, I heard the sounds shift and felt the furniture subtly take on a new shape and I thought that I was riding in a miracle."

They rode Arabou's miracle train into the Old West and escorted him to his hotel. When Arabou had gone to his room, Tico and Miriam excused themselves to return to the Oceanic. Korda stayed behind, pretending an interest in the architecture. He walked down a rough board sidewalk toward what Jester informed him was the location of magnetic north.

Old West, Fortuna-style, owed as much to cinema as to history. The streets were dusty, but not muddy or covered with manure. In addition to Arabou's hotel, storefronts advertised dry goods, livery stables, a post office, and a photography studio. Saloons outnumbered honest businesses three to one—odds Korda suspected were not far out of line with history.

Jester indicated a saloon down where a street petered out into sagebrush. The sound of a honky-tonk piano playing a ragtime piece several centuries out of date for the setting leaked, along with bars of yellow light, through the slats of the swinging door.

"That's the place, Pardner," she drawled.

"The saloon," Korda said. "I don't suppose that for once things are going to be easy and magnetic north will be quietly out among the sagebrush and cactus."

"Sorry, Pardner," Jester answered. "I've triangulated the readings and it's in the saloon."

"Oh, well," Korda sighed. "I couldn't expect anything else. Come on, let's check the lay of the land."

"Right beside you, Pardner," Jester said. "Keep your six-gun low and loose. I sense trouble."

"Jes . . ." Korda said. "Don't overdo the act."

His boots echoed with an inspiring solidity as he swaggered up the board walkway and into the saloon. He swung the doors open and was almost disappointed to find that no one paid much attention to his entry.

The hour was late and the saloon almost deserted. A man in a wide-brimmed cowboy hat, white shirt, red bandanna, and jeans sat playing the upright piano. Four men in dark shirts, hats, and jeans sat playing cards at a small table about midway into the saloon.

"I'm bartender as well as entertainment at this hour," the piano player called over his shoulder. "At least for another hour, I am."

"What happens in another hour?" Korda asked, walking over to the piano and leaning against it.

The piano player looked up and smiled. He had an honest face that reminded Korda somewhat of photos he'd seen of the older Roy Rogers.

"Shift change," he said laconically. "Then I catch some shut-eye until tomorrow night. Things'll be quiet until the Regatta is over, but we never close."

"Never?" Korda said, arching his eyebrows in surprise.

"What about to clean or restock?"

"Nope," the piano player said. "We just work around the card games. There's always at least one. I don't think I've ever seen that table empty—new players drift in and out, but the game keeps going."

"AND GUESS WHERE MAGNETIC NORTH IS, PARDNER?" Jester scrawled on his readline.

"They never leave?" Korda asked.

"Just about never," the piano player clarified. "Sometimes they fold for a few minutes and go for a smoke. Once somebody accused the dealer of cheating and there was a break while the bodies were cleared away. Guess that's about it. Get you a beer?"

"Sure," Korda said. They walked together over to a classic polished wooden bar. Korda sat on one of the stools and set his feet on the brass foot rail. He wondered if anyone ever used the polished spittoons that were set around the room.

"Draft good enough?" the piano player asked.

"Great," Korda said, handing him his credit slip. "Draw yourself one while you're at it."

"Thanks, but I'll settle for a sarsaparilla," the piano player answered. "I've got a lunch date tomorrow. Don't want to deal with a hangover."

Korda lifted his mug, sipped, and discovered that the beer was quite good. He took a larger swallow. Behind him, he heard the card players muttering occasional comments.

"Give me two." "Pass." "Fold." "Two pair beats pair."

"Ante up."

The rules of the game, its fine points, its peculiarities returned from memory as he sat drinking his beer. Sounded like they were playing standard five card draw. He hadn't heard anything he couldn't handle.

"Think they'd deal in another player?" he asked the piano player, sliding him his empty mug.

The piano player chuckled. "They're always glad for another victim. You play poker?"

"A long time ago," Korda said, remembering marathon games two centuries back when he'd been working on the terraforming of Persephone. "I got pretty good. I bet it'll come back."

"Well," the piano player said, "that's a bet I won't take—don't see the percentage in it for me. Go on over at the start of the next hand and put your ante in. Fortune be good to you."

"Thanks," Korda said.

The piano started up again, this piece vaguely reminiscent of old movies where the idealistic Eastern dude takes on the outlaws. Korda couldn't help feeling as if a soundtrack was being provided for his scene.

Striding over to the table, he paused where he could watch the play without snooping on anyone's hand.

"WHEN YOU PLAY," Jester offered through the readline, "I COULD TAKE A LOOK AT WHAT THE OTHER PLAYERS GET AND RELAY THE INFORMATION TO YOU."

"*No thanks,*" Korda replied. "*I don't think these guys*

would take kindly to cheating dudes. I wouldn't be at all surprised if the rule was shoot first and ask questions later."

"Brrr," the PDA answered. "Savage!"

The dealer turned slightly in his chair. "Ante up!"

"That's my call," Korda said.

He pulled a chair into the space two players had made for him. Even this close, the shadows of their hat brims effectively hid their faces. They sat with their hands loosely folded on the table in front of them. Although there were mugs of beer on the table, no one moved to drink. Korda found the entire situation unsettling.

"What's the ante?" he asked the dealer.

"Five credits," the dealer answered. "Game is five card draw, nothing wild, no house rules except one."

"What?" Korda said, trying to match his tough tone of voice.

"No messing with probability," the dealer said. "That's a hanging offense—if we take the time to find a rope. Otherwise it's a shooting offense. Get it?"

Korda swallowed. He couldn't help but remember the probability driver setting on his UT. He hoped that possession alone wasn't enough to get him shot. He ran his credit slip through the anachronistic reader in the center of the table and a chip dropped out. He added it to the heap on the table.

The hand he was dealt was a mess—not even an ace high. Korda folded immediately and let the others play out the round. The player directly across from him won with a pair of aces that beat the next best—a pair of threes.

Korda kept playing, folding frequently, winning an occasional hand, taking his turn when the deal rotated to him. The other players were deadly serious. No one cursed, cheered, or commented on the action. The mugs of beer remained untouched. Korda was getting dry, but the intensity of the other players was such that he felt as if he couldn't move.

He was beginning to believe that there would never be an opportunity for him to set up the resonance tracer when he saw the player across from him—the same who had won the first hand—slip an ace from his sleeve. It was smoothly done. Korda doubted that he would have noticed if he hadn't been looking directly at the player when he made the substitution.

The player won the game with a short straight. When it was his turn to deal, he won again, this time with a royal flush. Korda decided that he had to act.

"Wait a sec," he said, putting his hand over the pile when the player would have swept them in. "I want to check the cards. I thought I saw something—"

"Cheating?" the winner said. "That's a serious accusation, friend."

Korda felt his heart pounding, but he couldn't back down now.

"It is," he said, "but I think we'll find that there's an extra ace in the deck—an ace just like one of those that's sitting in your winning hand."

The player to Korda's right wordlessly reached out and

took up the deck. He thumbed through it, letting each card fall face up on the table. The winner drew a six-shooter and angled it at Korda.

Korda didn't let his gaze leave the falling cards, confident that if he did the incriminating ace would somehow be palmed. He felt the barrel of the gun staring at him like an extra eye.

Two cards from the bottom of the deck, the Ace of Diamonds showed. There was a stir from the other players.

"There's already an Ace of Diamonds showing," said the player to Korda's left.

"Drop, Sugar Pop!" Jester yelled.

Korda did so just in time to avoid the deadly crossfire that blossomed from the guns of the other four players. The table fell to its side, scattering cards, beer, and poker chips in all directions.

When the thunder of gunfire faded, Korda pulled himself to his knees. The air was blue with smoke and smelled of gunpowder. The cheater was dead, his chest a ruin of red holes. His hat had fallen off. Horrified, Korda saw that his features were those of a zombie, skin shriveled to bone, fleshless lips pulled back from yellowed teeth.

"Time for a smoke," one of the other players said.

They clomped away in a group. Korda couldn't bring himself to check if they, too, were zombies. Trembling, he got to his knees.

"Second time this week," the piano player said. He had put on a fringed leather jacket and was obviously on his way home. "Boy, I'm glad that this time it happened at the end of my shift. The next guy can clean up—I'm out of here."

Korda stared after the swinging door, knowing that he should have asked questions, too stunned to do so. He caught a faint odor of cigarette smoke on the wind.

"Sugar Pop," Jester said, coming to hover in front of his face, "you'd better get the resonance tracer set up before the players come back. I don't think they'd like having you in the middle of their game."

Korda hurried then and when the reading was safely relayed to Jester's system, he folded the machine away. The relief bartender had come in while he was finishing up and was setting up a new game on another table. When Korda rose, he slid the table over so that the endless poker game would once again cover magnetic north.

"Want a beer?" the bartender asked companionably, getting a push broom from behind the counter.

Korda looked at the zombie poker player on the floor, heard the clumping footsteps as the others returned.

"No thanks," he said. Unconsciously, he echoed the words of the piano player. "I'm out of here."

Jester insisted that Korda take a nap, arguing persuasively that Cristo must know of the Regatta and that he would probably time his attack so that it came either during the race, when most of the Cardinal Points would be busy, or after the tourists had left Fortuna.

Korda knew there was a flaw in her logic, but he was too tired to find it—reason enough for him to get some sleep. He retired to his room at the Black Pyramid, told Jester to wake him if stasis fell or in six hours, whichever came first, and then crashed into a deep, dreamless sleep.

He awoke refreshed and knowing what he had been too tired to see the night before. As he showered and cleaned up, he explained his worry to Jester.

"If Cristo learns I'm here, it may change his plans," he said. "Our profession is a small enough one that he probably knows me—either personally or by reputation."

"You did say his style seemed familiar," Jester commented. "Go on."

"Cristo may deduce that I've been sent after him," Korda continued. "He must realize that the shutdown of Urbs and Aurans couldn't go unnoticed forever."

Jester bobbed once—her attempt at a shrug. "I don't know. From what we've learned, Urbs didn't do a lot of business with other universes. The saboteur's luck ran out when those merchants showed up when they did. Aurans was equally isolationist."

"True," Korda stopped, his comb halfway through his wet hair. "Jester, you don't think I'm being vain, do you? Am I stupid to assume Cristo will have heard of me? I have been retired for a while."

The PDA rested on his shoulder. "No, Sugar Pop. I don't think that's vain at all—I think it's constructive paranoia, something that organic brains do far better than electronic ones. Still, there are a bunch of tourists here for the Regatta. Maybe Cristo won't hear about you."

Korda pulled on a clean shirt and fastened his bottled time out of sight below its hem.

"What I would do, in his circumstances, is get a printout every so often—say, every twelve hours—on every ship to come into Fortuna. I'd scan the list for possible pursuit."

"And your ship has been called the *Jester* for a long time, hasn't it, Sugar Pop?" Jester said.

"That's right," Korda answered. "Even before I finished the programming for you, I called my personal vessel the *Jester*. I thought that too many people in my business took themselves too seriously. After all, we're just doing with lots of fancy gear what nature does all on her own."

Momentarily, he heard the clacking of pool balls in his memory.

"So Cristo," Jester said, "would have a pretty good chance of knowing that a ship with Old Terran registry bearing the name *Jester* would be yours. He could double-check that easily enough."

"Right," Korda said. "So we need to get to work. You contact the others and make certain they're okay. I'll get the direction finder and start narrowing down our options. Want to make a bet with me?"

Jester giggled. "That's a serious thing here, Boss."

"I know," Korda said. "I'm willing to bet the direction finder is going to lead us straight into the Black Pyramid. That's Alachra's central base of operations and he wouldn't want the world key too far from his main protections."

"No bet," the PDA answered. "I've too much respect for your human intuition."

The direction finder did indeed confirm Korda's guess. However, after they had pinpointed the reading from several different angles, they were confronted with a new problem.

"I'm not really surprised," Korda said, "but access to the world key doesn't seem to be available in public areas."

"There's a nest of tunnels behind the walls," the PDA said. "I can't scan very deeply, but what I do see is enough to confirm that we could go around like rats in a maze while the Cardinal Points tracked us down. The direction finder is only so good in a maze—what we want could be right next to us, but if there is baffling of any type, it will guide us the long way around."

Korda nodded. "And there will be baffling, I'm sure of that. Clia T'rifit had a good reputation. I can't believe she would have neglected a precaution so obvious."

"Well," Jester said, "I guess we just wander around looking for access points and trying to find one that isn't too well guarded."

Korda frowned. "I hate the delay, especially since I suspect that Cristo is well ahead of us, but I don't think we have much choice. If we draw off some of the security staff to chase us, then we're doing him a favor."

"Remember what Alachra said," Jester added. "He said that the way you would be most obvious was if you didn't play any of the games. The same would apply to the saboteur. Let's go down to one of the main gaming floors. You can play and I'll do some scouting."

"Sounds good," Korda said. "Maybe if I sacrifice a few of Alachra's credits, my luck will turn for the better."

"That's the spirit, Boss!" Jester cheered.

Korda let Alachra buy him a club sandwich, an iced tea, and a handful of chips for the slot machines. Then he hauled his lunch over to an elaborate slot machine shaped rather like a planet with several concentric rings of neon.

Jester commented that she thought the machine looked cool, but for Korda its advantage was that it had a table for his sandwich and a clear view of a major security post at the far side of the room. Korda figured that if there was any problem, the guard on duty there would be contacted and maybe he could send Jester to eavesdrop on the message. It was a weak plan, but, for the moment, it was the best he could come up with.

Taking a bite from his sandwich, Korda fed a few chips into the slot machine.

The genius in the design of the slot machine became obvious as soon as he began to play. Like many sophisticated machines of its type, it paid off almost at once, then teased him with occasional trickles. However, its true magnificence was in the physical design. The same loops of neon that had attracted Jester's admiration now centered him on the machine. If he glanced to either side, their glare drove his attention back to the game.

"I wonder if Clia T'rifit designed these, too," he said to Jester, "or if Alachra has some masters of human psychology on staff?"

"I'd bet the latter," Jester said, examining the machine. "This has a manufacturing date of this standard year. Odd . . ."

"What, Jes?" Korda said, dropping a few chips in.

"I had figured that Alachra would have a manufacturing plant here in Fortuna," Jester said, "but this is stamped with the hallmark of someplace called Dyce."

"And Dyce," Korda said, forgetting the slot-machine, "is the name of one of the other God's Pockets universes. They really are in each other's pockets, aren't they?"

"That's a terrible pun, Boss," Jester said. "Still, I am forced to agree with the import of what you've said. Obviously, one of the ways that the God's Pockets consortium protects its privacy is to trade as much as possible among its own units."

"Good plan if you can make it work," Korda said, "and from what we've seen, I guess they can."

He played for a time, alternating taking bites of his sandwich with feeding chips into the slot.

"Looks like I'm going to run out of sandwich and chips right about the same time," he commented. "Lady Luck doesn't seem to favor me today."

"Why not use the probability driver?" Jester whispered in his ear. "I'd like to compute how much it affects the odds. I've been keeping track of your play so far."

Korda hesitated. "I'd hate to cause any trouble."

"Aw, c'mon, Boss," Jester said. "Cheating is only cheating if you get caught."

"You have a point," Korda said, "but if some defense system shoots me, you're going to regret this."

From the sheath on his belt, Korda drew the universal tool and activated the variable setting. Obediently, the solid metal rod shifted shape, becoming a device about eight inches long, etched with stylized representations of the suits on a deck of cards.

He touched it to the slot machine, felt an energy surge, and then fed a chip into the machine.

The neon rings lit, swirling like Saturn doing a hula. Bells rang, heavenly music played, and a flood of coins poured out of the slot. Korda bent to insert a bucket to catch them, sliding the probability driver back into its sheath as he did so.

"Satisfied, Jes?" he said.

"That was sure interesting, Boss," the computer replied, "but it doesn't give me enough data to draw any real deductions. Try it again!"

"I'm not certain that's a good idea, Jes," Korda said. "The Cardinal Point at the security post across the room seemed awfully interested in the commotion."

Jester brought her PDA down in front of him. Korda was absolutely certain that if she had eyelashes she would bat them at him.

"Please, Rene? For me?"

He sighed and surrendered gracefully. Again he touched the probability driver to the machine and fed in a chip. Again the heavens pealed, rings gyrated, and chips (a smaller amount this time), flooded forth.

This time, however, he felt a hand on his shoulder. He glanced over and up. A Cardinal Point, identical as far as he could tell to West, towered over him.

"Excuse me, sir," she said. "It has come to our attention that you are using a device to alter probability. Please be warned that if we detect further use of it, you will be shot in full sight of the other patrons."

Korda blinked—he wasn't precisely surprised by the warning, but there was something about the guard's bored delivery that gave him chills.

"Of course," he said, trying to be as charming as possible. "I was just testing it. My name is Rene Korda and I'm here—"

"I am aware why you are here," the guard said. "Your mission does not excuse you from obeying the law. Thank you for your cooperation in this matter."

Korda gestured to the buckets of chips around his feet. "Do you want to confiscate these?"

The guard shook her head. "You cheated fairly to get them. You may retain them. If they are too awkward for you to carry, the clerk will convert them to your credit account. Good Fortune follow you."

"And you," Korda said. When the guard had departed, Korda looked up at the PDA. "Now do you have enough data, Jes?"

"Not quite," she admitted, "but this will have to do. The odds of your being killed are too high to take an additional risk."

"Gee, I'm so glad to hear you say that," Korda said sarcastically. "Let's go trade these chips in. I'm not interested in taking the risk that stealing is considered an acceptable form of cheating on Fortuna."

Jester hovered as he gathered up his winnings. "I'd give odds that it is. Want to bet?"

"With you, Jes?" Korda laughed. "I'm not stupid enough to take those odds."

Korda had just finished trading in his winnings when Jester gave a glad cry and darted across the casino.

"Hi, Arabou!" she chirped. "How's your luck?"

"Very good," the blind trader replied. "First, I have found you and secondly, I have an interesting anecdote for Rene. If you are here, he must be near."

"I am indeed," Korda said, coming to join them. "How on Fortuna did you figure out where to find us?"

"I asked one of the Cardinal Points," Arabou said. "They knew precisely where you were."

Korda chuckled. "I'm not surprised. Jester got me into a bit of trouble with one of them. Did I hear you have some information for me?"

Arabou nodded. "I do indeed. Shall we find a quiet place to talk?"

"Sounds good," Korda said. "There's an ornamental fountain in the café across the hall. It should block out any eavesdropping. We can even get some lunch if you're hungry."

"I've just come from lunch with my friend Sam," Arabou said, allowing Korda to take his arm and guide him to the café, "but I would welcome a demitasse."

In the Fountain Café, Korda ordered Arabou a small cup of the thick, oily coffee the desert merchant preferred. To keep Arabou company, he ordered himself some calamari sautéed in olive oil with pimentos. Jester checked for listening devices while they waited for their order. When they had both her assurance and their food, Arabou began his account.

"When I was having lunch with my friend Sam, he decided to amuse me with an account of a rather colorful incident at the saloon where he works the late shift as bartender and piano player. Arabou took a tiny sip of his coffee. "From his description, I realized that you, Rene, were the 'dude' involved."

"Hey, Arabou, wait a minute," Jester interrupted, her concern for Korda overwhelming her limited understanding of the very human concept of manners. "You're blind. How did you know Sam was talking about Rene?"

Korda did not chide the computer. Her approach might be rather tactless, but he had been struck by the same point.

Arabou, however, did not appear offended. In fact, he seemed rather pleased.

"I recognized Rene because of you, little imp," he said. "When Sam described the dude as being accompanied by a smiling sphere that whispered in his ear and appeared to advise him, I knew he must mean you. Miriam has described you to me and Sam's description tallied with hers on all salient points."

"Sorry for asking," Jester apologized, "but it did seem kinda strange."

"Not at all," Arabou said. "You look after Rene. I would not expect less of you."

Korda finished chewing a tentacle. Spearing another, he asked, "So your friend Sam told you about my encounter with the zombie card players. What else did you learn?"

"Something quite interesting," Arabou said. "Earl, Sam's relief at the saloon, joined us in time to hear Sam's tale and he took it upon himself to supply the sequel, describing in hilarious detail how you ignored a fortune in poker chips scattered on the floor in order to set up a small machine and take a reading of some sort. Sam got quite excited then—it seems that a few days ago a young man came into the saloon and had a similar encounter with the poker players and . . ."

He paused, deliberately playing for suspense. Korda humored him.

"And?"

"And, just as you had, the young man set up a small machine." Arabou folded his hands complacently across his belly. "This young man did pause to take the chips, however."

"Our saboteur," Korda said softly. "He was there!"

"Indeed," Arabou looked positively delighted with

himself, "and he was not there alone. He was accompanied by a young lady Sam happened to know. She is the lead singer for a band here in the Black Pyramid Casino. I thought that you might be interested in this, for if she is still keeping company with Mr. Cristo, she may know where he is."

Knowing that Arabou could not see his smile, Korda reached over and squeezed the old man's hand.

"Wonderful!" he exclaimed. "Cristo may even be hiding out with her while he waits for the Regatta to end. We'll go scout out the place. Do you know what the band is called?"

"Tophet Khan," Arabou said. "They are a neo-jazz band. I would be interested in hearing them play if you permit me to accompany you. Their glifnod player, Glifnod Garu, is famous even in Aurans."

Korda rose. "Wait here. I'll go find out when Tophet Khan is playing next and see if we can get tickets."

He came back a few minutes later and slid back into his seat.

"Good news," he announced. "Tophet Khan plays in a few hours. I bribed the ticket manager and learned that they will be setting up now. He gave me a couple of backstage passes. We may be able to talk with the lead singer before the show starts."

"And if Cristo is hanging with her," Jester added, "we may be able to nab him!"

"That's right." Korda turned to Arabou. "Did Sam describe Cristo to you? The photo that Alachra's security people had only showed a fairly average fellow with brown hair."

Arabou frowned. "That is strange. I did ask, for I recalled your dissatisfaction with the description you had. Sam said that this other dude had light blond hair and fairly strong features. He mentioned the nose and eyebrows particularly."

"Well," Korda said, getting to his feet, "we could be on a wild goose chase, but this beats sitting at a slot machine waiting for something to happen. I've settled the tab. Shall we go and listen to Tophet Khan?"

XVI

Tophet Khan was jamming when Korda and Arabou arrived in the nightclub. The roadie who tried to muscle them out retreated at the sight of the backstage passes—the handful of chips Korda handed him didn't seem to hurt either.

Korda led Arabou to a table off to one side of the stage and then, taking a seat next to him, studied the band. It was a four-piece ensemble of which not one member was human.

The keyboard player was an enormous, bulbous alien who resembled a heap of gray mashed potatoes with arms and hands. Sitting ringed in its instrument, rather as if the potatoes had been set inside a thick slice of pineapple, it played with astonishing dexterity, unlimited by such restrictions as joints or handedness.

Compared to the keyboard player, the angular robot who played a combination drum kit and stringed instrument of some sort seemed almost normal. It was constructed of tubular metal sections fastened together in an approximately humanoid shape. Its triangular head swiveled to the beat and served as a percussion instrument as well.

Seated on the floor at the point of the stage's apron was the glifnod player. Purplish in coloration and humanoid in shape, he had four arms. The light of his glifnod—a purely electronic instrument resembling a selection of pastel Easter eggs connected by thin pieces of wire to a central tree—reflected from his faceted orange eyes.

Korda had heard glifnod recordings, but he had never seen one being played. The combination of flashing lights coordinated with corresponding sounds was almost hypnotic.

Turning to the lead singer, Korda decided that she looked exactly like a fairy—a fairy as rendered by an artist of Old Terra's Victorian era, but elongated and then dressed in a beret and a nearly transparent, iridescent shift. Her indigo blue butterfly wings beating in time to the music, she tapped the tambourine that was the standard prop for such performers and wailed melodiously.

While waiting for the piece to end, Korda started to whisper a description of the musicians to Arabou, but the trader politely waved him to silence.

"I wish to listen," Arabou explained. "The presentation is very interesting—they sound well-rehearsed. Glifnod Garu is not as good as I had been led to believe, but then legends have their best performances to live up to."

Korda waited for the end of the set, then, when the lead singer called for a five-minute break, he approached the stage.

"Excuse me, miss. Are you Simeen Ishbrendu?" he said, hoping he was pronouncing the name from the program correctly.

"That's me," she said fluttering to the edge of the stage. "Autographs usually get signed after the show, but if you have your program I can do it now."

Korda promptly handed her his program. It would not do to insult her by telling her that he had something else to ask her. Anyway, it might make a nice souvenir for Arabou to take back to Aurans with him.

Simeen Ishbrendu waved to the other band members. "Hey, cats, scrawl your Hancock on this mark's program, would yah?"

None of the other performers seemed loath. Glifnod Garu even carried it over to Lari the Masher so that the keyboard player wouldn't need to lumber across the stage.

Korda accepted the signed program back with a grateful smile.

"Sam told us you'd be nice," he said as an opener.

"Sam?" Simeen seemed slightly confused.

The rest of the band—except for Glifnod Garu, who was resetting one of the eggs in his glifnod—had drifted backstage. Simeen seemed inclined to follow them, but Korda kept up his pose as the bright, eager fan and she was too polite to tell him to get lost.

"That's right, Sam—the piano player at the End of the Walk Saloon in the Old West," Korda said. "We asked him what band would be good to catch and he said we shouldn't miss Tophet Khan. My friend knew your stuff, but I'm just a rube."

Simeen seemed to realize for the first time that Arabou was blind. Fluttering her wings, she drifted off the stage and went to shake his hand.

"Always great to meet a fan," she said. "Have you ever heard us live before?"

"I have not," Arabou admitted, "but I have all of your albums."

The conversation drifted into exotic music trivia for several minutes. Korda was glad Arabou was having fun, but the conversation wasn't helping him find Montgomery Cristo.

Finally, Simeen glanced at her discreetly hidden watch.

"It's been utterly great to talk with you, Arabou," she said. "Hang for the show and I'll see if we can get you a demo of our next release."

"Why, thank you, young lady," Arabou said, his tones courtly. "If I did not know that you already have an escort, I would ask you to do me the favor of a private dinner. Still, perhaps I can invite you both to share a meal with me."

"You mean the chap I was with at the Old West?" Simeen laughed as if the idea was extraordinarily silly. "He's just a pal. I'd go out with you. You're cute."

Arabou's round face reddened, but he seemed honestly pleased.

Korda cut in. "Do you have any idea where the fellow you were with is? When Sam described him, I thought he might be a business associate of mine."

Simeen folded her wings, her expression suddenly guarded. "I doubt that, whoever you are and whatever you do. Anyhow, don't you have anything better to do when you're on vacation?"

As Korda struggled for a suitable answer, he suddenly noticed that Glifnod Garu had dropped his instrument and was heading out one of the nightclub's side doors.

"Jes, after him!" Korda yelled. "Garu's our man."

The PDA zipped away and Korda ran after them. Garu got out the door, slamming it behind him quickly enough to block Korda but not enough to stop the PDA.

"I'M AFTER HIM," Jester reported. "HE'S HEADING FOR AN ACCESS CRAWL SPACE. HE'S TURNING . . . . HIS FORM IS SHIFTING. HE'S DROPPING THE EXTRA ARMS . . . . HE'S GOT A GUN!"

There was a break in the transmission. Korda got the door open and headed down the curving corridor toward the sound of footsteps. He heard a crackling noise.

"BOSS! I'M HIT—"

The transmission cut off suddenly.

Rounding the corner, Korda came across the ruins of Jester's PDA. It had been seared by an energy weapon of some sort, its turquoise and purple paint bubbled, its delicate interior circuitry broken.

He froze, anger hot in his veins. Rationally, he knew that Jester was fine, that only the PDA had been broken, but the irrational core that is at the heart of every civilized man, that a universe designer must touch to create, that part riled and raged at the murder of a friend.

"BOSS?" His readline came alive. "HEY, BOSS? ARE YOU ALL RIGHT? ANSWER ME, RENE!"

"I'm fine," he answered, speaking to the air, in his relief not bothering to subvocalize. "Send another PDA immediately, Jes."

"ONE IS ON THE WAY, SUGAR POP," the computer promised. "DON'T GO AFTER THAT GUY UNTIL I GET THERE, OKAY? FORTUNA CENTRAL WON'T LIKE ME BLASTING THROUGH THEIR AIRWAVES LIKE THIS."

"I'll wait," he said.

Hearing footsteps behind him, he turned quickly, his shattered PDA still in his hand. Simeen Ishbrendu was running down the corridor, Arabou right behind her.

"Rene, what is wrong?" Arabou asked. "Are you hurt? I smell something burnt."

"I'm fine," Korda said. He held out the PDA, though he knew Arabou couldn't see it. "The bastard masquerading as Glifnod Garu burnt Jester's PDA to keep her from tracking him. She's sending a replacement. I'll go after him as soon as it gets here."

Simeen stared at the burnt PDA, horror evident on her delicate features. "That guy had an E-weapon on him? He said he was just dodging a debt . . . . I was hiding him until after the Regatta. He said he had a sure-thing bet on the race. I figured it wouldn't hurt, if he was going to pay."

"He was going to pay," Korda said, "though maybe not in the currency you imagined. I wonder what game he's playing?"

"I wish I could help," Simeen said, "but I don't know much more than what I told you. Monte came to the show, chatted me up, we went dancing, stuff like that. He seemed edgy, but when he told me about the debt, I could understand why.

She leaned her forehead against the wall, her wings fanning a slight breeze. "I was in a bind. Glifnod Garu got kicked out of the universe for running up too big a tab on the blackjack tables. Our contract runs until after the Regatta ends. Monte could play the 'nod, not as good as Garu, but good enough. Seemed like an answer to both our problems, y'know?"

"I do," Korda answered.

His anger was cooling. This Montgomery Cristo was a careful planner. He might even have arranged to have Garu deported so he could hide with Tophet Khan. One thing was certain. When the new PDA arrived, Korda wasn't going charging down a service corridor after him. He'd be setting himself up for a fall.

Arabou was stroking Simeen Ishbrendu in the narrow space between her wings. The singer was becoming less agitated, but she couldn't stop muttering.

"What are we going to do? If we don't play tonight, we'll be in trouble with the casino, but we can't go on without a glifnod—not on such short notice."

"Well, my dear," Arabou said. "I may have an answer for you. How long until show time?"

"An hour," Simeen said. "Do you know a glifnod

player?"

Arabou grinned. "Would I do? I'm not an expert, but I can play and I have faithfully listened to all of your albums. My ear is very good and I have perfect pitch. Shall I request an audition?"

Simeen brightened, her fear and anxiety draining away. Flapping her wings, she started dragging Arabou after her.

"Come on!" she said. "If Monte didn't bust the 'nod when he dashed out, we can make this work. No offense, Arabou, but a blind 'nod player will be a great draw . . . . Most need the lights to cue them on what to play."

Korda trotted after them. Jester's PDA would be coming into the nightclub to link up with him and there was no advantage to staying in the service corridor.

Cristo might have broken the PDA, but Korda was going to break something that had been protecting Cristo thus far—he was going to start breaking rules. Cristo was going to find out what it was like to have Rene Korda angry and on his heels. Somehow, Korda didn't think Cristo was going to enjoy the sensation.

They left Arabou warming up with Tophet Khan. Miriam and Tico—brought up to date with a quick call—had promised to hurry to the nightclub. Arabou and Simeen Ishbrendu were among the handful of people who knew about Cristo and the danger he represented. Korda wasn't going to leave them unguarded.

"What's up, Boss?" Jester asked.

"We're heading up to what the direction finder showed us earlier is the closest service corridor to the world key," Korda said. "It's under guard, but I'm counting on you to draw off the guard while I get through. If I lose you, you find me. Get it?"

"You bet, Boss!" she said. "You're playing hardball, now, aren't you?"

"He shot you," Korda said. "That upped the ante as far as I'm concerned. We now know he's armed and willing to use his weapons. We also know that he's a good shot—a PDA isn't much of a target, but he hit yours dead on."

"So you're after him because you know that he's armed and dangerous," Jester said, her tones hesitant.

Korda understood instantly. "Yes and no. I'm after him because he took a shot at my friend. He may figure that it was just a PDA and PDAs are replaceable, but that doesn't change that he gave you a shock."

"Rene," Jester said softly, "you do care, don't you?"

"What do you think?" Korda grinned.

Arrival at their destination saved him from any further conversation in that vein.

They were in about the middle of the Black Pyramid Casino. This floor was dedicated to craps tables, roulette wheels, and games of twenty-one. Although it was not as noisy as the areas with the slot machines, there was the hubbub of conversation, the zip of the spinning wheels, and the clatter of tumbling dice.

At the far end of one section, alongside a sliding double door, one of the Cardinal Points stood behind the counter of an efficiently designed security station. She wore a holstered weapon and one big hand rested protectively over a control panel. Her eyes restlessly scanned the room for any trouble. Korda did not doubt that she also got regular updates from the audio feed discreetly connected to one ear and the monitors built flush with her countertop.

"There's our target, Jes," Korda said, secreting himself behind a broad pillar and trying to look as if he was just interested in watching the spinning of the nearest roulette wheel. "Can you draw her off long enough for me to get the door open?"

"You bet!" Jester laughed. "I'll pay the forfeit if I can't!"

Korda had expected her to perform some aerial acrobatics to distract the Cardinal Point's attention, but he had reckoned without his computer's creativity—or her pent-up unhappiness about what Cristo had done to her PDA. Unlike Korda, she was more upset that the shot might have hit her human than that her mechanical extension had been broken.

"Round and round I go," she cried, neatly flipping the ball out of a roulette wheel, "and where I stop, no one knows!"

She skipped from number to number, black to red, stopping as the operator stopped the wheel, then hoping out and choosing a new number. While the gamblers, according to their bets, cheered or protested or argued with the operator, she whisked herself away.

Setting up enough of a breeze with her passing that she scattered cards to the floor, she joined a dice game, swallowing one die and then placing it with care to create an acey-deucy combination. When the croupier reached for her, she dove straight up, smashed a hole in one of the neon decorations, and went whizzing through the empty tube.

The Cardinal Point had left her post as soon as the shouting started at the roulette wheel. In the general chaos that followed in Jester's wake, she lost track of the PDA and completely forgot her desk.

Korda found it almost too easy to open the door and slip through. The service corridor was featureless gray with mesh steel flooring that rang slightly under his boots. Just as the door was shutting, the PDA dropped from a neon tube and squeaked in.

"How'd I do, Boss?" Jester said happily.

"Great," he said, shaking his head. "Good thing I have a positive credit balance with the casino. You were something they didn't gamble on."

He took out the direction finder and oriented himself. The PDA, meanwhile, had drifted up to examine the cameras monitoring the corridor.

"Walk fast, Boss," Jester said. "Once we're out of line of sight, we're going to find that Mr. Cristo has done us a favor."

Korda obeyed, climbing down a ladder and then crawling through a service tube before coming to a corridor just slightly taller than he was. Now he could walk more quickly.

"What has that bastard done that I should be grateful for?" he asked, once they were well away from any but a chance encounter with Alachra's security staff.

"He came well prepared for this job," Jester said. "The cameras are being fed dummy information. Even when the Cardinal Points notice, they won't be able to do much. His backup defense fries the cameras entirely."

"I guess he didn't opt for that right away because he'd hoped to get a head start without anyone the wiser," Korda said.

He'd come to a cross corridor. The direction finder told him to turn right and then pointed to an access hatch. This proved to lead to a crawl space that Korda wriggled through with some difficulty.

"Too much good food since we got here," he joked. "I wish I felt I had time to take a more civilized route, but the most direct way is the best now."

The PDA, which had no problem with tight spaces, only grinned. Jester was leading the way, her flashbeam on low in case they stumbled on a guard or an ungimmicked camera.

Korda lost track of time as he climbed ladders, took elevators, and hurried down corridors. His sense of direction was less affected. Jester's PDA confirmed what his internal compass told him. They were penetrating well below the Black Pyramid, somewhere off to one side.

"I guess the good news," Korda said, "is that since time

hasn't stopped we're either on Mr. Cristo's tail or ahead of him."

The PDA shone its light on a fresh scuff mark. "My guess is on his tail, Boss, as much as I'd like to believe otherwise. Still, he's not going to have much time for mischief even if he does beat us to the world key. Right?"

"I hope not," Korda said, "but we'd better stay alert for traps."

This slowed them some, and Korda wondered if he was wasting time—nothing blocked their progress. Still, the rattling of the pieces of the broken PDA in his pocket reminded him that they could not afford to forget caution.

At last they came to a door so ordinary that they would not have given it a second look without the direction finder's insistence that their path lay through it. The door's metal surface was painted the same utilitarian gray as most of the corridor and was unmarked.

Korda hunted for a latch or lock, but found nothing. "Your turn, Jes," he said.

"Right, Boss!" The PDA bobbed down. "Got it. Hidden behind the surface metal. It's magnetically keyed— I should be able to—"

The door clicked slightly and then slid to one side. In front of them was an office furnished so prosaically that Korda blinked. There was a desk with a comfortable chair behind it. Two more chairs faced the desk. A sofa with a long coffee table scattered with magazines occupied one wall.

The room was decorated with paintings and sculptures,

many of them almost certainly priceless originals. However, art lover though he was, this time Korda did not spare a glance for them. His attention was captured by the muscular young man who stood behind the desk.

The young man had blond hair and gray eyes. His nose was prominent and his eyebrows bushy. In his hands he held a three-dimensional representation of a pyramid, the sections glowing and marked out in various bright primary colors.

When the door had opened, he had looked up, then glanced at the energy pistol that rested on the desk, but had let it lie. He waited until Korda was in and the door shut behind him.

"Rene Korda," he said. "I knew that once you were after me, it was just a matter of time before you caught up. I had hoped to stop time, however, so we'd have a chance to talk. You got here too soon."

"Why would I want to talk with you, Montgomery Cristo—or whoever you are?" Korda growled.

Montgomery Cristo laughed softly. "Whoever I am, indeed! I am surprised you don't know me already."

He closed his eyes for a moment and his features melted and shifted. Korda recognized the rare psionic discipline called false-facing and then he recognized something else.

The young man's features were resolving into those of someone he knew. His nose was smaller, his eyes a piercing hazel. Long brown hair was drawn back into a neat ponytail at the nape of his neck.

"Do you not know me, Old Teacher?" the young man said, his tone slightly mocking.

"Milo!" Korda whispered. Then in a firmer voice, "Milo! What are you doing here?"

Milo twisted a section of the pyramid he held in his hands. "I'm shutting down this universe, Teacher. Wouldn't you like to know why?"

XVII

Y ou know I do, Milo," Korda said sternly.

His tone was calm, even slightly pedantic, but his mind was racing. Milo?

Milo had been one of his best students during the time about thirty years ago when Korda tried to pay his debt to the profession by passing on the knowledge he himself had learned from people like Charlie Bell.

Most of the students dropped out when they realized that full mastery of the art of universe creation and design took at least a century—although the rewards and opportunities to practice would begin much sooner, within two decades or so. Milo had been one of those rare talents who looked as if he would beat the averages and take mastery in as little as five decades. He had discipline and possessed a deep well of odd knowledge that helped him perceive the intricacies of universe design.

Then, after about five years—barely enough time to learn the basics—Milo had dropped out of the course and out of sight. Rumors said that he'd met a girl—that she was rich, that her parents were, that she was pregnant, that Milo had eloped with her and her family had assassins on his tail so he'd been forced into hiding.

Not believing the stories—for one, Korda had never noticed Milo pay any woman more than casual court—Korda himself had privately looked for the younger man, but could find no trace of him. Ultimately, Korda's respect for individual privacy made him abandon the search. Milo's disappearance receded from his attention to become one of the small mysteries that he pulled out, mused over, and then forgot again.

"Yes, Milo, I want to hear your story," Korda said, aware that Milo was watching him with a cool impassivity that did not hide a predatory gleam in his hazel eyes.

"Then help me put Fortuna into stasis," Milo said. "I want to have time to tell you my story. Alachra's Cardinal Points are searching for us, but it's a sure bet that Alachra never revealed the precise location of this room to them."

"They may have bottled time," Korda countered.

"I am certain that some of them do," Milo replied, "but not all of them, and even those who have bottled time will need to watch how far they range. We can sit within the sphere of one bottle while I fill you in and so conserve our resources."

Jester had remained unwontedly quiet, but when Korda glanced up at her, she bobbed a shrug. "I've been monitoring what communications channels I can and I don't think anyone is even close."

"Will you help me, Teacher?" Milo said.

Korda studied the other man. If this was Milo, he did want to hear his story, to have the mystery resolved after so long, but something was still troubling him, making him unwilling to accept Milo's plan.

"How do I know you really are Milo?" he said. "I have seen you change your appearance here—earlier you were Glifnod Garu. How do I know this isn't another disguise, something you set up when you knew I was after you?"

Milo chuckled, seemed to relax slightly as if he now was certain that Korda would listen.

"How about I tell you something that someone else wouldn't be likely to remember—something from our common experience that wouldn't have been written up in any of the biographies of the great Rene Korda?"

Korda nodded. Milo had always enjoyed needling Korda about his past successes—about his fame as the best of the human universe designers. For the first time, he wondered if Milo had realized that Korda was slowing down even then, heading for retirement. Could the acid jokes have been meant to stir him into action again, to keep him from getting too comfortable?

"Go on, Milo," he said, struggling to hide his thoughts, to hide the surge of liking he felt for the younger man.

"Back when I was in your class—after the deadbeats had dropped out," Milo began, "there was a girl in our class. A perky little blond. I always thought she was sweet on you and I thought you might be a bit sweet on her—though of course you were too professional to date a student."

Korda felt a blush creeping up from below his collar,

but he didn't interrupt Milo.

Milo grinned. "Her name was Courtney. You always called her 'Miss.' She always called you—"

"Stop!" Korda said, holding out his hand. "That's enough. I'm certain you are Milo. Someone might have gotten the students' names from the registrar. The rest . . . I believe you."

"Don't you want me to finish?" Milo said. "Courtney always called you—"

"No, that's enough, really," Korda said lamely.

"Sugar Pop?" Jester said.

"That's it exactly," Milo said, mistaking Jester's words as an attempt to finish his sentence rather than an address to Korda.

"Please!" Korda said to them both. "I believe you are Milo. As you pointed out, we may be running out of time. Let's get this universe shut down!"

Shrugging, a faint grin at having flustered the great Rene Korda still lurking in the corners of his mouth, Milo extended the multicolored pyramid to Korda.

"It's a puzzle of some sort," he said. "I'm stuck—it changes in some strange fashion. I'd guess, knowing something of how Alachra thinks, that it's tied to some odd rule of probability."

Korda set the pyramid on the desk. "You've apparently grown so accustomed to using your own wits to solve things, Milo, that you've forgotten that tools provide some excellent shortcuts."

He took out his UT and punched for the probability

driver. After tapping it against the pyramid, he reached out and followed the impulse to twist one section, align it with another, twist again, and so forth until the pyramid unfolded flat on the desk.

As soon as it flattened out, an array of controls was visible. Korda tapped them in a sequence he felt rather than knew and there was a popping noise as the wall behind the sofa vanished, revealing the world key controls.

Jester zipped in ahead. "The floor is a bit wet, so walk carefully. I'd guess that it was filled with water to baffle scanners into thinking this was a solid space. Sure baffled me!"

Milo paused a moment before following Korda and Jester into the control room. Once the shutdown sequence was well under way, he glanced over at Korda.

"Didn't you feel that using the probability driver was a less than elegant solution?"

Korda shrugged. "Maybe, but let me put it to you this way. You're on the bottom floor of a house and you need to get to the attic. Which is the more elegant solution—using the staircase or cutting holes in the floor and climbing up through them?"

"I see what you're getting at. Thanks—Teacher." There was no sarcasm in Milo's tone.

Korda turned away to hide his smile. Milo was clearly brilliant, but sometimes that brilliance could be blinding.

After the universe of Fortuna had been put into stasis, Korda and Milo returned to the office and took seats on the sofa close enough that one unit of bottled time set between them would keep them both out of stasis. Jester assured them that the cognac in the crystal decanter on the sideboard was an excellent vintage—something of an art piece in itself.

While Milo poured a splash for each of them into balloon snifters fine as soap bubbles, Korda subvocalized a quick request to Jester that she contact Miriam, Tico, and Arabou and reassure them that he was alive and on the job. Then he turned his attention to Milo.

Korda knew he'd always think of the other man as younger—indeed, he couldn't be much more than sixty or seventy even now—but there was an aura of age and weariness in Milo's eyes that a lifetime course of prolongation drugs could not hide. However he had spent those years, Milo's life had clearly not been a peaceful or gentle one.

Taking a small taste of his cognac, without any further introduction, Milo began his story.

"I was born in the Ciswig system, on the planet Pasqua. It was a good place to grow up. Back when my parents were small, the system had been purchased by a group of venture capitalists who sunk their money in having one planet—Pasqua—terraformed into something of an idealized, pastoral Earth. There were forests, wide strips of agricultural land, mountains, oceans . . . . Well, Teacher, you get the idea. You've designed places like Pasqua often enough."

Korda nodded. "I have—and Milo . . . why not try

'Rene'—it's my name and you're welcome to use it. After all, we are friends."

Another sip of cognac covered Milo's momentary shyness. "Thanks, Rene. I appreciate you're accepting me as a friend—even before you hear why I've done what I have."

"Well," Korda said. "I haven't said that I approve— but I want to hear your side before I do something as pompous as say I approve or disapprove. Fair enough?"

"Fair enough," Milo answered. Then, clearing his throat, he continued. "The Ciswig system's economy was largely based around exploiting the system's mineral and metal resources, but not in the usual fashion. The colony's founders had learned something from the history of other colonial ventures. They were determined that Ciswig would not export raw materials for others to grow rich on. Instead, they built factories on both of Pasqua's moons and the colonists turned out finished products.

"By the time I was born, Ciswig was flourishing. I lived on Pasqua with my parents and my grandmother Dolby until I was twelve. Then everything changed."

Korda had been remembering why the name Pasqua had sounded familiar while Milo spoke, but he kept his silence and subvocalized for Jester to do the same. If his guess was right, Milo not only needed to talk, this was the first time he was permitting himself to tell about a horror that all of civilized space spoke of in hushed whispers, a horror to which Milo might be the only eyewitness.

"I was twelve when the pirates made their attack—the slaughter that has been named the Pasqua Wipeout," Milo said, his expression suddenly vulnerable. "My parents were at work—my father on the moon Felix, my mother as director of urban planning in the nearby city of Rhett. I was standing out in the yard watching the skies. Rhett had a spaceport, so I was familiar with many designs of spacecraft, but on that particular day there had been more activity than I'd ever seen before.

"Innocent that I was, I had no idea that we were being invaded, that the bright flash I had seen a few hours before up on Felix was my father dying along with the factory he ran. Communications were jammed. Houses on Ciswig were usually built with acres of land between them—there was room, and with personal hovercars from our own factories widely available there was no need to cram together. The look on Grandma Dolby's face as she came out of the house, a suitcase in her hand, was the first hint I had that anything had gone wrong.

"'Milo,' she said sternly, 'come with me. We can't wait for your parents.'

"I obeyed," Milo continued with a slight smile. "You didn't argue with Grandma Dolby when she used that tone of voice. She'd been a Ditzen Commando—a colonel—and she could put a command snap to her voice that made your feet move before you knew that you had agreed. She drove our family hovercar into the hills outside Rhett and then into the mountains. As we drove, she explained to me what was happening.

"Pirates had come to Ciswig, she told me. They had been trouble for a while, but our people had always been strong enough to fight off their little raids. Our continual refusal to pay them protection or to give up our goods without a fight had made us an example to other systems. More and more systems were rallying, were refusing to be cowed. For being an example of courage, for refusing to let the pirates rob us or to use the Ciswig system as a jump-off point for other raids, the pirates had decided that we must die."

Korda put his hand on the younger man's shoulder. "Milo, I know something of the history of that event. If you don't want to go into the details, I can review my databanks."

Fiercely, his lip curling as he fought not to weep, Milo shook his head. "No, Rene. I have to tell you how it was for me—that way you will understand not only what I have done but what I have become. Please! Time has stopped for everyone but a small handful. Let me tell you how it was."

Jester cut in. "No sign of pursuit closing, Boss."

Korda squeezed Milo's shoulder once more and then let his hand drop. "Milo, I wasn't trying to stop you from talking. I was trying to save you a painful telling."

Managing a small, unconvincing grin, Milo finished his cognac and set the snifter down. "Thanks, Rene, but I've lived with this pain for most of my life."

"Talk then," Korda said. "Jester will warn us if anyone is getting close."

"Good," Milo rubbed his hands across his face. "I'm beat. It's been a long road Grandma Dolby set my feet on. She got me away, you see, up into the mountains where caves and tunnels remained from the earliest days of the colony, when mining was still done on Pasqua itself. She saved me, but she didn't spare me. From a shielded area, she had me watch as the pirates destroyed Rhett—and my mother.

"On a viewscreen, we watched the pirates herding people from isolated areas into transports. I learned later that most of them were sold in the Slave Warrens of Galloo. Later, I hunted down a few of these slaves, hoping to find allies among the survivors—and learned that before being sold they had been mindwiped. After all the cities had been looted and bombed flat, the people and crops taken or killed, the pirates finished their conquest of Pasqua by meltmining it from orbit."

"Meltmining!" Korda exclaimed. "That wasn't in any of the reports."

"Probably lost in the rest of the horrors," Milo said. "It almost meant the end for Grandma Dolby and me. The tunnels in which we hid were right in a metal-rich area. When the first heat rays came down, she realized what they intended and got us into the car. We hid in the bottom of an ocean for a week.

"Now remember, all we had was a family sedan and the supplies that Grandma had packed—not exactly a recipe for survival. She used drugs from her kit to keep me under so I wouldn't use too much air or realize that

I was starving to death. She couldn't give herself the same luxury.

"Her commando implants were still in place and she reactivated them, although at her age she could no longer tolerate their demands. With those implants, she was able to scout, to find us food, and, when the pirates finally left, to keep us both alive. I firmly believe that her death was as much by the pirates' hand as if they had cut her throat, for she could have lived at least another century in peace."

Milo dashed away tears he didn't seem to realize that he was weeping. "After the pirates left, Grandma took us back onto land. We lived for six months in that burnt-out ruin of what had once been one of the most beautiful and prosperous worlds in Universe Prime. During that time, Grandma collected whatever information she could about the pirates.

"From armor and ruined vehicles, she confirmed the commanders' identities. From a chance scrap of a log, she garnered a hint as to their destination. All the while, she was dealing with her own grief, her sense that she should have saved the rest of her family and friends with me. I wasn't much help. My week of near starvation combined with shock weakened my system. I caught a virus—probably a bit of leftover biological weaponry the pirates had used—that nearly killed me.

"Gradually, I recovered. About six months after the Wipeout a tramp trader who hadn't heard the news came in-system. Grandma signaled him and we were rescued.

She paid for our passage to a nearby system where her sister lived. Then she set about planning our revenge.

"Her first hope was that she could find the pirates' main base, but this was quickly dashed. Research confirmed that not one but seven different pirate fleets had taken part in the Wipeout. She wouldn't go to the Terran Regional Government with her findings because experience had shown the colonies that the pirates often paid government officials to slow investigations or pass on information."

Korda frowned. "I seem to recall that after the Pasqua Wipeout, the Terran Regional Government instituted a crackdown on pirate activity. The pirates have never regained their foothold since then."

"Grandma had her own theory about that crackdown." Spinning his brandy snifter between his fingers, Milo paused. "When she couldn't locate the pirates on her own, she made friends of some of the TRG troops who were going after the pirate bases. From them she learned that their raids were being based on inside information."

Jester was quick to catch the implications. "You mean someone was fingering the pirates for a fall. Gee, I wonder who would profit from that? Maybe the people who got the benefit of the Pasqua Wipeout?"

"You and Grandma Dolby think a lot alike, Jester," Milo said. "She deduced that after using their fleets to rape Pasqua and the rest of the Ciswig system, the pirate chiefs quickly realized that those same fleets had become a liability rather than an asset."

"I can see why," Korda said. "First, the fleets would want their share of the loot. More dangerously—from the pirate chiefs' point of view—far too many people knew their secret. Someone might decide to buy amnesty by giving evidence to the TRG."

"The TRG was also offering a substantial reward for information," Milo said. "I don't doubt that the pirate chiefs themselves collected it for turning in their own people.

"What all this meant to Grandma Dolby and me was that we needed to focus our search on a few people rather than on fleets. Grandma knew that vengeance would probably take longer than she had left to live. Therefore, I must be the avenger."

Milo set his glass down, looked as if he would rise and pace, then noted the limitations of the bottled time and leaned back again.

"She put me on a course of education designed to turn me into a one-man army against the pirates—but martial skills were not enough. I had to be able to find the pirates and, when I did so, neutralize their defenses. We had a feeling that they would take refuge in pocket universes, so, when I was ready, I became your student, Rene."

He bared his teeth in a humorless grin. "Even here, I'd be willing to bet you never realized that your quiet student was a death-arts master trained by the warrior priests of Galbron or that he could shift his features into a dozen different guises. I have acted with the Royal

Shakespeare Company to great reviews, walked the busy halls of the Terran Regional Stock Exchange, and smuggled exotic cargoes through the heavily guarded asteroid belts that surround the Religious Alliance Worlds."

"And all this to avenge the death of Pasqua?" Korda said.

"All of it," Milo asserted. "I am the last of the people of Ciswig. My life is not my own. It belongs to those who died because they had the courage to resist the pirates."

Korda gazed into the single amber drop of cognac that remained in the bottom of his glass, but it did not offer him any vision of the best course of action. He knew that Milo was waiting for him to ask the next question, the self-evident question, and he knew that if he did he would be accepting that on some level Milo had the right to do what he was doing.

Vendetta.

A pretty word for an ugly course of action. But was it any uglier than what had been done to the Ciswig system? The answer to that question was easy. It was not. Milo and his grandma claimed to simply be attempting to be agents of justice in a universe—in many universes—that would close its ears to their plea.

Had they been wrong for not trying to work within the system instead of outside it?

Quite possibly. But Rene Korda was a man with three centuries behind him. He had lost the automatic belief that the system worked for everyone within his first five decades, briefly regained it when he reached a point where the system catered to his needs, and then lost that belief again when he saw that the system accorded his new fame and wealth honors that it did not grant everyone else.

He asked the question for which Milo was patiently waiting.

"And the owners of God's Pockets?"

"Are the seven pirate chiefs," Milo responded promptly. "They took their money and had private universes designed, one each to suit their particular tastes. I believe that the initial design work was in place before the Pasqua Wipeout—they intended their long course of murder and betrayal in advance."

"And now?" Korda asked.

"I have found their secrets. My plan is to go to each pocket universe, shut it down, and then, when all are in stasis and they cannot reinforce each other, return and collect my enemies."

Urbs and Aurans—Korda felt uncomfortable when he realized that he was going to need to tell Milo that some of his work had been undone. He waited, letting Milo finish outlining his plan.

"Those pirate chiefs I can capture I will put in digital storage on the *Shrike* and bring them, along with copies of all the evidence that Grandma Dolby and I collected, to the Terran Regional Government. Enough time has passed that I believe the pirates lack allies there."

Korda cleared his throat. "And what about those you cannot capture, Milo?"

"Then they die, as Pasqua died, as all of the Ciswig

system died," Milo answered, his hazel eyes hard as marble. "Actually, they will die more pleasantly, for I have no taste for torture—only for revenge."

"'Revenge is a dish best served cold,'" Jester quoted, then added. "After all these years, this dish is getting rancid."

"No, Jester," Milo said. "I prefer to compare this to a fine wine—something that needs to age to perfection before being consumed."

Korda looked around Alachra's private lair, and his imagination tinted all the beautiful pictures with blood, sculpted all the figures in bone. Was this the filter through which Milo had seen his entire life?

"I only hope, Milo," Korda said at last, "that when you open this bottle, you won't find that the wine has turned to vinegar."

Milo nodded, something in the lines of his face telling Korda that he had not overlooked the possibility. Then he brightened.

"Does this mean that you aren't going to try to stop me?" he asked.

"I doubt that I could," Korda said levelly. "I am talented, but I am not a master of the death arts, nor have I trained my entire life for this one cause. I might delay you, but short of killing you I could not stop you."

Milo frowned. "I had hoped that you would at least understand why I do what I do."

"I do," Korda admitted. "I accept your story as true and I accept your right to your mission. Forgive me, but three centuries of essentially law-abiding existence make one a bit set in one's ways."

"THE KEY WORD THERE," Jester wrote on his read-line, "IS 'ESSENTIALLY.' DON'T BE SO POMPOUS. I WANT TO HELP HIM, SO I KNOW THAT YOU DO, TOO. TELL HIM. WE MAY HAVE STOPPED TIME, BUT WE WON'T BE SAFE FOREVER. ALACHRA MAY NOT BE ABLE TO FIND US, BUT OUR SHIPS ARE IN PLAIN SIGHT—ARABOU, MIRIAM, AND TICO WOULD MAKE GREAT HOSTAGES."

Korda shivered. He had been so caught up in Milo's story, in the silence of the universe beyond their little bubble of time that he *had* forgotten how vulnerable they were. He doubted that Milo had and mentally awarded the younger man kudos for his patience. He also understood why Milo had been so patient.

"You need me," he said bluntly, "not just because I could stop you or delay you, but because this job is too big for one person. Right?"

"Right," Milo said. "I need an ally and I respect you and trust your ethics."

"Before you trust me too far," Korda said, "I should tell you that I've been trailing you through Urbs and Aurans. Both universes are active again. Deter and Dwistor are not trapped in stasis waiting to be collected like ripe apples for your basket."

"Damn!" Milo swore. "I thought I had them!"

Korda held up a hand. "I think you underestimated how paranoid the pirate chiefs were. Even though decades have passed since the Pasqua Wipeout, both of them were equipped with bottled time and some formidable personal defenses. I doubt if they feared you or someone like you— I suspect that what they fear is each other."

Milo nodded. "True. Having joined first to destroy a solar system, then to betray their own followers, they must live in a constant awareness of how vulnerable they are."

"Vulnerable," Jester said, "even in a private universe. I guess this is what they mean when they say that the wicked flee where none pursue."

"Except," Milo said, staring at the floor, anger visible in every line of his tense body, "that I pursue. Rene, I understand why you did what you did. I made a misjudgment with those universes. I was more afraid of news traveling ahead of me than I was of those I meant to capture. I might have pulled it off if the Regatta hadn't delayed me here—I don't know . . . ."

Korda touched him lightly on the arm. "Milo, you are past the time where you can pause for recrimination and analysis. Let's move on Alachra. Then we'll decide what to do next."

When Milo looked up at him, Korda was surprised to see a momentary brightness as of tears held back glittering in the other man's eyes.

"Then you're with me, Rene?" Milo said, gratitude evident in his voice.

"I'm with you," Korda said.

XVIII

They crept back through the service corridors with Jester flying ahead on high guard for added security. Although they passed the occasional stasis-bound technician or guard—and once a pair of staff members frozen in a covert tryst—they did not see anyone who could do them harm.

"I don't like this," Korda said. "Alachra is too careful not to hedge his bets."

"Two-to-one they're waiting for us at the *Shrike*," Jester said. "Shucks, I'll give you even better odds than that. I'm feeling lucky."

Korda chuckled. "You won't find any takers there, Jes. Tell me what you have to report."

Jester spun happily. "I had to try, Boss. It's the spirit of Fortuna."

"Report, Jes," Korda said more sternly.

"Right," she said. "I've been in contact with Tico and Miriam and they're hiding in the bay where the *Shrike* is parked. Several of the Cardinal Points, all armed and all with bottled time, are there. Arabou and Simeen are near the *Jester* and they confirm my own readings that the *Jester* is also under guard."

"Simeen?" Milo interrupted in surprise. "Simeen Ish-brendu, the lead singer for Tophet Khan? What is she doing there?"

"Didn't ask," Jester said. "We're keeping radio contact to a minimum in case it gives the others away. Maybe she wants to get you for leaving the band in the lurch."

Milo frowned. "I didn't plan to, but Rene showing up and asking all the wrong questions made me feel that I had better clear out."

The PDA dropped to hover by Milo's face, her omnipresent grin a counterpoint to his grimness.

"Lighten up, Milo. I was just teasing you," Jester said. "My analysis of the situation is that Simeen demanded that Arabou let her come with him and that he agreed. He is blind and the stasis would have robbed him of most of the audio cues he uses to navigate."

Milo nodded and glanced over at Korda. "How did you ever program a computer to tease?"

Shaking his head, Korda shrugged. "I'm not certain that I did. I was trying for a responsive AI and Jester developed far more personality than I ever expected. Her sense of humor is exhausting at times, but I'm afraid that if I tried to edit I'd lose the valuable initiative factor."

"Boss!" Jester said, horrified. "It's not polite to talk about editing a person—especially in front of her!"

Korda grinned. "Just teasing, Jes."

Jester had no answer for that and Milo smiled.

"Not so much fun getting teased as giving it, huh, Jester?" he asked.

"Actually," Jester's tone was wistful, "I like when Rene teases me. It makes me feel like a person."

Her tone shifted to businesslike. "Boss, I've been scanning layout diagrams and if we climb the ladder in that service shaft it will take us directly up to the hangar bays. It exits near Irish's office. Analysis says that the Cardinal Points will be watching the access points from the public areas. This shaft is used mostly for large cargo."

"Let's do it!" Milo said. "It's quite a climb, but the elevator might alert them. I'm not certain how carefully they monitor their readouts most of the time, but I'm certain that they will be now."

Korda knelt in front of the access panel and removed its screws with his UT. The service shaft was unlit, the metal-rung ladder vanishing into darkness above.

He motioned for Jester's PDA to go first and light the way. Milo insisted on going next and, considering the other man's training, Korda did not argue.

"I wonder if their readouts will even operate in stasis," Korda said, once they were climbing. "Stasis must interrupt some of the relays."

"True," Milo said, "but if we have probability drivers, they might also. What if they altered probability to make it more possible for the signal to get through the areas of stasis? I don't want to gamble on those odds."

"Interesting point of art," Korda said.

They continued discussing the finer points of stasis,

the use of bottled time, and designing alternate physics within a universe as they climbed.

Were it not for the utter silence of everything outside their own sphere, for the fact that the sound of their boots against the metal rungs came flat and contained, Korda might have forgotten the crisis. Milo had a fine mind, and even if its paths had been shaped by Grandma Dolby's training, Korda could sense the artist who struggled for life beneath the warrior's watchful gaze.

Jester informed them that they were closing on the hangar bay and they fell silent. Their plan had been crafted during the early stages of the climb, now all that waited was to see how much of it would survive implementation.

No one was outside the service shaft when they forced the door open. Korda held out a hand to Milo.

"Luck," he said as he shook it.

"Never a thing to overlook on Fortuna," Milo replied, returning the handclasp. "Luck to you."

Korda broke right, Milo left. The first stage of the plan was deceptively simple. When Milo signaled that he was in position, Jester would begin to activate various of the *Jester*'s external systems. Their hope was that this, combined with Korda showing himself, would draw some of the guards off of the *Shrike* and enable Milo to reclaim his ship with minimal risk—and minimal killing of Alachra's personnel.

Their four allies had been briefed via comm bursts from Jester. Tico and Miriam were to join Milo; Arabou and Simeen would come with Korda.

"Ready, Jes?" Korda asked when his ship was in sight.

Three Cardinal Points, all indistinguishable from West or her clone at the security desk, stood alert and deadly, blocking all access to his ship.

"Waiting on word from Milo," Jester responded. "He had to skirt a cluster of in-stasis techs so he wouldn't bring them out."

Korda waited. He was tranquil, with that peculiar calm that only comes when everything that can be done is already done. Jester's two soft-spoken words were simply the gentle push that moved him into actions already begun.

"Now, Boss?"

"Do it, Jes," he responded.

With a flurry of lights around her bow and coursing up her folded aerial stabilizers, the *Jester* came alive. There was a slight rumble that anyone familiar with starships would recognize as take-off jets beginning to warm up.

The Cardinal Points clearly knew what the sound meant and, with the first show of emotion other than annoyance that Korda had seen on any one of their number, they backed away from the ship.

On the far right, one spoke into a collar-mounted commo unit—apparently those bow ties were functional as well as decorative, concealing a powerpack suitable for punching through the layers of buildings on Fortuna.

"South has just told the guards by Milo's ship what I'm doing," Jester giggled. "She's ticked. A couple of others are coming to check things out."

"My cue," Korda said. "Don't forget your part."

"I'm already on it, Boss," the computer responded.

He stepped around the bulkhead where he had been concealed and strode toward the *Jester*. The Cardinal Points glanced in his direction as he approached, but did not neglect their more general watch.

"Stasis fall," Korda said by way of greeting, "just as Alachra and I predicted. If you will let me aboard my ship, I have some equipment there I'm going to need."

"Why has your ship come active?" the Cardinal Point Jester had identified as South asked, making no move to permit him to board.

Korda looked surprised. "Because I called ahead and told her to. If the saboteur is spotted departing I don't want to waste time on warm-up. In fact, you anticipate my next request. I want the bay doors opened."

"We have our own pursuit craft," South said. "If the saboteur departs, he will no longer be your concern."

Korda paused, appearing to ponder. He subvocalized to Jester.

"How is it going?"

"NOT SO GOOD. I'M TRYING TO ISOLATE THEIR CONTROL FREQUENCIES AS I DID WITH DWISTOR, BUT THEY ARE WEARING FULL HARNESSES, NOT JUST A SINGLE UNIT. THESE THREE ARE ON THREE DIFFERENT FREQUENCIES AS WELL. I MAY NOT BE ABLE TO PULL ANYTHING OFF QUICKLY ENOUGH."

Korda nodded, as a signal to Jester that he understood,

but he tied it into his response to the Cardinal Points.

"Yes, I see what you are saying," he said, "but are your pursuit vessels equipped with bottled time? If not, they will be unable to function."

South looked honestly startled. "I had forgotten. No, they don't have bottled time. We once discussed it with Alachra and decided that it was unnecessary. Alachra's personal ships do have it, but we have been unable to establish contact with Tracks to learn his whereabouts."

She turned to her two subordinates. "Northeast and Northwest, I want you to get Irish, then go to the central control for the bay doors. Your bottled time may be necessary to activate the equipment."

Northeast saluted sharply. Northwest appeared to be about to protest when the Cardinal Points who had been lured away from Milo's ship came down the corridor. Seeing that South would not be left alone with Korda and his unpredictable ship, she saluted and headed off with Northeast.

"*How many are left with Milo?*" Korda subvocalized to Jester.

"TWO," came the prompt response. "HE CAN FLOOR THEM EASILY."

"*Remind him that he needs to wait until we have someone ready to operate the bay doors,*" Korda said.

"NO NEED, BOSS. MILO KNOWS ALL ABOUT WAITING."

Korda knew this was true. He returned his attention to South.

"Are you going to let me aboard my ship?" he asked. "If I don't have my gear, I'm going to be at a disadvantage against the saboteur."

"Didn't you carry it with you when you went out into Fortuna?" South asked.

"Not all of it," Korda lied. "I was told to act like a vacationer. That's hard to do with a variable frequency photon dissimulator hanging from your belt."

"VARIABLE FREQUENCY PHOTON DISSIMULATOR?" Jester queried across his readline. Korda could almost hear her giggle.

South appeared more impressed by his techno-babble than Jester had been. She frowned.

"I will consult with East when she arrives. If she agrees, we will let you aboard."

East came up at this moment.

"Where are Northeast and Northwest?" she queried.

"I have sent them to activate the bay doors," South said. Efficiently, she explained the situation to East.

Korda listened, trying to use body language to project the impression of impatience and artistic hauteur. He may not have had Milo's experience on the stage, but he thought he did a fair job. The two main Cardinal Points looked less confident than he had ever seen them. Clearly, they were torn between maintaining strict security and the fear that Alachra would be angry with them for interfering with an expert on the job.

"Northeast and Northwest radio that they are in position," one of East's assistants reported. "Irish has the bay door mechanism ready to be activated."

"I'VE FOUND THE OVERRIDE, BOSS," Jester reported almost immediately. "MILO AND ARABOU HAVE BEEN TOLD THAT IT'S ALMOST TIME TO DANCE."

Korda stepped forward. "Are you going to let me aboard my ship or am I going to have to use my external security system to clear you off? I have been sufficiently patient! Now, let me do my job."

In response to Korda's harangue, Jester slid back panels to reveal small laser mounts around the ship's exterior.

"Security system activated," Jester announced through the PDA. She snickered rudely. "Scan shows that the Cardinal Points have reflec woven into their skintights so I've upped the gain to compensate."

The four Cardinal Points exchanged nervous glances.

"Good girl," Korda said, almost absently, his attention on the guards. "South, I am not asking anything but to be permitted to do the job that Alachra agreed I could do. Let me get my equipment and we can concentrate on the real problem."

"Very well," South said. "Of course, we could hold you hostage against your ship's behavior. Don't think that you've intimated us."

Korda was nodding polite agreement when Jester spoke, her voice so full of subdued fury that even he felt a twinge of atavistic fear.

"Don't believe it, South," the computer said. "You hurt Rene and I blow up every one of you. Then I go and get *your* boss to even things out. Understand?"

South blinked and motioned the others away from the *Jester*. "Yes, I do. My compliments, Mr. Korda, on your security programming."

Korda nodded. "I assure you, it was nothing."

He walked briskly to where the ship's doors were opening for him.

"Thanks, Jes," he said, once he was aboard.

Jester's hologram twinkled into existence on the bridge holopad. She blew him a kiss.

"Think nothing of it, Boss, but I meant every word. By the way, part two of the plan is now in action. I might be able to tie into the bay's external monitors if you want to watch."

"Sounds good," Korda said. "Arabou and Simeen ready to come aboard?"

"As soon as the way is clear," Jester assured him. "And I'll clear the way if I must. Now, here's Milo!"

The bridge screen lit with a view of the hangar bay in which the *Shrike* was under guard. As Korda watched, a pile of packing cases off to the left of the ship—the side away from the access port—toppled and fell over. Then a repair robot started rolling across the floor.

"That's Tico and Miriam's part," Jester said as the remaining Cardinal Points oriented on the disturbance without leaving their posts.

Milo erupted from his concealment on the side of the hangar bay closest to the *Shrike*'s access port. With a beautiful flying kick, he knocked the weapon from the closest Cardinal Point's hand, then pivoted and knocked her out with a sharp blow to the side of her head.

"The remaining guard has just radioed South and East," Jester reported.

Korda nodded, knowing this was why Milo had not simply taken both guards out from cover.

Jester had split the screen so he could see the view outside his ship as well. South was motioning her cohort back toward the *Shrike*. He poised his hand over his own comm link, anticipating South's call even as it came.

"Korda, saboteur has been spotted trying to gain access to his ship," South said crisply. "We are going to intervene. If he gets past us—"

"I'm ready," he interrupted. "Good luck."

When the Cardinal Points had trotted away, Arabou and Simeen dashed from cover. They were holding hands, although as far as Korda could tell Arabou did not need guidance.

Jester opened the door, welcomed the pair aboard, then directed them to the galley.

"Strap in," she advised. "If the plan works, we're about to depart."

Korda could hear his passengers' soft conversation before he slid the bridge door closed, but his attention was for the action on the screen. Milo had taken out both guards and was motioning for Tico and Miriam to get aboard the *Shrike* before the approaching Cardinal Points could close.

The honeymooners obeyed him, although Tico

looked a bit nervous—no wonder as he was trusting both himself and his love to a man who, mere hours before, they had regarded as an enemy.

Once they were aboard, Milo stood in the airlock and aimed a single shot into a drum of cleaning fluid. This erupted nicely, forcing the Cardinal Points back long enough for him to get the *Shrike* buttoned.

"I've overridden the hangar bay controls and opened the hatches both for us and for the *Shrike*," Jester announced happily. "Getaway is clear."

Korda sagged back into his seat, relief flooding his tense muscles.

"Let's get out of here, Jes. I'll pilot so you can deal with the doors. Get me a deep scan of the system. We want Alachra."

Jester did not reply. She could have handled piloting along with the rest, but she didn't insult her human—after all, they worked best as a team.

"We're clear of planet Fortuna's gravity," she announced a few moments later. "The *Shrike* is also clear. Milo is calling."

"Put him through," Korda said.

Milo smiled at him. "Rene Korda, you are one sneaky son of a bitch."

"Me?" Korda said.

"You or that computer or yours," Milo said. "Tico and Miriam just informed me that Jester tight-beamed the full text of my explanation about Pasqua to them. While they were waiting for their part in the show, they reviewed it.

I've been assured that I can count on them."

Korda chuckled. When Jester had suggested informing the others of what they had learned, he had agreed. Not only would it assure the Auransans that Korda had not been coerced into working with Milo, but he had hoped it would win the saboteur some sympathy.

Milo had been a solo operator for too long—he needed to remember that the universe held potential friends as well as potential enemies.

"Glad to hear that," Korda said. "I thought you were praising my clever escape."

"That plan wasn't half bad," Milo replied with a wink. "I must say, I really underestimated the value of an AI. You wouldn't be nearly as effective without her."

Korda found himself at a loss for an answer—after all, what Milo said was true—but Jester giggled.

"By the way, Great and Powerful Makers of Universes," she said, "I have located what I believe to be the *Jolly Roger*, Alachra's ship. It is under bottled time over near the racecourse."

"Does it appear to be piloted?" Korda asked.

Jester's hologram frowned. "Data insufficient for absolute certainty on that matter. Ship's motion could be being maintained by autopilot. However, if you would allow conjecture, the alignment of the various ships in stasis suggests that the Regatta was about to begin."

"In that case," Milo commented. "Alachra should be aboard. Let's tight-beam him. I don't want to scatter what we have to tell him all over the system."

Korda agreed.

Jester added, "For effective tight-beam communication, we will need to close to line of sight. However, we still should be out of range of any weapons systems."

"Do your scanners detect that the racing boat is armed?" Korda asked in surprise.

Jester shrugged. "We're too far out to be certain, Boss, but if Alachra is anything like Deter or Dwistor we'd have to be really dumb to expect him to be unarmed."

"Good point," Korda said. "Closing, Milo?"

"I'm right with you," Milo said. "I'm taking the *Shrike* up to a forty-five degree angle with your plane. That should make it harder for any one weapon to hit both of us."

Korda stretched in his chair. "I'm glad both of you are so paranoid. I'm so tired that I'm overlooking all sorts of basic tactics."

Jester studied him, a worried line between her eyes. About a minute later, Simeen walked onto the bridge, a cup of coffee and a sandwich balanced on a tray in one hand.

In order to move with more freedom within the confines of the ship, the alien woman had her wings furled behind her. They crested over her head like an indigo plume.

Korda grinned ruefully to himself. He kept encountering beautiful women but none of them seemed interested in him.

"Your ship's computer said you needed to eat," Simeen

said, her expression bemused, "but she didn't want you to leave your post."

"Thanks," Korda said, accepting the tray and snapping it to the arm of his chair. "Are you and Arabou up-to-date on what's happening?"

Simeen nodded. "Jester has given us a channel to the ship's communications and activated a screen. Arabou shared with me the contents of Milo's confession. Wild, isn't it?"

"Wild," Korda agreed. "Do you mind that we're after Alachra?"

"Starry, starry nights! No way, cat," Simeen said. "He's one bad note, that one, if half what Milo says is true. I'm not a Cardinal Point, devoted to him. I'm just a singer in a band who does gigs in his casinos. If he doesn't learn I was along for the ride, I should be able to go back and pick up where I left off. Arabou's going to stay and play the 'nod for a while. He's a swinging cat, that Arabou."

Korda sipped his coffee to conceal a smile. There was something about the blind trader stumbling into an exotic romance just at the time when his daughter's marriage might leave him feeling useless that appealed to him.

"I'll go back to the galley now," Simeen said. "Rock it to Alachra, Korda."

"I'll try," he promised.

"We've closed to tight-beam range," Jester reported. "There may be some scatter at this distance—especially with both us and the *Shrike* contacting him—but it would take someone looking for it to find it."

Korda tabbed Milo. "You want to handle this, Milo, or should I?"

Milo looked uncertain. "This is the first time I've actually spoken face-to-face with one of the pirates. I wonder if I can keep myself together?"

"Give it a try," Korda advised. "You're going to need to do this again. I'll listen and cut in if things seem to get out of hand."

"Thanks, Rene."

Jester had put on her operator's headset. "He's placing the call. *Jolly Roger* responding, automatic setting. Wait! Alachra's picking up now, audio and visual. I'm putting it on the screen, split, so you get both halves of the call."

Korda leaned back and finished his sandwich and coffee, ready to intervene if Milo needed him.

"Alachra," Milo said, "my name is Milo. I have come to take you before the Terran Regional Government in connection with the Pasqua Wipeout. Will you surrender or do I need to disable your ship and come in after you?"

"Milo . . ." Alachra said slowly. "I thought we wiped every survivor. I see we were wrong."

Milo seemed shaken that Alachra did not even try to deny his complicity in the Wipeout. Clearly, he had expected protest or argument.

"You never got me," Milo said. "Now, will you surrender? I promise that you will have an opportunity for a fair trial."

Alachra reached for his cigar and puffed on it. Korda checked the readings, but the *Jolly Roger* was not moving, nor did the scanners show indications of the power surge that would indicate a hidden weapons system being brought on line.

"Surrender?" Alachra said. "Hmm. The odds between us are hardly even in a fight. Your ship was well-armed, I recall, and I see that the *Jester* is hovering high guard. Still, I could probably hurt you badly if you came aboard. I have West and a few other Cardinal Points here to even the odds some."

Milo nodded. Alachra's calm acceptance of the situation seemed to have steadied him.

"True," he said. "Though I have allies as well. In a boarding action you couldn't hope to cover every section and we could just hull you and come in that way."

Alachra blew a smoke ring. "What do you say to a bet?"

"A bet?" Milo said, surprised.

"That's right, a bet. This is Fortuna." Alachra showed his horsy teeth in a broad smile. "I was really looking forward to this race. If you and Korda can beat me in the race, I promise to surrender peacefully—as long as you agree to return the universe of Fortuna from stasis. If you fail, you give me a chance to get out of Fortuna and into hiding. What do you say?"

"How long would you want for your getaway?" Korda asked.

Alachra thought for a moment. "What do you say to

the amount of time it takes for you—without any interference from anyone in Fortuna—to reactivate the universe."

Korda considered. Now that he and Milo knew the tricks, reactivation should go fairly quickly. He nodded his agreement.

Milo did also, but he hesitated before accepting the bet in full. "What is the race route?"

Alachra pressed a button and a glowing map of the asteroid belt near the sun appeared on both Milo and Korda's screens. The racecourse was picked out in a fluorescent pink that matched the streak in Alachra's hair.

"There," the centaur said. "The finish line is an automatic beacon. Any of our ships passing close enough should activate it with our bottled time and register a win. What do you say?"

"Rene?" Milo asked.

"Your call," Korda said. "I'm just the backup for this."

"Then I accept your bet," Milo said. "We win, you surrender. You win, you get a chance to run—and only that. I won't give up trying to find you."

"I didn't expect you to," Alachra said, grinding out his cigar. "That's why I didn't even offer it as an option. Get your ships into position. I'm going to rise to a slightly higher plane so we don't accidentally activate any of the ships in stasis—or any of the newsies."

"Good idea," Milo agreed.

"When you're ready," Alachra continued. "I'll fire a unit of bottled time to the starter beacon. We'll have ten seconds after that to start."

The *Jester* and the *Shrike* maneuvered to starting positions alongside the *Jolly Roger*. A thin flare of green emanated from the bow of Alachra's ship and burst near a rhomboid shape off to one side. It began to spin on its lower point, flashing the colors of the spectrum in declining order.

"One one thousand," it counted. "Two one thousand."

Jester giggled. "Alachra has a weird sense of humor."

"Let's hope he has a sense of honor," Korda said, his hands poised on the piloting controls. "Milo is taking a big chance here."

On the count of eight, the *Jolly Roger* leapt forward.

"He jumped the gun!" Jester shouted as Korda sent the Jester in pursuit.

"'On Fortuna,'" Korda quoted grimly, "'cheating is only cheating if you get caught.' I suspect Alachra considers this a fair cheat."

Over the comm link, he could hear Milo cursing steadily. All thoughts of radio silence were forgotten now as they whipped their ships through the obstacle course of the asteroids—each of which moved slightly as the *Jolly Roger*'s bottled time awoke it from stasis, creating another hazard for the following ships.

"We're going to lose if we don't do something at least as clever," Korda said to Jester. "Our ships have more power, but Alachra's has a tighter turning radius and he knows the course. Tight-beam Milo to stay in close pursuit, I'm taking us up to even the odds."

Not waiting for a reply, Korda angled the *Jester* out of the plane on which the race was being run. Sighting ahead of the *Jolly Roger*, he located a promising asteroid.

"Jes, load a missile with bottled time," he ordered, computing the aiming trajectory, "and fire the instant it's ready."

Korda felt the faint tremble in the ship as the missile was loaded. Alachra was closing on the asteroid. If he passed it before Korda's missile arrived, all Korda would have achieved was assuring that he and Milo would lose the race.

"Firing, Boss!" Jester said.

"Drop us down to the racecourse," Korda ordered, "and take over piloting. I'll shoot any rocks out of our path."

As he raised his gunnery controls, he saw his missile smash the asteroid into chunks. As he had hoped, Alachra slowed and swerved to avoid impact.

"*Shrike's* automatic gunnery has taken out the nearest hazard to Milo," Jester reported. "Milo is now in first place."

Korda nodded, his own attention directed toward clearing a path down which Jester could take them. He could feel the hum of the engines as the computer pushed up the speed. Normally, the powerplant could handle gunnery and high speeds without strain, but the bottled time added another drain. Korda hoped that they would not burn out before they passed Alachra.

"Alachra is reorienting on the course," Jester reported. "Boss, cease fire! That rock is a mine! Don't shoot it!"

Korda swiveled his gunnery orientation away. Alachra was more clever than he had thought. He must have realized what Korda intended as soon as the missile flew and dropped a few mines in even as he swerved the *Jolly Roger* clear of the explosion.

"We're ahead, Boss!" Jester squealed. "Milo is closing on . . . Milo has passed the beacon . . . . Cutting unnecessary systems—"

Her voice vanished along with the lights. The omnipresent drone of the life support system vanished. Korda felt himself drifting from his chair, only his lap belt holding him in place.

Then, almost as quickly as they had vanished, the lights and gravity returned. The life support's quiet noise filled the background.

"—to gain power for final thrust," Jester finished.

Korda glanced to the screen. They were passing the finishing line beacon, the *Jolly Roger* a half length behind but definitely in third.

He cheered. "We did it!"

Alachra signaled. When the call came on screen, his eyes were shining.

"That was a fine race!" he said. "Fine ships and excellent tactics. Now, in accordance with Fortuna's law, I surrender to Milo's custody. My Cardinal Points have been ordered to leave you and your associates unharmed. I will eject myself from the *Jolly Roger* in a life bubble. I bet you will pick me up."

Milo nodded. "I accept your bet and your surrender, Alachra."

Korda flew high guard while Milo retrieved Alachra. Then they returned to the planet Fortuna to reactivate the time flow and make arrangements for Arabou's stay.

The Cardinal Points, although clearly unhappy about Alachra's defeat, scrupulously honored his word. Arabou was permitted to transfer the credits from the others' accounts into his own. With that sum in addition to what he would earn as a glifnod player, he would be comfortable on Fortuna.

Leaving him to say his good-byes to Tico and Miriam, Korda joined Milo in conversation with West.

"Alachra has commanded that the universe continue to run as normal in his absence," West informed them. "However, once you two depart, you will not be granted re-entry visas."

Thinking of Alachra imprisoned in digital storage on the *Shrike*, Korda could only agree. The pirate had kept his bet, but there was no reason for him to want to host his captors in the future.

"I can understand," he said. "Take good care of Arabou for us."

West actually smiled. "I will. He's the coolest cat with a 'nod since Glifnod Garu!"

❖ ❖ ❖

Once outside the universe of Fortuna, Milo brought the *Shrike* alongside the *Jester* and came aboard. Miriam and Tico came with him. They gathered in the *Jester's* galley.

"The *Shrike*," Tico said diplomatically, "is an impressive vessel, but we would prefer to travel on the *Jester*. It has a bit more space."

"And we missed Jester," Miriam twinkled.

Jester spun on her holopad. "I missed you guys, too."

Milo shook his head, still amazed at Jester's over-abundance of personality. If he noted certain similarities to a young woman who had once been a classmate, he was tactful enough to keep his thoughts to himself.

"Now," Korda said, passing around a tray of drinks, "we need to make plans as to where to go next. I've agreed to help you, Milo—"

"You can count on us as well," Miriam said, squeezing Tico's hand. "Aurans will not be safe for us for a time and now that we know what Milo is doing, we want to help."

Milo spun his beer bottle between his palms. "There are still six pirates at large. My guess is that Deter and Dwistor will have made themselves scarce. I say we should leave Urbs and Aurans active and concentrate on the other universes."

"Very well," Korda said, somewhat stiffly. He still felt awkward when he thought about the effort he had put into undoing Milo's work.

"From information hidden in the world keys on Urbs, Aurans, and Fortuna," Milo continued, "I can pinpoint three other universes—Jungen, Cabal, and Verdry. Dyce, the last one in the God's Pockets roster, remains elusive. My guess is that the pirates had a hierarchy of their own and only those in prearranged cells knew the location of each other's universes."

"That's clever," Miriam commented. "That way they needed to trust each other only so far."

"Alachra must have been a thorn in their sides," Tico said, "since he made the location of Fortuna public knowledge."

"Still," Korda said, "the others could not be located without the coordinates the other members of his cell possessed. They probably found Alachra's behavior a nuisance, but not a threat."

Milo pushed a notescreen to the center of the table. "I gathered the partial coordinates for a fourth destination as well. My hope is that when we visit the world keys on Verdry, Cabal, and Jungen, we will find the rest of what we need to pinpoint the location of Dyce."

"Good so far," Korda said. "Let's combine the notes I have from the Terran Regional Representative with your research and discuss our next target."

A screen lit on the galley wall. Jester manifested her hologram nearby. This time she wore a long academic gown—trimmed in yellow and pink. A mortarboard perched on her hair at a rakish angle, looking ready to slide off at any moment.

She gestured at the screen with a long, thin pointer. "Class, if I might have your attention—"

An unfamiliar noise broke into her speech. Tico and Miriam jumped and Korda wheeled on the source. With delighted surprise he realized that Milo was laughing— a rich, full laugh that sounded as if it had been bundled within his chest for far too long.

Wiping tears from his eyes, Milo swallowed his laughter enough to talk.

"I'm sorry," the vigilante said, still chuckling. "It just occurred to me that even Grandma Dolby could never have anticipated Jester. Somehow, I think we're going to find those pirates—they simply won't know what hit them!"

Jester smiled and cupped her chin in one hand. "Really, Milo! Can't you pay attention even for a moment?"

Postlude

In the outer reaches of the universe of Fortuna, Deter on the *Endgame* and Dwistor on the *Lawrence* strained their communications scanners to the limit to catch the fragmenting signal of the conversation between Alachra and his enemies.

"The fool!" Deter raged. "He as much as admitted his complicity in the Pasqua Wipeout."

Dwistor frowned. "I heard. I am more disturbed that we now have confirmation that someone knows enough to blame the owners of the God's Pockets universes for that crime."

They watched on long-range scanners as the race was won, saw Alachra surrender, and slipped away when the universe was returned from stasis. There were too many ships, all preparing to take part in a Regatta that they were not aware had been interrupted, for the two pirates to feel safe.

Once outside the universe of Fortuna, they conferred.

"We cannot warn O'Ryan directly," Dwistor said, "not without the full coordinates of Dyce. I have done business with him indirectly, however. We can send a warning and an update to the others."

"Yes," Deter agreed. "Let us do so. Then what are your plans?"

"I still want the head of Rene Korda," Dwistor said dramatically, "and now to that I add the head of Milo of Pasqua."

"We could go into hiding," Deter said. "We would be able to rebuild our fortunes by plundering Urbs and Aurans first."

Dwistor sneered. "Does the great warrior run at the first sign of a powerful enemy?"

"Not at all," Deter said. "I simply state an option."

"There is no other option," Dwistor replied. "Death to our enemies, then concern about mere material fortunes!"

"I agree," Deter said. "Messages are being drafted even as we speak."

They hung there in the darkness of the void outside Fortuna. With their engines shut to minimal and a nearby drifting asteroid to conceal their mass, for all practical purposes they were invisible.

When the *Jester* and the *Shrike* emerged from the universe of Fortuna, the confident crews within never had a warning that their enemies kept watch on them and marked their course as they headed off to their new destination.

Hardback

In The 1st Degree: A Novel $19.95
Dominic Stone

The 7th Guest: A Novel $21.95
Matthew J. Costello and Craig Shaw Gardner

Paperback

Hell: A Cyberpunk Thriller—A Novel $5.99
Chet Williamson

Masterminds of Falkenstein: A Castle Falkenstein Novel $5.99
John DeChancie

The Pandora Directive: A Tex Murphy Novel $5.99
Aaron Conners

From Prussia with Love: A Castle Falkenstein Novel $5.99
John DeChancie

Realms of Arkania: The Charlatan—A Novel $5.99
Ulrich Kiesow
Translated by Amy Katherine Kile

Realms of Arkania: The Lioness—A Novel $5.99
Ina Kramer
Translated by Amy Katherine Kile

Star Control: Interbellum—A Novel $5.99
W.T. Quick

Star Crusader: A Novel $5.99
Bruce Balfour

Under a Killing Moon: A Tex Murphy Novel $5.99
Aaron Conners

Wizardry: The League of the Crimson Crescent—A Novel $5.99
James Reagan

X-COM UFO Defense: A Novel $5.99
Diane Duane

FILL IN AND MAIL TODAY

PRIMA PUBLISHING
P.O. Box 1260BK
Rocklin, CA 95677

USE YOUR VISA/MC AND ORDER BY PHONE
(916) 632-4400 (M-F 9:00-4:00 PST)

Please send me the following titles:

Quantity	Title	Amount
_____	_____	_____
_____	_____	_____
_____	_____	_____
_____	_____	_____

	Subtotal	$_____
	Postage & Handling	
	($4.00 for the first book plus	
	$1.00 each additional book)	$ _____
	Sales Tax	
	7.25% California only	
	8.25% Tennessee only	
	5.00% Maryland only	
	7.00% General Service Tax Canada	$_____
	TOTAL (U.S. funds only)	**$_____**

❑ Check enclosed for $_____(payable to Prima Publishing)
Charge my   ❑ Master Card   ❑ Visa
Account No._____ Exp. Date _____
Signature _____
Your Name_____
Address _____
City/State/Zip _____
Daytime Telephone_____

Satisfaction is guaranteed—or your money back!
Please allow three to four weeks for delivery.

THANK YOU FOR YOUR ORDER

JANE LINDSKOLD is a science fiction writer and former English professor. She co-created *Chronomaster* with science fiction legend Roger Zelazny. Her novels include *The Pipes of Orpheus*, *Marks of Our Brothers*, *Trumps of Doom*, and *Brother to Dragons, Companion to Owls*.